Big Time

Also By Rus Bradburd

All the Dreams We've Dreamed:
a Story of Hoops and Handguns on Chicago's West Side

Make It Take It (short stories)

Forty Minutes of Hell:
The Extraordinary Life of Nolan Richardson

Paddy on the Hardwood: a Journey in Irish Hoops

Big Time

Rus Bradburd

Etruscan Press

Etruscan Press
Wilkes University
84 West South Street
Wilkes-Barre, PA 18766
(570) 408-4546

 **Wilkes University**

www.etruscanpress.org

Published 2024 by Etruscan Press
Printed in the United States of America
Cover design by Logan Rock
Interior design and typesetting by Aaron Petrovich
The text of this book is set in Oculi.

First Edition

17 18 19 20 5 4 3 2 1

Library of Congress Cataloging-in-Publication Data
Names: Bradburd, Rus, 1959- author.
Title: Big time / Rus Bradburd.
Description: First Edition. | Wilkes-Barre, PA : Etruscan Press, 2024. |
  Summary: "Big Time is a subversive anti-sports novel that skewers the
  lofty place of athletics on American college campuses"-- Provided by
  publisher.
Identifiers: LCCN 2024011135 (print) | LCCN 2024011136 (ebook) | ISBN
  9798988198567 (trade paperback) | ISBN 9798988198581 (ebook)
Subjects: LCSH: College athletes--United States--Fiction. | LCGFT: Novels.
Classification: LCC PS3602.R335 B54 2024 (print) | LCC PS3602.R335
  (ebook) | DDC 813/.6--dc23/eng/20240318
LC record available at https://lccn.loc.gov/2024011135
LC ebook record available at https://lccn.loc.gov/2024011136

Please turn to the back of this book for a list of the sustaining funders of Etruscan
Press.

"When I feel like exercising, I just lie down until the feeling goes away."

Robert Maynard Hutchins,
University of Chicago President, 1929-1945

For Connie Voisine and Alma Bradburd...

and for Antonya Nelson and Barry Pearce

Chapter 1

The smell of artificial butter made Professor Eugene Mooney queasy. What choice did he have, though, when the authentic stuff was so expensive? Two hours before game time, he felt vaguely nauseated as the corn popped and the first industrial-sized batch emerged. The sick feeling would last well past the opening kickoff, and probably another three hours. Or at least until they sold out of popcorn.

Mooney and his remaining History Department colleagues were operating concessions at Coors State University's football stadium for the first time. He'd prepared for their new gig by reverting to what he did best: meticulous research. All week, library books had sprawled across his dining room table. He was filling another box when a man in battle fatigues leapt over the counter with a piercing howl. Startled, Mooney jerked his hands into the air as though it were a stickup. Popcorn scattered across the floor.

It was Peter Braverman, his best friend from History.

"Typical," Braverman said. "Our esteemed Professor Mooney is prepared for everything except battle." Braverman sometimes spoke as if a documentary film crew were trailing him. He brushed the spilled popcorn off Mooney's chest and his tone softened. "Hey, you okay, Eugene?" he asked, squeezing his shoulder.

Mooney fumbled for a snappy retort, but all he could manage was, "You almost gave me a heart attack."

"How do you like my getup?" Braverman asked, gesturing at his camouflage trousers and slouch hat. He said they were marketing tools to bring attention to his first book. His gaunt face and frame fit well with battle fatigues, Mooney had to admit, but selling their own books at a Silver Bullets football game was humiliating.

"You should wear a sombrero to promote your book," Braverman said, crunching over the spilled popcorn.

"A sombrero with this?" Mooney was sporting a number 10 jersey to honor quarterback Trevor Knighton.

"You know who looks good in varsity gear?" Braverman asked. "Varsity players."

Mooney was about to answer, but Braverman didn't give him a chance. "Everyone looks good in battle fatigues," he said. "That's why your war machine government hasn't needed a draft since Vietnam. This outfit does their recruiting." He paused then said, "Man, it smells weird in here." He reached elbow-deep into the popcorn machine anyway and jammed a handful into his mouth.

Last week, almost exactly a year after the University's rebranding, History had gotten the good news—they were no longer assigned to stadium bathroom cleanup, responsible for toilets that smelled far worse than the artificial butter. Instead, they had been granted control of the fifteen concession stands during football games, something they hadn't even applied for. The opportunity to take over concessions was a total surprise to everyone in History except Eugene Mooney, but their dwindling faculty had just six days to set it all up.

Mooney had tried to toss a high five to Braverman at the announcement, but he was rebuked. "Celebrating a sellout?" Braverman said. "Not me."

Mooney didn't see it like that. With their new assignment, History would survive, maybe even thrive. A colleague from

Accounting estimated they might earn $100,000 each football game. Basketball wouldn't be as lucrative on a per-game basis because its arena seated only 18,000. Then again, the team played at home more often. They would know more when the department met on Monday to total their take, which would then be pooled for salaries. With any luck, they might even approach their pay scale from before the rebranding. Unfortunately, other departments hadn't experienced History's resurrection, a fact Mooney had tried to bring up at that same meeting.

"It's too late to save English, but Philosophy might still survive," he had said at the meeting. When he spoke, his colleagues usually listened since he was the senior member. Years earlier, his fourth book, *Arriba, Amigos: Pancho Villa's Appropriation of Salsa as Signifier in Coopting the Mexican Underclass* (University of South Dakota Press), propelled him into his position as a full professor, one of the few left in History.

"So I'm suggesting," Mooney added, "we consider sharing our new concessions revenues with struggling departments."

It was quiet for a moment, then he was booed by everyone except Braverman. It was the first time Mooney had ever been booed. Things had certainly become less collegial since the rebranding.

Next, predictably, History could not agree on a menu. Bitter fights erupted. Mooney had had to intervene when Braverman called a Modern European scholar "a food Nazi," but in the end, the sacred principle of academic freedom prevailed: the professors would determine their own menus.

Mooney's final suggestion—that he and Braverman work as a duo—was greeted with enthusiasm. They all knew Braverman would offend customers if left unmonitored, and nobody else wanted to work with him anyway. Mooney had considered it a rare win until the meeting broke up and Braverman steamrolled him with his demand to peddle their own books along with the popcorn.

Mooney and Braverman had plenty in common besides being professors at the big state school in Colorado—maybe too much. They'd been hired the same year, 1997, over two decades before the school rebranded. Soon after arriving on campus, each had been dumped by his spouse—Braverman in the aching aftermath of a stillborn daughter. Both were enamored with the anti-war protests and civil rights movements of the 1960s. Mooney had two older brothers who had been genuine radicals then, but Braverman was actively involved, even after the end of the Vietnam War, in his teenage years. "I did my part" was his mysterious mantra. They were now in their late fifties, although Braverman often acted like a junior high school kid with anger issues. Running partners for a few years, they covered five miles most mornings until Mooney's knee went bust. He adapted by lifting weights at a local health club, but over time he'd ballooned up to 230 pounds. Braverman, protestor thin, still ran.

Mooney and Braverman agreed the school's overemphasis on revenue sports was appalling. Where they strongly differed was on the remedy.

Braverman wanted to blow shit up. He'd harangue whoever was nearby, post angry missives on the school's Faculty Talk email chain, and sneer at the professors who, like him, had remained. He could do righteous indignation better than anyone. He refused to accept that football and basketball were more valuable than physics and biology. Mooney still took pride in their department despite the depressing developments, and he believed one need only apply the right pressure on the right levers within the complex democratic structure already in place. Braverman was like a human museum piece, a link to 1960s' protest movements. When teaching his classes on the Vietnam War, he constantly namedropped to flash his radical credentials at the kids, and sometimes he did it to Mooney.

Mooney loved Braverman anyway, admired his idealism, which he mostly found amusing.

Their new concession stand was small, cold, windowless, and solid concrete, not a place you'd ever want to be stuck in. While Braverman set up the soft drink machine, Mooney sat in the corner and reviewed what he'd learned, should customers have questions.

Mexican history was Mooney's field, but he'd had to educate himself about popcorn's prominent past. Cortez, after invading Mexico in 1519, found popcorn among the native Aztecs, who used it for ceremonial decoration and food. The ancient Peruvians made popcorn, too. In the bat caves of central New Mexico, archaeologists uncovered ears of corn that had been carbon dated from the year—he fished a notecard from his pocket for the correct date.

Mooney's research into culinary history and the psychology behind it indicated that a subtle buttery smell attracted customers who weren't even hungry, so he rigged up a cheap box fan to spread the phony aroma. When another batch of popped corn spewed out, he put down his notes and filled more red-and-white striped boxes, arranging them into rows. Someday they'd introduce an extra-large bag. This was the sort of strategic thinking now integral to his job.

Dozens of other departments were working at the stadium as well, but not English. Mooney felt awful that English had been eliminated by Football, but they had put themselves in jeopardy by refusing to switch with History and take on bathroom duty. They had to assume some responsibility for their own demise.

The only survivors of the purge were two poetry professors because, it was rumored, one poet was planning to retire, and the newly hired poet was something of a pop star whose classes were already overflowing. They were now known as the Poetry Department and had a humble new gig hawking game programs until kickoff.

In fact, when Mooney arrived that evening, a pod of poetry students, and probably their two faculty members, had been posted outside the stadium, getting ready to sell the programs. Mooney had purchased one from what might have been a grad student, dreadlocked and dressed like a retro-hippie. Selling programs was simple once the first issue was edited and published, and if a couple dozen students pitched in, Poetry didn't require a big staff. It wasn't the worst early-season gig, but profits would evaporate as the fans memorized the players' names and programs became unnecessary—although sales could likely be counted on to keep a two-person department afloat.

Mooney fired up the popcorn machine for one more batch, then took a peek at the program. The poets had employed a— well, a poetic tone. One player was described as "...a mythical force of nature whose velocity would elicit tears of envy from the Gods of Sparta whilst a chorus of human passion from the Coors State aficionados doubtless will lift him above; woe be it to the mortals whom he shall battle in imminent clashes." No, that wasn't written by a poet, he thought, it must have been a recently fired Medievalist. The Poetry Department was taking advantage of the work that had been completed before English had been canned. He closed the program and noticed a sticker on the front. "Fishes live in the sea, as men do a-land; the great ones eat up the little ones." William Shakespeare—Compliments of the English Department. Yes, Poetry was obviously recycling parts of last year's programs; they'd have to be careful about plagiarism.

* * *

With the corn popped and the fountain drinks ready, Braverman said he needed help carrying the other snacks into the stadium. They left their post and walked the empty concourse to the delivery dock. Boxes of candy, pickles, and his new book, *Hell No! We Won't Go!* were crammed into the trunk of Braverman's beloved 1972 Volvo. He'd conned his way past parking attendants (aka Urban Planning professors) distracting them by discussing the possibility of solar-powered lights at the stadium. They'd eventually let him pass but insisted he move the car immediately after unloading.

Braverman treasured his Volvo, the only car he'd ever owned, the only material possession he was proud of. His ranch house gutters were decaying, his lawn was desolate, his office was a disaster, he never bought new clothes, but he was passionate about his Volvo.

After they stacked the boxes at the delivery door, Braverman checked to make sure the Urban Planning profs weren't around, shut off the hazard flashers, and zipped his Volvo into a primo vacant spot, right next to the stadium.

"Bad decision," Mooney said, pointing to the sign. Coaches Only.

"They're already in the stadium. And how many football coaches can there be?" Braverman asked, waving at the vacant spaces. It was a rhetorical question because Mooney and Braverman knew the answer. Besides the head coach, the university employed twenty-five assistant coaches. Also, eight strength coaches, six directors of football operations, four film coordinators, three dieticians, two steroid counselors, two social media advisors, and an academic coordinator. That didn't count the dozen graduate assistants. One staff member for every two players, basically. Until recently, Football had ten academic support workers, but because the team had accumulated a GPA over 3.0 during their first year as the Coors State Silver Bullets, they rechanneled their resources into more weightlifting coaches.

Mooney feared that the Volvo, with its "Save Tibet" and "Bernie Sanders" bumper stickers, could be towed, but before he could warn him again, Braverman said, "Nobody would dare. The car stays."

This kind of civil disobedience was how Braverman rebelled, so Mooney said nothing. They hoisted up the bulky boxes and headed back to the stand. The gates would not open to the public for a few more minutes, and the only people walking the stadium concourse were Criminal Justice professors in their electric-yellow vests. They served as ushers, frisked fans, and policed the campus. Complaints about excessive force were common. They had gotten big heads because their enrollments were up and so many athletes majored in Criminal Justice.

Mooney and Braverman wobbled past two of the guards coming from the other direction. One carried a Taser.

"Need help?" one guard snickered without slowing his stride.

"Go fuck yourself," Braverman said over his shoulder.

"Hey, Fatso," the other guard yelled, "you better return that jersey to Trevor Knighton, it's almost game time."

Braverman was about to lash out yet again, but Mooney told him to cool it. Some professors had degenerated into trash-talking each other after academics had been castrated. Braverman was the worst. Or the best, depending on your viewpoint. Mooney was sensitive about his weight, but infighting was bad for university morale, and he prided himself on never losing his cool.

After they dropped off the boxes at the concession stand, Mooney walked the concourse, making notes of their History colleagues' menu listings. He wanted to avoid an accidental price war, but how could he compare popcorn to a pastrami sandwich? Or a Baby Ruth to a bowl of hummus? Each stand had a single professor flanked by two grad students, and their menus were confusing. What the heck were Cold War Nuggets? What exactly were Pillars of Western Civilization w/ Cheese? Well, his colleagues were trying, and it wasn't Mooney's place to complain. The acquiescence of their own History faculty made Braverman crazy, but it was good they were keeping an upbeat attitude about the challenges ahead.

When Mooney returned, Braverman was arranging their book displays. He unfurled an American flag with the peace sign in place of the stars, a replica of his new publication's cover. He duct-taped the flag between the pickles and popcorn machine, then listed the prices on the poster board. Naturally, he put his new book first, Mooney's next, then the snacks. At the bottom it read:

Academic Special!!!
Large Coke
Popcorn
One book (your choice)
$25

"Good luck with that one," Mooney said. The popcorn machine hid a modest stack of *Arriba, Amigos*. Mooney had hoped Braverman would forget to bring his book. No such luck.

While the two professors often bickered like brothers, that morning on the phone Mooney nearly got his friend to admit that new books wouldn't save History. This concession stand assignment might.

Mooney hadn't told anyone, not even Braverman, how History got the concession stand assignment, or exactly why

English had been punished. He had learned—from quarterback Trevor Knighton—that an English instructor had given an important football lineman, a Croatian kid, a "C" in an intro-level class. That set off a firestorm within the football offices which, along with English's refusal to clean bathrooms, led to their closure. By chance, the English Department's screwup occurred during the same semester Trevor Knighton had enrolled in Mooney's Intro to Mexican History class.

As a freshman on the field last season, Trevor was more potential than product, but Mooney believed he had bolstered the kid's sense of himself. Trevor had taken a strong, if immature, interest in Mexican history, and one day he yelled, "Remember the Alamo!" at the conclusion of class. Mooney had called him aside for a chat.

"Look, Trevor," Mooney told him, "as an African American athlete, you should be sensitive to issues of identity and national origin. Can't you see how shouting that phrase might be offensive?"

That was how Mooney learned of the kid's inquisitiveness, if not a valid excuse for shouting in a lecture hall: Trevor Knighton's mother was born in Mexico. He'd enrolled in Mooney's class because he wanted to make his mother happy. Mooney couldn't remember a student ever voicing concern about his mother. He began to mentor Trevor after class occasionally.

Now as a sophomore, Trevor was the starting quarterback, and in the team's first road game he'd thrown a school-record six touchdown passes. Two days after that game, Trevor came by to visit Mooney, and the professor and the quarterback chatted, wandering around campus for two hours. Mooney was honored that the team's new star even remembered him, and he didn't see the point in burdening a blossoming student with the ethical complications of the school's rebranding. It certainly wasn't Trevor's fault, and besides, Mooney couldn't expect to get him involved.

The professors were still setting up when they realized simultaneously that a man was walking away with an armload of their full popcorn boxes.

"Hey, asshole!" Braverman yelled. "You gotta pay."

When the man, not twenty yards away, turned around, Mooney knew instantly that Braverman had made a mistake. Hadn't Braverman noticed the stretch pants and rubber cleats? Mooney had seen the football coach's face dozens of times on TV. With his black hair slicked back, his trim waist and classic features, he looked like Al Pacino in *The Godfather*.

"Sorry, Coach," Mooney called out. "We assumed you were a professor."

The man balanced the popcorn boxes, dug into his pocket, and dropped a handful of change, which clinked on the cement floor.

"That's not necessary, sir," Mooney said. He wondered why a coach would be cruising the concourse. Pregame nerves probably.

"These boxes are for all the coaches," the man said, as if that justified the pilfering. "We could smell it popping way down in our lounge."

The aroma was working? That took the sting out of the theft for Mooney. Braverman, however, seemed to think it was time for a stare-down. The coach smirked before he strode away.

"Just one more insult," Braverman muttered. "I can only take so much. You watch, Eugene, I'll turn this goddamn place on its head. I'll eat all one-hundred yards of turf, use the goalposts for toothpicks, and shit green for a month."

Mooney suppressed a laugh. "You've got to choose your battles, Peter," Mooney said for the umpteenth time. "What pacifist goes around picking fights?" He flipped through his game program to see who they'd offended, then let the program fall to the floor as the coach's coins had moments earlier. "Now you've done it," he said. "That was Tom Maniscalco." The name didn't appear to register with Braverman. "Tom Maniscalco is our goddamn offensive coordinator," Mooney said. "The top guy, besides our head coach."

Rather than back off or apologize, Braverman shook his arms as though preparing for a boxing match. He said, "You're my witness, Eugene. If they offend my morality just one more time, one more, I am warning you. I might really mean it this time. I'm going to lead the movement to overthrow Football and take our university back."

"But History is headed in the right direction," Mooney said. "We'll make money tonight, and if we keep it up, changes might eventually—"

Just then, the PA blared a welcome. The gates opened, fans streamed in, and soon their concession stand had a long line of customers.

They ran out of popcorn midway through the second half. This was a good problem, Mooney thought. They'd been caught short, but not by much, and week-old popcorn was practically inedible. They slid the candy bars to the front of the counter, followed by the book displays. Braverman, who'd finally cooled down, draped his peace flag over the popcorn maker to discourage buyers.

Minutes later, Mooney was surprised to see Braverman sell five of his books, all to one woman. At first glance she looked like a student, sporting dreadlocks and a tie-dyed skirt, but her

sun-worn face suggested otherwise. She might have been thirty
or she might have been forty. She fumbled for folded money in
her sports bra, which caused Braverman to nudge Mooney with
his forearm. Braverman offered to sign her books, but she didn't
seem to make the connection—the author of *Hell No! We Won't
Go!* was also selling Cokes and candy.

Braverman stared after her as she slid away. He said, "I love
dreadlocks on white women. Is she listed in your program, too?"

Mooney realized that he'd bought his program from her. She
was probably the new poetry professor.

They might have sold more candy, but Mooney's curiosity
about the score overwhelmed his business sense. Braverman
crammed the cashbox into his backpack; they locked up and
climbed up to the Standing Room Only area. By that time, the
Silver Bullets were winning by 53 points, so Trevor Knighton
was already resting, goofing on the sidelines with his teammates.

The lone break in the tedium of the blowout was the fans'
reenacting the Coors State tradition of "the Groundswell," the
local version of the Wave. Fans sprung to their feet in unison,
row-by-row, to create the illusion of a tsunami that went
bottom-to-top before snaking back down the next section.
Nobody took notice when Braverman refused to participate.

"It's interesting to see everyone working on game day,"
Mooney said after the Groundswell fizzled. Agriculture had
made the field a vivid, if unnatural, green. Across the way,
Computer Science controlled the new Jumbotron, a state-of-the-
art gizmo that constantly ran commercials for Coors. Everything
was running smoothly, but Mooney couldn't help but worry
about the survival of his fellow academics. All it would take was
one inaccurate game stat and Math might be axed.

When the game ended, Criminal Justice guards pointed
100,000 fans to the exits. Below them, Consumer Science

professors swept up, followed by the recycling teams from Environmental Studies. "You missed one," Braverman called to a professor, pointing at a plastic cup.

Mooney didn't think it was funny, and although he didn't know the guy, he reached down for a few cups, stacked them, and dropped them into his bag.

Mooney offered to stay and keep Braverman company until the parking lots emptied. With the Volvo parked right next to the stadium, he'd no doubt be trapped in traffic for at least a half hour. Braverman relished a battle, but he had no patience for battling traffic.

"I hope we see that dreadlocked girl again," Braverman said.

"Dreadlocked woman," Mooney said. "Hey, we've got time, let's go down onto the field, shall we?"

"No, thanks," Braverman said.

"Oh, come on. We'll get close to the enemy, and you can gather intelligence."

Braverman made a face, but he stood, and they went against the grain until they got to Row One. Agriculture professors were already down on the field, reseeding with perennial rye grass to bolster the Bermuda. It truly is a beautiful field, Mooney thought, and a moment later he said so out loud. He hadn't been so close to the gridiron since his junior year of high school. He'd never revealed to Braverman or Trevor Knighton that he'd played prep football his first three years.

"You want to wait for a selfie with Trevor Knighton, too?" Braverman asked.

"Why not enjoy ourselves?" Mooney said, as if to an unreasonable teenager. The truth was he would like to see Trevor, but not under these circumstances, when he was sure to be mobbed by autograph hounds. "We can still fight the power, as you like to say, on Monday. Come on." He slapped

Braverman's backpack, and the cash box inside rattled. "Maybe that's the sound of our future," Mooney added.

They started down the last steps to the grass, but yet another Criminal Justice professor appeared. "You got a pass? Players and their families only, pal," the guard said. "Rules are rules."

Mooney thought it might be the same guy who had called him "Fatso," but he smiled and turned around, putting a hand to Braverman's chest to get him to comply. Braverman grumbled the entire way as they shuffled up the stadium steps, easily beating Mooney to the top. There, Braverman counted their cash in the cool Colorado night while Mooney caught his breath.

When they got back to the Volvo—or, rather, the empty parking place where the car had been—Braverman went bonkers. If empty threats were publications, Braverman would be a Regents Scholar by now, but the violent tone in his voice was very different this time.

"Eugene, I am taking an oath, here and now, in front of you." Braverman said. "Football has crossed the line."

Mooney tried to calm him, but Braverman was like a keg of beer with a broken spigot.

"Mark my words," Braverman said, "Football and Basketball will be begging for mercy when I get done."

Mooney tried to intercede, but Braverman was off again.

"You're either with me or against me, Eugene, and if our friendship means anything your decision will be a no-brainer." He stood on the cement parking block where the Volvo had been, hung a fist in the air, and launched into an obviously-rehearsed-yet-rambling, expletive-laden speech—although Mooney was his only audience, as usual.

Braverman referenced Malcolm X, Patrick Henry, and Fidel Castro. It was quite a moving speech, Mooney had to admit, so he waited patiently, nodding and applauding in appropriate spots until his friend was finished.

"Listen," Mooney finally said, "you're reacting out of emotion. Give it a few days. You've always parked illegally, and the Volvo could have been towed dozens of times before we even rebranded. And look at all the money we made tonight. I bet our colleagues did just as well."

"That's the third time you mentioned the money." He stepped down from his cement parking block and added, "You're a sellout."

Mooney felt the shame rise in his face. "We can still work within—" Mooney began, but he began to stammer.

"The revolution is on!" Braverman roared. "It started right here and now. Let's remember this as the opening salvo, when the fascists drew first blood and we both decided enough was enough."

Mooney feared another speech, but instead Braverman's tone softened. "I guess I need a lift home, Eugene," he said. "Where'd you park?"

"In the History lot. I'll drive you home. But really, Peter, think about it over the weekend. I mean, what are you going to do, overthrow the president?"

"Maybe I will," Braverman said.

Chapter 2

Trevor Knighton usually loved Sundays, but the pain in his arm had him worried. After last night's win, he was unscathed, not even a scratch, which was unusual for any quarterback. But he stayed late in the stadium's parking lot to sign autographs for local school kids, and they took turns climbing all over him and posing for pictures. Some of them were pretty chunky, and the stress from those fourth graders hanging off his shoulders while he scribbled his name had given him an ache in his right forearm.

The trainer would insist Trevor come in for treatment, but the whirlpools were surely brimming with bruised linemen. And being perceived by the coaches as injured or soft might affect their confidence in him. He figured he'd keep ice on it, they could treat him Monday if it got worse. Maybe the trainer might demonstrate some pen grips that caused less discomfort.

At the kitchen table, Trevor was experimenting with signing his name left-handed when he heard his roommate, Sasha Dimitrievic, upstairs. The agonized creak of his bed frame, the belches and groans, the long piss with the bathroom door open.

Sasha appeared on the stairs a moment later, his shorts sliced up the sides to make room for his massive thighs. His legs were unmarked because, unlike the other linemen, he didn't bruise. He gave the bruises. With a final burp, he stepped off the landing, his ever-present horn-rimmed glasses in place. Sasha declined the popular sport goggles, preferring white athletic tape around the back of his shaved head to keep his regular glasses secure under his helmet. Before they took the field for practice or games, Trevor wrapped the makeshift half-headband onto Sasha's bare skin, where the tape left a raspberry-colored rash.

Trevor smiled to say good morning and adjusted his ice bag to keep it from sloshing all over the place.

"No eye in team," Sasha said, adjusting his glasses. He was from Croatia, but this wasn't his typical malapropism or fractured English. Rather, it was his standard greeting to Trevor, like a secret handshake. The expression came from their coaches' cliché, *There is no "I" in TEAM.* Sasha had been confused until Trevor wrote down the hackneyed phrase to explain.

Trevor had his own response: "Four I's in Dimitrievic."

Sasha smiled. "Four eyes," he said. Nobody thought Sasha's clunky English was funnier than Sasha himself. "I am a four-eyes!" he was delighted to admit. Trevor spent a lot of time helping Sasha, correcting his pronunciation and syntax. He loved Sasha's playfulness. The only time Sasha got upset was when anyone asked about the Serbo-Croatian war. He was born a few years after the conflict ended, but his family had suffered, and his own father had been tortured. Trevor didn't know the exact details, but Sasha got so emotional about the "Homeland War" that Trevor promised never to bring it up again.

As usual, Sasha went right for the box of Wheaties.

"Whoa, don't eat," Trevor said, just as his ice bag ruptured and leaked all over the kitchen table. He tossed it in the sink but left the small puddle on the table. No more autographs this week, he decided.

"We have more groceries?"

"My dad's taking us for omelets."

"I remember," Sasha said. "Now, warmed up I will get for breakfast. Cheers, big ears." He poured a massive bowl of cereal, sliced up two bananas, and doused it all with organic Half & Half. The extra calories helped keep his weight above 300 pounds.

Trevor and Sasha were awake earlier than usual because the lawn and gardening guys—professors from the Agriculture Department—had revved up their mowers and weed whackers at 10:00 a.m. Trevor didn't want to hurt anyone's feelings, but he'd have to insist the Ag profs respect Sunday as a day of rest. Or at least wait until a decent hour. Typically, the football stars had a parade of weekend well-wishers and visitors.

Trevor settled back with his cranberry juice and began posting on social media, typing with just his left hand. He was one of thirty players in a Computer Science class whose semester-long homework project was to make public their thoughts after every game. Before he'd finished the required 50 words, there was a sharp knock on the door.

Trevor stood and peeked out through the peephole. The professors from Human Nutrition were back, although the roommates already had enough food for a Denver Broncos team banquet. For a moment Trevor hung his head, as if a referee had called him for illegal procedure. What to do? He cracked the door an inch.

"Great game, Trevor," one of them said.

He pretended to cough. "Sore throat," he gasped. "Just leave everything there."

"We'd rather bring it inside," the other professor said.

"I think I'm contagious," Trevor said and coughed again. "Just leave it."

The first professor reached into a shoulder bag for an 8" x 10" photo.

"Of course," Trevor said, ignoring his promise to himself. He groped his pajama pants pockets for a pen he didn't have. The professor had one handy and Trevor signed quickly. He flinched as pain shot through his throwing arm.

The professors thanked him and left the brown grocery bags in a neat row on the porch. "If those filets thaw, you'll have to eat them soon," one prof said. "Grass-fed beef."

Although Trevor appreciated the steaks and seafood, loved the organic vegetables, even Sasha couldn't eat that much. Besides, there'd be an elaborate training table at dinner, so this visit felt a bit invasive. At least the Family and Consumer Sciences professors waited until the apartment was empty on Mondays before they started cleaning.

This Sunday would be busier than usual because Trevor's father was in town.

The fact that Trevor was the first great African-American quarterback in Coors State history meant the world to Ben Knighton. Trevor's father took great pride in "the Movement," and he probably imagined a place for Trevor in school history if not the history of the civil rights movement. Trevor, however, identified more with his Mexican-born mother. Sure, his father had caught thousands of his practice passes, drilled him on complex footwork exercises, taught him the basic reads—but it was his mother he'd always opened up to. Even now that he had emerged as the team's star, his mother's advice, while never sports-related, felt more relevant.

Trevor had attended a racially mixed high school in Dallas and was not a top recruit nationally. He was 6'4" though, and Coors State's offensive coordinator had an eye for potential. In fact, Coors State was the only major school to offer him a football scholarship. The sexual attention on campus, easy grades, free gear, weekly steroids, groceries, and comped meals around town made him a little skittish, but there was no point in fighting freebies. He'd been an unassuming kid in high school, but the way everyone fawned over college football players caused a strange transformation in Trevor. He'd behaved obnoxiously as a freshman, acting out in class, being overly suggestive to women on campus.

Without any single event shaking Trevor out of this, he'd decided this year he'd stop acting like a jerk—it just wasn't him— even if he couldn't convince the entire campus to stop treating him like a hero. He didn't, however, want to spoil his college fun by over-thinking. He continued to collect comped stuff from the coaches, professors, and around town, but he gave away food to his pep-band neighbors. Extra swag got handed out to his classmates.

All sophomores had to declare a major by January, and their coach was pushing for a new one for Trevor, Online Studies. Trevor had already taken five online classes, and his homework got completed by a tutor he hadn't met. The coaches complained openly about how their tutors wasted time by writing papers from scratch and not being more efficient. The tutors felt they had to be extra-careful about recycling the same essays, research papers, or business writing memos. One actual in-person class for Trevor had been Eugene Mooney's Mexican History, which turned out to be his favorite.

Maybe it was Sasha Dimitrievic who had made the quarterback reconsider his behavior their freshman year. Sasha was bemused and perplexed by all the stuff football players got, the fussing and attention. He'd been a strong influence on Trevor.

Sasha was also a decent artist with a pencil, and he sometimes scrawled quick sketches for a laugh. And he was handy around the apartment. He'd fixed their washing machine with just a screwdriver, finally bending the steel door with his bare hands to adjust the tripping mechanism. (Trevor would have been perfectly happy to call the Family and Consumer Science professors for help.)

Sasha had come to Coors State directly from Croatia. Over the years, dozens of college basketballers called the now-fractured Yugoslavian states home, but Sasha was the first Croatian-born Division I football star in the nation. He was the team's center, and their friendship aided their uncanny timing on the field. That was a big reason Coors State was already 2-0.

Everyone on the team knew Sasha's background because Trevor Knighton had boasted about (and, yes, embellished) the story.

Tom Maniscalco, the same coach who'd found Trevor, had been vacationing in Croatia, on his way to Italy. Lost and in need of a drink, the coach stopped in a village called Pokupsko after seeing banners for what turned out to be the town's annual Plum Brandy Festival. The weekend's finale involved a centuries-old tradition, a complicated fifteen-mile horse race that weaved through nearby villages, forests, and fields.

Sasha Dimitrievic had won the competition—with the slack-jawed coach looking on—after his horse suffered a broken leg, and he dragged the stunned steed the final ten meters. The dramatic finish was now the stuff of legend around campus, and Pokupsko, probably. Trevor constantly relied on the story to introduce Sasha to young women at parties. Trevor wasn't in Croatia when it happened, naturally, but he told the story as if he had been. Sasha heard the other riders approaching, Trevor would say, and he dug down deep for the strength to drag the horse for thirty yards (the distance kept growing), and finally carried the horse on his hip (Trevor's latest editorial addition) across the finish line for the victory.

It wasn't so very far from believable. Sasha had inherited his incredible strength from his great-grandfather, who was known as "The Croatian Samson." This strongman had made a living lugging huge loads of timber on his back and claimed his power was a gift from the Slavic war god Gerovit. Although the great-grandfather was too big to even consider getting on a horse, at each Plum Brandy Festival in the 1930s, the man had been pitted against a young ox in a crude version of tug-of-war.

Sasha had never lifted a weight in his life before coming to Coors State, but after a single year of training he could bench-press nearly 600 pounds. He was a genetic freak who disdained the steroids placed in his locker every Monday, although he kept quiet about it. He claimed his strength was aided by his ability to sleep deeply—he'd occasionally doze off at odd times, although never in class.

Sasha also aspired to be the first Croatian-born football star to graduate with honors. On placement tests, he'd shown an impressive proficiency in math and science, and his scores let him leapfrog past intro classes at Coors State.

But at the start of this year, their second, Sasha made a curious choice. Instead of one of the sciences, he said he wanted to major in English, certain that this was the best way to master the language. It was still a bit early to declare a major, but he was anxious to do it before the Winter Quarter, which would soon be approaching.

The "C" Sasha got in freshman Composition was bad enough. The bigger problem was that English was now defunct, and he had to select another major.

Sasha's struggles in Composition had first led him to seek help from Trevor's father. Ben Knighton had himself been an English major who taught high school briefly before earning his fortune in the tech industry. At their monthly breakfasts,

Trevor's father would unfold simple English grammar worksheets, and they'd hunker down while Trevor perused the sports pages.

Now, through a mouthful of Wheaties, Sasha said, "No practice with grammar today. Not sleep so good again and I need bigger help from your Papa." Sasha was a compulsive planner. He'd already picked out and packed up Christmas gifts to mail to his parents back in Pokupsko.

"You're still worried about what to major in?"

"Now I return to Croatia someday without Honors diploma in English because department is kaput," Sasha said sadly.

"You realize you could get straight A's in Criminal Justice," Trevor said. "Or any of the sciences, knowing you."

"I wanted English major."

"Coach told me the new Online Studies major would be a box of chocolates."

"English major," Sasha said again, like a kid who refused to admit Santa Claus wasn't real. Then he paused. "Box of chocolates is metaphor?"

"My dad will know what to do," Trevor said.

The LeSabre was the only cafe in town that would cook Sasha's sausage-laden six-egg omelet. The others insisted on serving two separate omelets on two separate plates, which for some reason never satisfied him even if it was the same amount of food. The young men chewed, grunted, passed containers of cream, jelly, and wads of napkins back and forth. Trevor experimented with using the fork in his left hand while his father tried to decipher the undergrad catalog.

Ben Knighton scribbled notes as the players ate. He was still the all-time statistical leader in several passing categories for tiny Knox College, and he was proud of his alma mater. He used to suggest Trevor could transfer if he was ever unhappy at Coors State.

Trevor thought, no TV appearances? No bowl games? Nine-hundred fans at the homecoming game? Bus rides while you studied with McDonald's on your lap? Forget it. Knox College didn't even have football scholarships, although Ben Knighton could easily afford the tuition for his son. After Trevor was named Coors State's starting quarterback, his dad's Knox-as-a-back-up option seemed obsolete and never again came up. Like most of the players' parents, he didn't mind the pomp surrounding the sport since his son was in the spotlight.

"It's clear," his father said looking up from the catalog, "that Sasha needs one more General Education class before he can declare a major." Ben Knighton began reading aloud. "Physical Education? Physical Science?"

After each possibility Trevor shook his head no, while Sasha remained stoic, slathering butter onto his toast, his mouth open, as though he'd suffered a concussion on a kickoff.

"Personal Health? Philosophy?" Ben Knighton continued.

Ben Knighton waited for either of the boys to speak. He finally said, "Sasha, there's also Poetry, but look here, Political Science. You're interested in politics, right?"

"Poetry," Sasha said in the pause. His voice had a clear lift as he repeated the word like a mantra. He studied the ceiling fans as if they were stars at midnight.

"What about it?" Trevor said.

"Poetry is a major?" Sasha asked, as if that was too good to be true.

"It's a small department it seems," Ben Knighton said.

"My family," Sasha said, "is long history strong men and poets. But nobody is both strong man and poet. I am cousin of Slavko Mihalić," he added with obvious pride. Trevor gave him a blank look, so he added, "Famous Croatian poet, but very weak and skinny. He dies in 2007." Sasha suddenly stood and clinked his water glass with a knife as if to toast the Most Valuable Player at a banquet. The clatter of the restaurant stopped instantly. In a deep voice, Sasha recited:

"*Izgubljen, za stolom, sred oceana*
mislim o sebi kao o pustoj hridi..."

By the third line, Sasha had every table's attention.

When the poem ended, the silence turned into applause. A waitress stopped at their table, cheeks flush and eyes glistening. "That was kind of beautiful." She blushed. "What was it?" A few people continued to clap. One called out for an encore.

Trevor turned to Sasha in wonder. "Yeah, what was that?" he asked.

"I'm not sure to explain," Sasha said as he took his seat. "The beginning of famous poem by cousin Slavko. I am thinking in English. Time-out," he said, forming the "T" with his hands. He closed his eyes and his lips moved slightly, then his voice adopted a gentle tone. "Lost, at the table," he said, "in middle of the ocean. I think of myself as a lonely rock." Sasha kept his eyes closed for a moment, to reside briefly wherever the poem had taken him.

"A lonely rock," Trevor said. "Right on, man. You're a lonely rock."

"You, too?" Sasha said. "We are both lonely rocks." The players grinned and exchanged fist bumps.

His father circled the new option—305: Introduction to Poetry Workshop. Sasha would still have to get special permission because they only had two professors and the choices were limited to upper-level classes this coming quarter. One would have to waive the prerequisite requirements—and sign in a non-native speaker who had stumbled to a "C" in English 101.

"To point out the obvious," Ben Knighton went on, "there's no guarantee Sasha could ace a 300-level class, either, but here's the course description," he said, a new energy in his voice. "Students will submit twelve of their own original poems in a workshop setting. All styles of poetry encouraged and welcomed."

"Even Croatian poetry, Dad?" Trevor wondered aloud.

"Poetry," Sasha said again. "Poetry is almost like English. Good news for me, my friends."

Ben Knighton said, "Email this woman and go meet her."

"Poetry is a woman?" Sasha asked.

His father underlined the name and slid it across the table to the boys.

Layla Sillimon.

Trevor wrote her name on a napkin. Sasha pulled the pen away and sketched wavy flowers on each side of her name. "No eye in team," he said.

Trevor figured the next step, just to be safe, was to run the idea of Sasha majoring in Poetry—and jumping into an upper-level workshop—by Professor Mooney.

On Monday morning, Trevor and Sasha ditched Intro to Criminal Justice, their only mutual class. Neither player liked to miss, but this one had an enrollment of 500, and they spent much of class time watching true crime television program reruns. Trevor figured nobody would care if they were AWOL. He wore his Pancho Villa T-shirt that morning as a tribute to Professor Mooney.

Mooney sometimes made Trevor a bit uncomfortable. For one thing, he never requested a photo or autograph. Most people either tried to give Trevor things or wanted gear from him, as though he were a Nike outlet store. Mooney could come off as a little weird, Trevor cautioned Sasha on the walk to the History building.

"Weird with a beard," Sasha replied nonsensically. Clearly his poetry recitation yesterday had knocked something loose.

"Let me do the talking," Trevor said, tapping on Mooney's door.

Instantly the door opened, as if the visit had been expected. "The conquering hero," Mooney said, and he motioned for them to sit.

Trevor understood Mooney was being ironic. "Professor," he began, "this is my roommate, Sasha Dimitrievic."

Sasha gave the professor a decisive nod. Instead of sitting, he went to a framed photo of Pancho Villa on horseback. Villa loved his horse, Trevor remembered. He'd scored bonus points on an exam for recalling the horse's name, Siete Leguas.

Mooney asked how he could help.

Trevor blurted, "Professor Mooney, you don't hate football, right?"

"Let's say that my feelings about the sport are complicated." So were the professor's feelings about Sasha, Trevor assumed, although this was the first time they'd met—Sasha was the anchor that inadvertently sunk English.

Trevor stammered through Sasha's backstory, then the reason for the visit.

Mooney agreed it was best to sit down with Layla Sillimon to make their appeal.

"Like I said, Sasha's English is getting better," Trevor said, adding quickly, "Is Miss Sillimon a good gamble? We want an easy teacher. I mean one who will be supportive and open-minded."

"You boys still have time to decide," Mooney said.

"Sasha thinks this is urgent," Trevor said. "And he wants to earn an 'A.'"

"Impressive," said Mooney. He said to Sasha, "Are you truly interested in poetry, son?"

Sasha nodded. He still hadn't spoken a word.

"It's an unusual plan," Mooney said, "and there must be immense pressure on Poetry now that the rest of English is gone." He moved to his computer. "Layla Sillimon," he said, "She's new to Coors State, but she's no kid. Who knows what she thinks of Football. Geez, I've actually crossed paths with her before. Let's see what we can learn from her bio. She's been on television a lot. A poet on TV. Who knew?" He stared at the screen for so long that the players moved behind Mooney to check out her photo.

She was pretty, Trevor thought, even with the combo of dreadlocks and pale skin. He told Mooney how poetry was part of Sasha's family's tradition, just like his superhuman strength.

"I believe you," Mooney said, glancing at Sasha, "but his English won't improve if he never speaks."

"He got a 'C' in Freshman Comp," Trevor admitted as though it had been his fault. "I'd better be honest."

"That's a big red flag."

Sasha swallowed and broke his silence. "Maybe you can feel up Layla Sillimon for me?"

Trevor started to sputter, but Professor Mooney saved him. "I know what your friend means," he said. "I'll do your research on Miss Sillimon."

Chapter 3

Layla Sillimon grew up in San Francisco an only child, abandoned by her father before she'd learned to walk. In her formative years, her hippie mom dragged her to a monthly poetry reading, and by the time Layla was a teenager she was a regular performer on the local slam scene. Even after earning a graduate degree from San Francisco State, she still lived with her mom, helping with their astronomical rent by waitressing for fifteen years.

Self-Portrait in a Funhouse Mirror from Stoned Venus Press was Layla's debut collection of poems. The book sold four hundred copies in the Bay Area, mostly after Layla performed at open-mic events. Everything changed one night, though, when pop star Taylor Swift read one of Layla's poems on a television talk show, holding the cover up to the camera. The collection went crazy viral, outselling all other poetry books that year. The book even got mentioned in *Rolling Stone*, *People*, and *Cosmo*.

Layla was savvy enough to understand the notoriety was mostly luck, and she might never have another hit poetry book. It made her laugh, really, just to say, "hit poetry book." Then a friend reminded her she was nearly forty, and the publication might be her ticket to an academic gig, one with financial security. Waiting on tables was exhausting, and besides, what else could she do with an advanced English degree?

Coors State University's job ad was the only one whose deadline hadn't passed. The school greeted Layla's application for an assistant professor's position with enthusiasm despite her scrawny teaching CV and the fact that the English Department didn't need yet another white woman. They were at a dreary crossroads because the number of English majors had shrunk to less than fifty.

During two days of on-campus interviews that spring, she was told repeatedly that English was being elbowed into obscurity by athletics, and she sensed the department's quiet desperation. San Francisco State didn't even have a football team, not that she was aware of. Clearly Coors State did things differently. She learned that its full-time English faculty had faded to just twelve professors in the year since the name change.

Layla's campus visit had been unremarkable until her required public reading. Other candidates had far more teaching experience and academic publications, but not a pop star's endorsement. Word got out on college radio, then on a slew of social media posts: Layla Sillimon was on campus and her poetry reading was open to the public. Rumors of a Taylor Swift appearance floated around cyberspace, and Layla was happy to let them float. An hour before the event, the location had to be switched to a 700-seat auditorium used for Criminal Justice lectures. Campus security was called in to manage the multitudes. After the seats filled up, a dozen white co-eds in dreadlocks came in and squatted cross-legged at her feet, looking exactly like younger Laylas at a folk music festival. The jam-packed room energized her, and she spontaneously sang the opening poem. After two encores and a crush of students seeking autographs and selfies, she noticed a clump of faculty gathered in the back, bickering.

The next morning, while she was packing to return home, Coors State offered Layla her first full-time assistant professor's job. Although the position would triple her income and provide health insurance, she freaked out a bit and requested a few days to decide. "I have to discuss the offer with my mother," she said.

That was sort of true, mostly because, in spite of the cost of living, she was comfortable crashing on her mother's futon in her Mission District apartment. Also, while Layla needed a real job, she could practically hear the virtue-signaling by her sister slam poets—her only real friends—blasting her for pursuing an academic career. She decided she'd do the ethical thing and turn the position down.

Back in the Bay Area, Layla was still unloading her backpack when her mom strode through the kitchen with a cardboard box and announced she was moving, immediately and permanently, to Belfast, Northern Ireland. "There's nothing here for us anymore," she said. "You're taking that job in Colorado."

Layla wasn't at all political, and she'd never believed her mom truly was, either. But her mother, whose maiden name was Cullen, claimed she was going to spend the rest of her career toiling for economic justice for poor working-class Catholic families.

What about us? Layla thought. *We're practically living in poverty, too.* And she nearly said something she wasn't certain she meant—"Can't I go with you, Mom?" But before she could open her mouth, her mother put her in her place, saying, "You're too old for these abandonment issues, Layla."

Still, with her entire life on hold, Layla stalled. She couldn't afford to be a de facto orphan in a pricey apartment. And a tremendous sense of guilt washed over her because she'd lashed out at her mother a month earlier, thumped a finger on her collarbone, and said, "Mom, your lifelong hippie lifestyle has been exactly that—a style." Was it her fault her mother was moving?

An odd thing happened after she called Coors State back to accept the job. She found herself longing not for her soon-to-depart mother, but for her father. She had no memory of the dude who'd dumped his toddler off at daycare the day he bounced, so why would Layla miss him now? She knew little about him, just that her mother referred to him as "that loudmouth" each time Layla had inquired. She'd learned as a teenager to stop asking about him, but she never stopped wondering.

The day her mom vamoosed, Layla probably made things worse. Instead of gushing with love and gratitude, as her mother stood curbside awaiting an Uber to the international terminal, Layla made the mistake of asking one last time where she could find her father.

An hour after her mother's flight departed, just as she feared, the Bay Area poetry police labeled Layla a turncoat. Some dickhead tweeted about her being a traitor, then that got retweeted a dozen times, but she decided then and there the haters could kiss her tattooed ass. She needed a real income and an affordable place to live.

She didn't want to wallow in self-pity, not as the best paycheck of her life awaited in Colorado, but the night before leaving California, feeling irrationally sorry for herself, she wept bitterly—she'd been deserted by her dad, and now by her mother. And abandoned by her poetry pals around the city, which stung. She was the kind of person who would participate in a drum circle just for the feeling of family.

The English Department got all-but-eliminated the summer before Layla arrived. She heard something strange about restroom-cleaning duties, and the salary wasn't going to be what she'd hoped. Perhaps because Layla's hiring had gotten a bit of media attention, the two poetry professors were allowed to remain—Layla and a stodgy old fossil named Wilson Keats, who was scheduled to retire soon. A two-person Poetry Department. The rest of English was...well, history.

Before they'd been fired, the English Department must have believed a popular poet with a following could boost enrollment and help improve its standing. That was probably why she'd been hired. The irony: they were "disappeared" before she'd even found an apartment. Layla felt terrible about the loss of English, but there was nothing she could do. She also wasn't shocked to learn Wilson Keats had been the man at the center of the argument at the back of the auditorium, and he'd tried to block her hiring. It turned out the now-extinct English professors all hated Wilson Keats, and if Keats objected to a proposal, the others were fully in favor. So Layla would have no natural allies on campus.

From day one, Layla had wanted to tell Wilson Keats to drop dead. At their first two-person faculty meeting, she mistakenly mentioned her classes were overflowing. Keats fumed. It felt like payback minutes later when he declined to endorse Poetry's new duties as assigned by the athletic department—writing, publishing, and selling the game programs for football. She'd been a gig-based worker for years, so the fact that her new salary would come from program sales didn't bother her that much. She'd get by, and rent was a quarter of what it was in San Francisco. Keats did agree to tally up the take from her program sales, and he'd be on hand at the games, but he refused to sell them himself. The whole setup was bizarre, but she wanted to be a joiner, a builder, and complaining about a chance for human connection felt counter-productive.

At the home opener, just a week after classes began in September, she wheeled a wagonload of game programs to the stadium, two dozen students by her side. Layla's poetry students were tech-savvy, and under Layla's guidance, they'd produced the new programs in just a few days, and some were already claiming it as their first publication.

Orchestra music floated above the parking lot since the Music Department had a new arrangement for game day, "busking." Musicians wandered from tailgate to tailgate, playing for tips. Layla appreciated it wasn't elitist classical music but the school fight song.

That evening, Keats pouted on the sidewalk in his folding chair, a pile of programs at his feet. He thumbed through a Wallace Stevens anthology and ignored the fans who streamed by. An impotent protest, Layla thought. He sold zero, never bothering to call out to a single passing pedestrian or potential customer. Talk about a wet Navajo blanket. At the first game, Layla couldn't collect the cash fast enough, and a half-hour before kickoff, she sold Keats's stack, too.

Layla spent much of her first week on campus signing Special Permission override slips to add student after student. Her classes should have topped out at twenty, but she had nearly fifty in each of her three sections. Criminal Justice boasted of overflow classes, but nobody else on campus was doubling enrollment caps.

Of course, fifty students made a poetry classroom quite a challenge. How could you run a workshop with so many?

"You can't," Wilson Keats told her one day in the hallway.

Okay, he was probably right. The only time this century. She quickly got the idea to have the students work in pairs to compose poems. That sliced fifty students into twenty-five and cut grading time in half.

She wanted to feel content at Coors State. She'd scored a legit poetry position. Gorgeous hikes and recreational marijuana were within walking distance. And she had a debut book under her hand-woven belt. Sure, she'd lost her mother, her father, and her so-called poetry friends in San Francisco, but that's why she truly appreciated her fawning students who were bound to become her surrogate family. Layla even encouraged them to post her classes on YouTube for people who couldn't afford college. She enjoyed teaching and the university setting, despite everyone's strange football addiction. She'd never been to an actual game until this job, but she surprised herself by digging the tacky weirdness. Nobody was being ironic dressing up like a can of Coors Light in silver with red trim, with matching shoes, earrings, and scarves. But that made it more ironic, right? An honest and authentic irony, not a cynical one so typical at universities. "Basketball is more fun," one of her poets told her. "You'll see. They run around in baggy-ass shorts, and they're not weighed down like puffy gladiators."

The only negative about the job so far, for real, was the disdainful glare of Wilson Keats. It took her a while to admit that Keats's rejection was painful, but his pathetic courses might as well have been titled "Dead White Guy Poets." His enrollments were so small that, combined, his students would have fit into Layla's only inheritance—her mom's old VW van—with loads of leg room leftover. She hadn't helped the relationship by Googling her senior colleague, finding Keats was not even his real name. It used to be Wilson Kirchplatz, a real fucking clunker. She spat out her peppermint tea in a burst of laughter when she discovered that. Kirchplatz! She didn't blame him for changing the name legally while still a grad student at Dartmouth. But then she learned the German translation for Kirchplatz was Church Place. Now that could have been a cool name for a poet. Way cool.

One day in the hallway she asked him, "Why didn't you change your name to Wilson Churchplace?"

Keats reacted like such a doofus, sniffing pompously, as though she'd teased him about his toupee. By the time Layla said, "Call yourself whatever you want," he had vanished down the hallway. Now I've done it, she thought. They'd hardly spoken since. Nobody held a grudge longer than an old pissed-off poet, especially one who was alive.

Chapter 4

On this brisk early-October morning, Layla Sillimon was prepped and ready to teach. Outside her office door was a row of students, seated in line. Here we go again, she thought. She'd sign some add slips, pose for some photos, jot down an autograph. Ten minutes, tops.

Last in line was an older dude in a football jersey. She motioned him to the front of the line because he was clearly in the wrong place. No point in making him wait. He was thick, with a white mustache that looked like a pair of toothbrush heads, and he struggled to get up. Layla feared there'd be a protest about him cutting the line, but the students seemed to understand that sometimes you had to give old people a pass. The students at Coors State protested the strangest things. Yesterday they had picketed the Chinese takeout in the student union which had begun charging for fortune cookies.

The man introduced himself as Eugene Mooney. Layla cleared off a wide spot on her couch. He glanced around for her light switch. She knew many people weren't comfortable living in natural light.

Without thinking, Layla dropped into her recliner and it fucking happened again—she went wheeling, ass over heels. She let out a whoop and landed with a thud, her feet in the air. The recliner was an extravagant gift from a fan in Sweden, and during the move from San Francisco, something had snapped in the chair's internal mechanism—a slight shift of weight would send her spinning backwards and she had to squirm and struggle to get right-side-up. Anxious about meeting somebody new, she'd forgotten the chair was broken.

"My goodness," Mooney said, "are you okay?" Then he added, "I like your shoes."

Layla's huarache sandals must have been about eye-level for him. She was already used to this—the male professors usually complimented her on her clothing. She didn't fault them because she often found herself regressing into her own social tic: acting ditzy out of nervousness, or maybe to seem less threatening to men. Now here she was, looking like a kook.

She couldn't see Mooney, but he had a warm, gentle tone. She reached out her hand and he pulled, but it didn't do much good. "Push down on the footrest," she said.

Mooney did, which uprighted her in the recliner. She thanked him, kicked off her sandals. Without thinking, she put the bottom of her bare feet against the sole of his shoes. It seemed like a good way to connect in the moment. He took his cue from her, kicked off his shoes, and soon they were barefeet-to-socks. It gave her a radiant feeling about him.

"And I like your pullover," Mooney added.

She thought he meant the recliner, or the near-backflip. A pullover? Then she remembered her top. "It's called a Baja hoodie," she said.

"I know," he said. "I teach Mexican history."

"It's honestly not even that old," Layla said, which didn't make sense, but she was rattled by the one-upmanship. Most professors hadn't tried besting her, because how many of them could say they'd been on Stephen Colbert's show? How many had gotten a personal letter from Jewel? And how many—

"I just meant I'd seen Mexican pullovers before. None as attractive as yours. No offense."

Layla thanked him. She didn't know what to make of this guy, but he sure looked silly in a football jersey. "Did you play football?" she asked.

"I'm friends with our quarterback," he said, twisting so she could see the name on the back. Knighton. "That's why I'm here."

She pulled a Sharpie from her denim shirt pocket. She'd never autographed a uniform, but she uncapped the black marker. "Stand up and turn around," she said. She should have stood first, because when he pulled away from the footrest, she whirled back in her recliner, landed with thud again, and this time she bit her tongue. It hurt like a roaring bitch.

"Oh, dear," he said, pushing the footrest back down. "Let's stay seated. I'm not here for autographs." Instead, he explained Sasha Dimitrievic's predicament.

"That's a gorgeous name," she said. "Sasha. It sounds like a breed of stallion."

"My gosh," Mooney said, "your mouth is bleeding." He handed her his handkerchief. "He's from Croatia," he added.

"I embrace all kinds of poetry," she said. "I'm not one of those English Only people. Sorry about your hanky," she added, handing it back. "Send Sasha over, we'll get him signed up."

"Great," he said. "I'll tell Sasha to stop by." Mooney pointed at her desk. "By the way, we've met before. At the football game. You're the tie-dyed woman."

"Am I?"

"You bought copies of *Hell No! We Won't Go!*" He motioned at the stack of Braverman's books.

"Oh," she said, and it clicked. "I didn't recognize you either. You're one of the popcorn men." She remembered the strange moment—a concession stand that sold books. The football mania was still new to her, but if it could be coupled with promoting books, maybe football wasn't so bad. She said as much to Mooney. "I bought a bunch," she confessed, "for Christmas gifts."

"I know the author appreciated that. Peter Braverman was the guy working with me. Thank you, Layla," he said, "and welcome to Coors State." He bent toward her feet, a humble bow. She realized he was holding the footrest down so she wouldn't flip again.

The next morning, Sasha Dimitrievic was first in line at Layla's door. He was a human oak tree, twice the size of Professor Mooney. Although he was a pleasant dude, Layla had trouble understanding him. He was witty, but often his comments were misplaced, like he'd memorized a bunch of phrases from American television and uncorked them at the wrong moment. And he rocked these blocky black glasses, like a performance artist's goofy prop.

But she could tell he was interested in poetry. When he recited poems in Croatian it made Layla a bit dreamy—such a lovely language, filled with feeling. She asked what the poems meant, but they nearly made more sense in Croatian. That was the thing about poetry: the reader decided the meaning. That's what drew Layla to poetry in the first place, the liberating lack of absolutes. Unlike Wilson Keats, she never believed you had to have a Ph.D. to enjoy a fucking poem. The reason her book had taken off was people related to the poems, not just Taylor Swift. She sat on the couch with Sasha—avoiding the Swedish recliner—and recited two of her own poems from memory.

When they were awash in the buzz of poetry recitations, Sasha commented about the curvy-lined design of the reclining chair.

"Don't sit in it," she warned. "You'll be sorry." For one thing, she thought, the chair could collapse under his weight.

"Sorry to sit?" he asked.

"It's broke," she said, and she showed him how the chair was now like a device astronauts might use to practice for zero gravity.

It weighed more than she did, but Sasha hoisted it up by the armrests. Then he held it in one hand to check underneath. His bicep bulged at this incredible feat of strength. "I find the trouble," he said. He placed the chair upside down on the carpet, squatted over it, and a minute later he pointed. "Broken lever. Spring is loose." He picked it up again and shook it to demonstrate. A thin bead of sweat appeared above his glasses.

She did hear a rattle. "Can you fix it?" she asked.

Sasha clucked twice. "Easy peasy lemon squeezy," he said. "Pretend I am not here. Go. Pretend." He shooed her to her desk, and she sat down dutifully, her back to him. She had plenty of emails to attend to and a stack of student poems.

It couldn't have been fifteen minutes later Layla turned around. The chair must have been repaired because Sasha was asleep in it. That was sweet.

A week later, Layla was in her office doing yoga. She held the Downward Dog for as long as she could before she collapsed on the carpet and rolled onto her back, dreadlocks splashing over her face. She'd been trying to incorporate yoga into her morning routine, in place of surfing news and poetry sites, as a way to deal with the stress of working with the jerk who called himself her colleague.

She wondered why Wilson Keats didn't have anything better to do than snoop around her classes. All she talked about during her job interview was helping students find their voices.

She must have said it a million fucking times, even used it as a response when it had nothing to do with the question. And now Keats was complaining about her teaching methods. She was also irritated because he must have been the one who had posted the sign near her door: Please Don't Congregate in This Hallway.

She didn't poke her head into Keats's class and yell "Boring!" because she didn't want to wake anybody. In fact, she had heard stories about Keats falling dead asleep in the middle of class.

His recent complaints stemmed from an assignment she'd given. Students were to bring in "found-poems" to class, then incorporate them into longer poems. Two students had used radio commercial jingles. Others lifted instructions from Layla's own syllabus. That was clever. One student integrated her last ten incoming text messages and spliced them together randomly into one poem. That was so cool.

The point was a poem could be generated from anything and didn't have to creep out of a coffin. The sooner a young poet learned that, the better, as far as Layla Sillimon was concerned. She suspected one student must have talked to him about her assignment, and Ol' Kirchplatz went right to her office to whine. He cautioned her about the rigors of academia, and she countered that many of her own best poems had begun with this exact exercise. Al Roker had even read one, "Why We Trippin', America?," aloud on *The Today Show*.

A lesser problem was struggling to keep track of her students, who were more interested in getting on television than immersing themselves in cool poems. Rather than ask her about her own work, influential books, or recommendations for outside reading, they wanted to know what Al Roker was really like. Or what the dressing rooms were like on Stephen Colbert's show. (The dressing rooms were wicked. Al Roker was a total sweetheart and a fantastic hugger.)

She was thinking about *The Today Show* the morning Sasha knocked again. The line was short, because of the negative karma from Wilson Keats's sign, but she expected the throngs to return when registration began for the Winter Quarter.

"I already signed your permission override," she said. "I'll see you in a few weeks."

What Sasha said next made her weepy with joy—he just wanted to talk about poetry. Imagine that. He'd even bought the most recent release of *Best American Poetry*, and he wanted recommendations. Mooney was correct about him. She motioned Sasha into the office, back to her recliner, which had been holding up just fine. She had forgotten already how to say his last name, and she asked him to repeat it slowly.

"Dah – MEAT – tree – A – vitch."

"It's such a delicious name."

"Thank you."

She said it slowly. "Dimitrievic."

"Four eyes."

"Excuse me?"

"Sasha is first name," he said.

"I remember."

"Sasha is short for Alexander. Like Alexander the Great."

"And what about Dimitrievic? Is that like huntsman or blacksmith? Warrior, maybe?"

"Son of Dimitri."

"I see," she said and motioned for him to sit. "What attracts you to a poem?"

She couldn't quite follow his answer. His family loved poetry? Or they wrote poetry? And they were very strong writers, or something. He used a Croatian metaphor about a horse. He said he loved imagery, she caught that.

"My cousin is famous Croatian poet," he said.

"Like, famous how?"

Sasha looked perplexed.

"On TV?" she suggested, smiling.

He said television was not as popular in Croatia as America. She asked him what Croatia was like.

"Almost like another country," he said.

She had to stop herself from laughing. Maybe he was being facetious.

"And getting better since the war," he went on. "Beautiful beaches. You can visit."

Now it was Layla's turn to thank him.

Sasha yawned, but she sensed he wasn't bored. Just comfortable. Last time she'd left him asleep in the recliner because she had to get to class. When she'd returned, there was no sign of him. "Do you want to sleep here again?" she asked.

Sasha didn't blush or seem the least bit embarrassed. She liked that. He was fascinated by poetry, but he didn't fuss over her, and he was one of the only students who didn't bring up her television appearances or Taylor Swift. "I've got to go to the library," she said, "but stay as long as you like. That's your chair now. Sasha's Chair, I call it."

"Maybe I wink forty times," he said, yawning.

Chapter 5

J ust four weeks into his sophomore season, Trevor Knighton was flying high. The team's Monday morning video session had evolved into a New Age confidence builder, and when the coaches turned the lights back on, he felt taller, stronger, better-looking. The game films were practically highlight reels, and the Monday sessions counted as a school-sponsored activity, so players were allowed to miss morning classes.

Afterward, all ten football secretaries teamed up with the Gender Studies Department to set up a breakfast buffet, complete with eggs cooked to order and a fresh-squeezed juice bar. Trevor and Coach Maniscalco always met privately after the meal, where they'd tweak plays, adjust offensive sets, and prepare for their next victim. Coors State was ranked in everyone's top 5 nationally and their schedule for the next few games would be less than challenging.

Trevor was fond of Maniscalco, the coach who had taken a chance recruiting him. Sasha felt the same. They showed their loyalty to their coach by tamping down any locker room detractors.

Maniscalco was a game-changer, on the field and on campus. Maniscalco introduced the university-wide policy requiring professors to get written permission from the coaches before assigning homework. Basketball quickly copied Football on this, and many teachers simply gave up, assigning the athletes no homework at all, rather than waiting for the paperwork. Maniscalco was also the brains behind the decision to stop referring to players as "student-athletes"—he insisted everyone use "athlete-students" in all printed material, press releases, and interviews.

Maniscalco had confided recently to Trevor that their head coach, Bill Anderson (who had been smartly investing his nine-million-dollar-a-year salary), had decided to retire while things were going great. Although Anderson was just fifty-five years old, he was going to announce his retirement just prior to their inevitable bowl game in December. Maniscalco was pining to be named as the next head coach before the university could run a national search.

"I'd like you to support me," Maniscalco told Trevor that morning.

"I always do," Trevor said. "Me and Sasha both, honest." He figured hiring Maniscalco was the likely scenario, anyway. The school would be foolish not to. "You think a reporter will ask me?"

But Maniscalco meant something else entirely. He wanted Trevor to go to the university president's office and insist he hire the offensive coordinator. "His name is Martin Cardly," the coach said.

"Why would this President Cardly care what I thought?" Trevor asked.

Maniscalco laughed so hard he apologized. He finally said, "You outrank him."

Now it was Trevor's turn to laugh, although his coach didn't. One hundred thousand paying fans per game, Maniscalco told him, with the average ticket price at fifty bucks, not counting the 2,000 students who camped out to get in free. "That's a policy I'm not in favor of, by the way," he said. "The students walk to the game, don't pay for parking, they smuggle in snacks? Wasted revenue." Maniscalco could get sidetracked with tiny details, but that was part of the reason he was such a genius for offense.

"Anyway," Maniscalco continued, "I know you're not Sasha, but you can do the math. Over five-million-dollars revenue per game. It takes less than two home games to pay the head football coach for the entire season."

Trevor let out a whistle. Maniscalco turned his attention to the rogue departments still resisting Football's primacy.

"Nothing is more desperate than a dying animal," Maniscalco said, "so the coaches figured we'd better squash dissent by offering some crumbs. We had to make sure you dummies stayed eligible." Selling food and drinks at the game amounted to a small percentage of the ticket revenue.

Trevor knew Maniscalco didn't mean anything by referring to the players as dummies. Football was big business, and although the players were not yet getting paid legally, the perks added up to a pretty extravagant lifestyle.

"But here's the thing," the coach said. "Only a few dozen universities make money off sports. I mean real sports, not the hobby sports like baseball and tennis. That's what keeps Coors State going. Now schools will aspire now to be us. We all know they can't be us, but it's what fuels the spending on our campus."

"Wait," Trevor said, "most colleges lose money trying to be something they can never be?"

"Exactly," said the coach. "The hobby sports are a waste. Two things ought to be done in private, and one is women's basketball. Get it?"

Trevor sat quietly for a minute. "I never knew our president's name before today," he finally admitted.

"He'll know yours, if that makes you feel better."

* * *

Trevor's timing was bad, crossing campus during the rush between classes. The shouts of encouragement were okay, but students often stopped him to pose for pictures, which provoked copycats, and Trevor got stalled in a way he never did on the field. After a half-dozen photos, he pulled his cap down over his eyes and broke into a jog.

The receptionist—an old skinny dude in a suit—seemed unsurprised to see Trevor. He mouthed a "Hello, Mister Knighton," while he covered his headset mouthpiece and held up a finger—wait one minute.

With a person on the phone still yakking, the receptionist abruptly hung up. "How can we help you today?" he asked, turning his attention to Trevor. The switchboard buzzed again, but he ignored it.

"I'm here to see President Cardy," Trevor said.

"Of course," the man said. "But it's Cardly. Let me take you upstairs."

The upstairs reception area felt familiar. Trevor soon recognized the furnishings from the old Football office—framed posters, monogrammed area rugs, and couches covered with the same style pigskin as a football. Evidently when the team upgraded, they'd sent their used furniture over to the president.

"Make yourself comfortable," the receptionist said. "Anything to drink?"

"Cranberry juice," Trevor said. That was his favorite. Football kept the locker room stocked just for him.

"I'm sorry," the man said. "What about a nice banquet-style lager from Coors?"

Trevor laughed. "I wish. We have a game this week."

"Water?"

"Bottled?"

"No."

Trevor said, "It doesn't matter."

The receptionist came back with water in a coffee cup. He shuffled a pile of papers and finally sat himself down behind the president's desk.

"Now," the man said, "how can I help you?"

Trevor figured he shouldn't be dismissed so easily, not after Maniscalco had claimed how simple it would be to get into the administrator's office. He measured his words and spoke kindly so as not to hurt the man's feelings. "I'd prefer to wait and discuss the matter with President Cardly," he said.

"That's me," the man said.

"Pardon?"

"I am the president. Martin Cardly."

Trevor sprung to his feet and apologized.

"Oh, sit, sit," the president said.

"I thought you were the receptionist," Trevor said.

"I am," the president said. "Budget issues mean many of us wear more than one hat these days." Cardly reached to adjust a hat that wasn't on his head, then pushed over what remained of his wispy white hair. Classical music floated in from an open window.

If this Cardly guy was fielding phone calls and fetching drinks, maybe he wouldn't be making important decisions like hand-picking the next coach. Finally, Trevor forced himself to say he'd come to endorse Tom Maniscalco.

"Oh, yes," the president said. "Coach Anderson is planning to retire." Cardly scribbled. "Okay, Maniscalco. New coach. Got it. Anything else?"

Anything else? Wasn't Coors State's next coach important enough to warrant a lengthy discussion? "Don't you want to know why, President Cardly?" Trevor asked.

"I'm sure you have your reasons. Good ones, I bet. Call me Marty."

"For one thing, he's the best qualified," Trevor started. That wasn't at all the opening he'd rehearsed. He'd planned to talk about innovative offensive schemes and move on to Maniscalco's rapport with their best players.

"Fine and dandy," Cardly said. "I'll announce it in a couple of days. I would do it sooner, but I have to write my own press releases."

Trevor resisted the urge to rise to his feet. Cardly might be fibbing. Announce it in a couple of days? For real?

"Now, if you'll just stand here," Cardly said, pulling out his phone to take a photo. Cardly fumbled with the timer. "My family simply won't believe you were here." He coaxed Trevor into a staged handshake and grinned. The camera blinked its countdown.

Chapter 6

One day that September, Braverman burst into Mooney's office and began waggling *Rocky Mountain High*, the school newspaper, in his face. When Mooney reached for it, Braverman changed tactics, using it to whack him on the shoulder. Mooney finally tore the newspaper away to stop the flogging and read the headline. The Philosophy Department had been shut down.

"We've got to fight fire with fire," Braverman said.

"Listen," Mooney said. "You used to disparage Philosophy as a bunch of passive navel-gazers. By the way, have you ever noticed firemen never fight fire with fire?"

"I'm a man of my word," Braverman said. "You heard my sworn oath after the fascists stole my Volvo. You have to choose a side. Aren't you tired of selling out, Eugene?" Braverman jerked the newspaper back out of Mooney's hands, as if waving it in his fist again bolstered his argument. "An out-of-control power structure sparked all those student protests in the 1960s," he went on. "When our revolution is over, Football will be finished."

Mooney sighed. Philosophy employed just five professors, fewer than anyone but Poetry. Philosophy had never taken on any duties because what could they do, practically speaking, for a football team? They would have been more helpful to fishermen in the Philippines, and now they were gone, just like the English Department. Well, actually, more gone. You could observe what was left of English—four professors who refused to leave campus even after being fired—in their forlorn tent city on the east lawn every day. They called it The Hamlet.

Braverman shook his head in disgust, as if Mooney had dropped an easy pass.

"Oh, don't look at me like that," Mooney said.

"Like what?"

"Like I'm supposed to do something."

"You said it, not me, Eugene. You're the only full professor in History. I'm still untenured after twenty years."

"That's what we should be concerned with," Mooney said. "Not Philosophy or Football, but your own future. You should be laying low now, not calling attention to your situation."

Braverman was at a crossroads. In the spring, he was due to learn whether he had achieved his bid for tenure—and a lifetime of job security. Since the rebranding, the faculty was unclear on how tenure would be determined. But if Football turned down Braverman's tenure application, he'd have a one-year grace period before he got dumped, his career as an academic over.

Of course, Braverman should have applied for tenure years earlier, but the problem had been his publishing record. Instead of publishing a book, as expected, he'd figured out a loophole. In 2003, when the school implemented an online system for tenure review, Braverman had shown Mooney a glitch. If he didn't fill in an Ending Date, his tenure application would never come due. In this way, he had flown under the radar for over a decade, until he was flagged last spring. He constantly raged about bureaucracy, but he could sure game the system when it was advantageous.

By midsummer, with the university forcing his hand, he'd self-published his first book. *Hell No! We Won't Go!* (PublishYou) was an oral history of draft card burning in the Vietnam War era. Nobody knew if Football would accept a self-published book for tenure. Most universities would not. Also, Braverman didn't exactly write the book so much as type it, transcribing four lengthy interviews, then slapping on an introduction. When he got tired of typing, he had switched to voice-activated technology. He didn't spend much time editing, so some laughable mistakes made it into print. One chapter was supposed to be titled "A Bad Omen," but came out as "A Bad Almond."

"I'll be fine," Braverman said nonchalantly. "I'm a survivor. I'll figure something out."

But Mooney knew his friend might be in real trouble. In 2012, Braverman had invested all his savings, and even borrowed against his retirement, to start a new recreational marijuana business. Although the industry thrived, somehow Braverman's partners did not, and he lost everything. He simply wasn't in a position to lose his job, too.

But if Braverman wasn't awarded tenure, he wouldn't be the first History prof to disappear. They'd lost nearly half their faculty, and the rebranding had damaged their younger colleagues' chances to find decent jobs. Still, they left in droves, either getting out of education altogether or taking less prestigious community college jobs. The exodus so far had reached nine professors; Braverman could be number ten. Those who remained were mostly loyalists who accepted the changes at Coors as the new normal. Like removing your shoes at airport security checkpoints.

"We have to be smart about this," Mooney said. "People like our popcorn. It's all over Facebook today."

"You've been saying we've got to be smart for a long time."

"And you think what?" Mooney said. "That we march into the Football office, take over the building, like our older brothers in the 1960s? Start a coup and assume the role of president?"

"Hell, yes," Braverman said, and he rose to his feet as if challenged to a fight.

Mooney took a deep breath. "My point is," he said, "we can't overreact."

"Another of your pet sayings," Braverman said. "You haven't overreacted ever. Remember the Doomsday meeting?"

A year ago, the Doomsday meeting—Braverman's name—took place in the History Department. On that fateful afternoon, they learned that everything would be worse than first imagined. The Coors conglomerate's contract, it was announced, had vital provisions besides naming rights. The billion dollars was to benefit only football and men's basketball. And there was more—the university president was cutting all funding for academics in twelve months. Other than minimum-wage salaries, nobody on the academic side would get another dollar from the administration. All staff and most of the secretaries would get dumped. There would be no money for research, travel grants, or test tubes.

That was when Braverman elbowed Mooney, leaned close, and said, "I'm out of here."

Mooney knew they were too old to get hired as professors at another college, but too young to retire. "We can't leave," Mooney whispered back.

"You mean we're screwed," Braverman said, loud enough that his colleagues turned toward him, and the room grew quiet.

The school's diminutive president, Martin Cardly, caught surprisingly little heat, even from the faculty, for brokering the deal with Coors. The pioneering Cardly had also separated their two moneymaking teams from the rest of the Athletics

Department, and minor sports—including all the women's teams—were reduced to glorified intramurals. The board of regents was delighted to be suddenly in the black. The name change sent ripples through the national media for two days, then it never came up again.

The teary-eyed department chair had ignored Braverman as usual. She explained how every department had a probationary period to become fiscally solvent by providing a service to Football and Basketball. They could set up a cash-based business at the games. Or they could negotiate with the revenue sports for services performed yearlong, be classified as "contract labor." Once a department's proposal got clearance from the coaches, they'd use whatever skills their professors might provide. Naturally, incomes would vary.

Mooney figured out that there was also a third option. They could get "disappeared." He didn't want that, so he took the lead, standing to speak in his usual calm and measured voice.

"Let's prepare, do our research," Mooney said, "consider our options, and figure out how to flourish like Chemistry." Just after the rebranding, Chemistry had gotten special permission to set up one tented tavern to sell their homemade microbrews on game days. Coors didn't mind, and Chemistry became the first department to demonstrate the necessary survival skills.

Just as Mooney took his seat to modest applause, Braverman stood, not to second Mooney, but to deliver a blistering tirade about the leap to big-time athletics. He didn't get far before several of their history colleagues shouted him down with free market platitudes, a rhetorical gang tackle. When Braverman sat, his legs were quivering.

An hour later, however, the History Department still couldn't come to a consensus, and they missed the next-day deadline for a proposal. Mooney feared the worst. Nobody anticipated a fourth option. Their contract-labor task had been chosen for them—bathroom duty cleanup at games for minimum wage, although they were encouraged to put out tip jars.

"The Doomsday meeting was ugly," Mooney admitted, "but we have to solve this puzzle. And why would I overreact when I've got you, my best friend, to do it for me? Listen, we can't simply go Che Guevara here. Think about the history of progressive movements."

"Right. Martin Luther King took a bullet in the neck."

Mooney gasped. He loved Martin Luther King Jr. Braverman knew invoking King's name in anything but glowing terms was hitting below the belt. Only the Mexican revolutionary Emiliano Zapata held the same place in Mooney's heart.

"Sorry," Braverman said. "You keep saying we need to out-smart athletics. But we have no choice."

"That's not a tangible argument: We have no choice. It's just an expression of your frustration. I need you to say, we have no choice but to do something-or-other. What's our plan? Have you done your research? And let me make it clear yet again. Ol' Eugene Mooney here is on your side, Comrade. I agree with you, athletics is a monster. But what's the best way to change the system?"

"Not by wearing that ridiculous Trevor Knighton jersey. I'm starting the revolution without you if you don't get changed."

Mooney felt his face get hot. This was the thing about Braverman, he would push, push, and push. That was exactly the mindset that ruined the anti-war movement in America during the early 1970s. Mooney knew all about overzealousness and how it could derail a worthy cause. The Vietnam War was over by the time he was sixteen, but the next year, when he attempted to support a radical movement at his high school in Chicago, things had backfired badly. He'd never shared the story with Braverman. He hoped he never would.

They hadn't known each other in college. When Mooney was at Swarthmore, Braverman attended Cal-Berkeley. Mooney had heard his stories, how Braverman, while he was still in high school, had once talked politics for hours with Mark Rudd of the Weather Underground. He'd briefly been the driver for Patty Hearst. Braverman could boast of a long history of radicalism, fueled by youthful indoctrination.

"When our young colleagues see you on campus," Braverman went on, "in a number 10 football jersey, what do you suppose they think?"

"I would hope they'd give me credit—"

"No credit," Braverman yelled. "No credit. They think you're shilling for athletics. What else would they think?"

"Trevor Knighton is just one kid, and he's my former student. By the way, his mother is Hispanic, and his father is African American," Mooney said, hoping to change the narrative.

"Really? Trevor also happens to be the best quarterback in school history. That's what *Rocky Mountain High* said."

"You're reading the sports page now?"

"Do you know what his percentage is on third-down conversions? It's amazing."

Mooney thought he was being sarcastic, but there was a sense of awe in Braverman's voice. "Okay, Peter, here's what I think it means when I wear Trevor's jersey. I call it reaching out, not selling out, reaching across the divide. Trevor Knighton used to act like a drunken frat boy. By the end of his first year in college, partly because I showed an interest in him, he requested outside reading. A student asking for more books? Who was the last kid to do that with you? Grateful Dead bootleg tapes don't count." Mooney was joking, but he instantly regretted saying it. He didn't want Braverman to think the jab was retribution for the Martin Luther King comment.

Braverman's "Dark Star Club" was a sensitive topic. He'd formed it on campus for Deadheads six years after Jerry Garcia died. The members were supposed to exchange concert tapes, but Braverman was the only person who owned any and he wound up being a sort of loaning library. By 2008, the club was just Braverman and a divorced, over-pierced forty-year-old woman, an undergrad who went by Luna. He had fallen hard for Luna and keeping the club going was probably only a vehicle to hang with her. A year later, she left school without warning, didn't even give Braverman a chance to say goodbye to her eight-year-old boy, with whom he was also enamored. He'd hardly dated since, and the Dark Star Club faded away. Dating a student was off limits, divorced-with-a-son or not. Although nobody in the History Department ever mentioned it, one of them might still use it against Braverman in his belated push for tenure. Professors could stash away their grudges for years, like bottles of wine.

"I don't listen to the Dead much these days," Braverman said, "and let's stay on topic. How is being a toady to Trevor helping our cause?"

Mooney needed to distract Braverman. Like a playful baby pit bull, his friend would not let go of his pant leg unless something sparkly got his attention. Mooney scanned his office. "Oh," he said, "I got you a book of poems. Here."

Braverman held the book at arm's length, one eyebrow arched.

"The author is a new professor on campus," Mooney added.

Braverman crinkled up his face. "*Self-Portrait in a Funhouse*

Mirror. That's the title? What would possess you to buy this for me?"

"Because the author bought five of your books. Remember?"

Braverman flipped it over to check out the author's photo.

"Her," he said. "The tie-dyed woman from the football game is a poet?"

"I met her earlier in the week."

"Why?" Braverman said. "How?"

Mooney stopped himself. If he said, *I'm trying to help Trevor Knighton's roommate find an easy class,* he'd get blasted again. He felt a rush of guilt. Maybe Braverman was right. Maybe he was kowtowing too much to Football. "It's a long story. I just thought you'd like the poems," he said, hoping that would satisfy Braverman. Fat chance.

"She liked *Hell No, We Won't Go?*"

"She didn't say."

"You didn't ask," Braverman said.

"Your books were front and center on her desk. She's going to give them as Christmas gifts. I'm sure she'll keep one for herself."

"Naturally she would."

"I'll take you to meet her," Mooney said offhandedly.

Braverman sat up straight, like a dog hearing the jangling of his leash.

"Not now," Mooney said, and Braverman immediately began to sulk. Mooney relented. "Okay, how about Wednesday at noon?"

Chapter 7

The following Wednesday, at 11:52 a.m., Braverman walked into Mooney's office without knocking—another annoying habit of his—wearing a sport coat.

"Ready when you are," Braverman said. "No hurry." His hair was neatly combed for once, tucked behind his ears, and for the first time in a week, he was not decked out in a track suit. Rather than spend money he didn't have to recover or replace his towed Volvo, Braverman was running everywhere he went.

"New sport coat?" Mooney asked.

Braverman said, "I got it twenty-five years ago. Layla knows we're coming?" He had all the restraint of a caged grizzly at feeding time.

"I emailed her and said it will be great to see her again."

"You'll slip away after she and I get to talking?"

"Absolutely not."

"Figure she's read my book yet?"

"I doubt it." Mooney knew *Hell No! We Won't Go!* wasn't the kind of book that would impress a poet. He shut down his computer, slipped on his windbreaker, fiddled with the zipper, then looked up. "You're wearing cologne."

"Brave Dragon."

"I've never smelled cologne on you before."

"Is it that strong?" Braverman had burned out his sense of smell after decades of smoking. Smoking anything.

"Use patchouli next time."

"Good idea."

"I was joking," Mooney said, and off they went.

Halfway to Layla's office, Braverman stopped suddenly and pointed. "Do we have to walk past that?"

An enormous Coors-themed pub had popped up where the bookstore once stood. This new student hangout, with forty flatscreen TVs, was known to be lax checking IDs. Giveaway nights with backpacks, bookbags, and beer cozies were popular. Mooney had heard that more pubs were in the planning stages. Coors State had recently been ranked one of America's top party schools. As student enrollments mushroomed, so did class sizes, putting more stress on the remaining professors.

They took a sharp turn to avoid passing the pub, with Braverman rabbiting the pace. Mooney gave a hard tug on Braverman's sleeve when they got to The Hamlet.

The four remaining English professors had made a pledge, a decision, after dismissing Football's bathroom duty offers just a month ago. They'd folded up their metaphorical tents and pitched real ones, inspired by the Occupy Wall Street movement.

Mooney thought the name was a smart choice. One of four remaining professors was a Shakespeare scholar, and they'd all been smart enough not to resign—they planned to collect unemployment, but that wouldn't last long. Two of the professors, the men, had sold their homes; the women professors were a couple who'd renounced the comforts of condo living. The quartet set up camp in the grass below President Cardly's window. The Hamlet also served as a base of operations for letters, tweets, emails, and meetings. Despite the continued online onslaught, it hadn't been mentioned in the news. Most of the university ignored The Hamlet.

Three of the English profs practically lived for committee work, couldn't shake the bureaucratic mentality. That August, the women had told Mooney they had come up with a plan to push back against big-time athletics. It involved four committees, and each prof chaired one: Planning, Outreach, Outcomes, and Advisory. But to plan, reach out, analyze outcomes, and advise what exactly? Perhaps it didn't matter; most of their time was taken up with meetings. Even Mooney, a believer in protocol, found English perplexing.

English had made small progress, though. Their Outreach Committee had contacted the Music Department, and two weeks ago, a group of grad student musicians began holding their daily baroque quartet practice in front of the tents. The music inspired the English professors to read aloud from Charles Dickens's *A Tale of Two Cities*. Mooney thought that was a wise move, reading from a novel about the French Revolution. It was an example, English insisted, of how committee work could really pay off. Often as many as six or seven students gathered to eat their lunch and listen.

Mooney preferred to pay his respects by observing the tent city from a safe distance. He'd already grown weary of how depressing it could be to talk to the occupants. Today, as Mooney and Braverman approached, the musicians were setting up their chairs for another go.

"Maybe Philosophy will join The Hamlet," Mooney said. "A show of force. I heard a rumor Philosophy wants to, but they insist on input in renaming the place. They want to share the identity, and English is hesitant. They're both going to form a committee to—"

"Committee?" Braverman scoffed. "Committee? With nine professors who don't even work for Coors State?"

Maybe Braverman was right. Or, rather, righter than Mooney was ready to admit. What sense did it make to follow university protocol if you've been effectively fired?

Philosophy's situation, however, was different from English's. Philosophy's professors had been arrested outside the stadium. And, they admitted on the spot, to selling pirated T-shirts. But that left a lot of unanswered questions, not the least of which was why did Criminal Justice take one Philosopher away in handcuffs and keep him overnight when he'd already confessed? There were some disturbing rumors about waterboarding, but surely that couldn't be right.

"That's exactly what's fucked up," Braverman said. "Can't English just do something real, instead of ad hoc committees, data analysis, and Dickens readings to chamber music?"

Mooney nodded, but he wasn't certain he agreed. The French Revolution was a great event for world democracy, so how could he fault English for reverting to democratic methods? And their colorful tents were certainly eye-catching. He had always been interested in human endurance, especially in the face of injustice, and here was The Hamlet, pointless and rudderless, but flourishing in a strange sense. He had to give them credit, even if Braverman would not. But was it a meaningful symbolic gesture, the tent city, if nobody paid attention?

"I guess to me it's still a powerful place," Mooney said, but he could hear the lack of conviction in his own voice, as if he were reading from a dated department memo.

The musicians were tuning up. One English prof, not twenty yards away, held out a steaming cup of tea, an invitation. Mooney waved her off and bowed gracefully, a "thanks, anyway." Strange how he admired their courage but worried about being seen with them.

"Sometimes I wish I could join them," Mooney confessed without thinking.

"Oh, come off it," Braverman said. "Aren't you on enough committees? Their unemployment benefits will run out, then what? And I've already asked you to join a fight, a better one. A real fight. You have no sense of how to make history."

"You have no sense."

"I'm glad Rosa Parks didn't listen to people like you," Braverman said.

"Rosa Parks had a plan. She wasn't acting alone, that's just how she appeared on the bus. She'd undergone extensive training." Mooney couldn't remember who was backing her in Montgomery, Alabama. Southern Baptists? SNCC? He'd look it up later. He'd wanted to name his first child—the one he never had—Rosa Parks Mooney.

The violin began to play, and the cello joined in on a soothing waltz. In that moment, Mooney had a revelation. That's what they needed at Coors State University, their own Rosa Parks. Braverman, was right, sort of, despite his guerilla-in-a-china-shop manner.

"When Martin Cardly and the coaches decide Mexican history and the Vietnam War are passé," Braverman said, pointing past the tents, "we'll be camped just over there."

"Will not," Mooney said. He didn't have the energy to keep formulating an argument. He was thinking about Rosa Parks.

"Will too," Braverman said.

"Will not."

"Will too."

"Will not."

Yes, Rosa Parks.

Mooney closed his eyes and imagined the bus with Rosa Parks coming to a stop right there. He and Braverman were standing on the sidewalks of Montgomery, under a canopy, out of the harsh sun. Mooney saw the bus driver hoist himself up, order Rosa out of that seat—it was for white folks. Braverman nudged Mooney, knowing what was next, and they looked on in horror and awe. The driver radioed the incident in, and minutes later two police cars pulled up. Mooney retreated from the wail of the sirens, stepping back until he bumped into the window of a diner. There was a sign in the window: Whites and Coaches Only. One cop had a nightstick in his right hand, Rosa Parks's collar in his left. Before they shoved her into the back of the squad car, she studied Mooney and Braverman for what seemed like a full minute. Unlike the Silver Bullets, Rosa Parks didn't need to perform a dance in the end zone after her game-changing move. Just standing there, in the grip of authority, she was full of grace, righteousness, and dignity. Just as Mooney raised a hand to salute, Rosa Parks winked at them.

"Who the hell are you saluting?" Braverman said. "The Hamlet?"

"I was just thinking," Mooney said, embarrassed. He'd never before had a daydream as vivid.

"Layla is waiting, let's go," Braverman said, but stopped. "Careful," he added, "you're going to get knocked for a loss here."

Briskly approaching from behind Mooney were a half-dozen football players, yukking it up, slapping backs. One barked repeatedly like a rabid dog. As they came closer, Mooney realized Trevor Knighton was in the middle. Of course—he was the quarterback. Where else would he be? This would be a good time to prove to Braverman the players were not all mindless louts.

"Rock and roll," one of them shouted at the musicians, and he mimicked a drummer, waggling his head and crashing the cymbals.

"Hiya, Trevor," Mooney called, raising a finger as the players passed. "I want you to meet my best friend, if you have a moment."

The pack didn't slow or stop their chatter, and Trevor hesitated—Mooney was pretty sure. But the quarterback kept up the pace, leaving Mooney looking like a fool with his arm in the air again.

"What gives?" Braverman asked. "You sure that was Trevor?"

"I thought he saw me."

"Why would he be so rude?" asked Braverman, with a hint of hurt in his voice.

These little pockets of tenderness were what endeared Braverman to Mooney. Just when you thought here comes another radical rant, he'd sound gentle and wounded. Mooney once again wondered if Braverman's aggression was all an act.

Braverman flopped a hand onto the back of his friend's neck and squeezed. "Don't worry about it, Eugene," he said.

Mooney's chest filled with a profound sadness. "Maybe Trevor was late," he said. "More likely it was peer pressure, which can quickly manifest itself in a mob setting. Even a star athlete is susceptible, I suppose."

"Forget it," Braverman said, "we've got a woman waiting." But their energy had dissipated, and they wandered into the English building like lost children.

No one was in line outside Layla Sillimon's door, but Mooney hesitated before he knocked. He feared another flare-up from Braverman and wondered if he should remind him yet again to keep calm.

Over the last year, Braverman's outbursts had become increasingly embarrassing. Last winter he'd erupted in anger at the basketball game's halftime ceremony—Criminal Justice Honor Roll students had dropped down on ropes from the rafters, military style, like academic ninjas, a ritual they repeated every few games. Braverman stomped up the steps cursing about fascism until Mooney finally caught up with him and convinced him to stay. Mooney hated macho gung-ho show-off stuff, too, but little benefit would come from a knee-jerk reactionary protest.

At Layla's door, he said, "Let me take the lead," and tapped twice. No response. "We'll leave a note and come back," he said, relieved.

Braverman was not as easily dissuaded. He hammered at the door with the meat of his fist.

"Raaajjjj." It sounded like a lawnmower struggling to start inside the office. The men looked at each other and shrugged. Braverman reached for the doorknob, despite Mooney's protest. Inside, Sasha Dimitrievic was passed out in Layla's recliner, head tossed back, his mouth wide open.

"Shhhh," Mooney said. "He's asleep."

"Who?"

"One of our football players."

"Obviously. He's as big as a Buick."

"His name is Sasha Dimitrievic. He's from Croatia."

As if on cue, Sasha's eyes opened. "Up and at 'em," he mumbled.

"Good morning," Mooney said.

Through a yawn, Sasha said, "I am sleeping with the professor in her office."

"My God," Braverman said. "Let's go back, Eugene."

"But she's not even your teacher until next semester," Mooney stammered, and he barred his arm to keep Braverman in place.

"Clearly he's going for extra credit," Braverman said. "There's no limit to how our faculty bows down to Football."

"No line to get in today," Sasha said, waving them inside.

Mooney raised a palm to his pal and whispered, "Relax, Peter. Sasha's still getting a grip on his English."

"More like a grip on his teacher."

Mooney thought for a moment. "Sasha, I'll bet you mean you're taking a nap in Layla's office. Is that it?"

Sasha spread his arms in another yawn. "No shit, Sherlock," he said.

"See, Peter?" Mooney said. "She's safe."

"Sure, we've got Hercules here guarding her gate, so to speak."

Mooney slapped Braverman on the back and told him to cool it.

Sasha raised his eyebrows. "Hercules? Son of Zeus. Thank you. You are funny fellow." He flexed his biceps in the midst of another yawn. Mooney thought he heard the player's T-shirt tear under the strain. Sasha shifted the recliner upright.

"Where is Miss Sillimon now?" Mooney asked.

"She comes back," Sasha said.

"We'll wait with you, if you don't mind."

Sasha pointed to the couch. "Pull up a chair."

Mooney gave Braverman a brief introduction—Sasha was a math and science whiz, but he was more interested in poetry. Layla was to teach the Croatian next quarter and mentor him.

"Right," Braverman said. "We have to help Football. Of course." To Sasha, he said, "What exactly is the political situation in Croatia these days?"

Mooney groaned. Everything was a test with Braverman, and asking difficult questions about politics was one way he administered this test. A week earlier, he'd harangued a waitress, pressuring her to start a workers' union in the cupcake shop near campus. She turned out to be the owner's daughter. Braverman's question now would prove Sasha was a boob, just another dumb jock. In this case, Mooney thought, it simply wasn't fair. How many kids could explain the political situation anywhere, and how many could do it in their second language?

Sasha considered the question for a moment, and he expressed a surprisingly nuanced view of what had unfolded after the old republic of Yugoslavia had split. His grammar was messy, but once you got used to his pacing and syntax he was pretty clear. He condemned Milosevic, but bemoaned the atrocities on both sides, the human face of a war that haunted the place years later. Sasha said what really rankled him was torture, and occasionally he had sleepless nights thinking about it. He described the lack of trust, the lingering suspicion. He'd lost an uncle and three cousins near Zagreb, an entire family wiped out. His English seemed to be improving, even as he spoke. When he finally finished, Mooney crossed his arms at Braverman as if he'd just beaten him in a game of chess.

Just then, Layla walked in with a backpack full of books. "Oh, a party," she said. "Did you make popcorn?"

Mooney was concerned she was mocking them, that they were known around the university for their concessions. Layla sat on her desk and switched on a lamp. "Somebody's wearing too much cologne," she said.

"This is my friend Peter Braverman, the gentleman who wrote that book you bought," Mooney said. "The five books."

Braverman stood and bowed like an English gentleman.

"I took a book home last night," she said.

"Well?" Braverman asked.

Sasha interrupted. "You write poetry, too?"

"You could say that," Braverman said.

"I loved your introduction," Layla said.

"I wrote that part," Braverman said.

"The voices are heartbreaking," Layla said, "I finished the first three chapters. War is such a terrible thing. Even if you didn't go and burn your draft card."

"Agreed," said Braverman. "It's about the horrors of war for the people who didn't fight."

Mooney could already hear Braverman on the walk back to History saying, *Layla and I have a lot in common. Neither of us fought in Nam, but we are both—.*

"Sasha knows more about war than we could ever learn from books, though," Layla said. "It's dreadful."

Braverman shifted and coughed.

"But you know," she continued, "most of our soldiers had admirable reasons for going to Vietnam."

Mooney cringed. A legit reason to murder Vietnamese peasants? He could keep quiet in a social setting after a comment like that, but Braverman couldn't. No way. Mooney searched the office and pointed at a poster on her wall. "Hey, is that a Miro? No, it's Matisse, right?"

Braverman was sniffling, the way he did before he went on a rant. "I suppose," he said, "that's true, our guys were only doing their duty."

Mooney was flabbergasted. Duty? He'd never seen Braverman surrender, certainly not about Vietnam. He'd needle him later. Or wait. Maybe it'd be best to let it slide. If he were to criticize Braverman, the old radical might never compromise again. Layla smiled, and something about that smile made Mooney realize that she was older than he'd first guessed. She was maybe forty. Born after the war ended.

"Hey," Layla said, "maybe Sasha would like to take one of Professor Braverman's classes, too. Sasha, have you heard of Vietnam?"

"They'd be difficult for a non-native speaker," Braverman said.

"In fact, here's an early Christmas present." She frisbeed a copy of *Hell No! We Won't Go!* to Sasha.

Sasha flipped the book over, noticed the author's photo and held it up next to Braverman's face. "Famous writer, yes," he said. "John Hancock, please," and handed it over.

Layla passed the remaining three books over. "Sign all these, okay?"

Now she's done it, Mooney thought. Nothing would give Braverman's ego a bigger boost than signing copies of his own book.

They hustled across campus back to History. Mooney took great satisfaction in truly connecting with a student, football star or not. While Sasha Dimitrievic probably wouldn't be enrolling in his Mexican history classes, Mooney still felt like he'd done a good deed. Layla had let Sasha enroll in her poetry workshop, and Sasha had been, in a word, inspiring.

Braverman was practically skipping.

"It's little moments like that," Mooney said, "which keep me returning to campus each day with hope, despite athletics."

"Agreed," Braverman said. "A productive meeting."

"And there are plenty more fascinating people on campus, if we only had the time to uncover them all."

"I doubt that. What an interesting person, though," Braverman said, swerving onto a different walkway than they'd taken before. Mooney was relieved. He wanted to avoid the new Coors-themed pub, but also The Hamlet. The tents would be too disheartening when both men were so upbeat. When was the last time both of them had gushed about the same student?

"Sasha is quite interesting," Mooney agreed.

Braverman laughed. "Not Sasha. I meant Layla. Wow. She's got it all, Eugene. What a woman. And very generous of you not to keep her to yourself."

"I'm afraid I wouldn't get to make that choice," Mooney said, embarrassed he'd misread his friend's reaction. Divorced-guy talk occasionally seeped into their conversations, sparked by a pretty waitress or a new professor. They were closing in on sixty, and it was Braverman who was always more interested in giving women another go-round. "She's older than I first thought," Mooney said. "I bet she's just a bit under forty."

Braverman said. "People under forty wouldn't know the first thing about Vietnam. She knew plenty."

"Indeed," Mooney said. "And she had a very mature view on why our soldiers, on a personal level, fought in Vietnam." He was just tossing that out, not necessarily goading Braverman.

"That's right," Braverman said. "They say the mark of intelligence is when a man can hold conflicting views in his head simultaneously."

"What about a woman?"

"You know what I mean," Braverman said.

"I'm prompting you to say exactly what you mean."

Braverman stopped to face him. "Here's exactly what I mean, Eugene. I feel like I'm stoned. Stoned on Layla." He strummed an imaginary guitar sang "Layla," and twanged out the lead from the 1970s' Eric Clapton song. "I bet she was named after the song came out. How old would that make her?"

"It would make you old enough to be her father, and that's a healthier way for you to think about her. Look, I wasn't trying to find you a romantic partner. I merely thought you'd enjoy meeting—"

"An interesting person."

"Yes," Mooney said.

"You're saying I should keep the horse in front of the cart," Braverman said.

"Something like that. Let's get a coffee."

Waiting for their orders, the post-Layla glow wore off, and Braverman began bitching again about the new Coors-themed pub. That's when Mooney noticed a copy of *Business Week* on a table. The cover featured their own President Cardly as one of their "Top Ten Innovators to Watch."

Braverman snatched it away from Mooney and read the article aloud, his voice charged with sarcasm. It predicted their school would one day be known as the trailblazer in an impending national trend. Large state schools would soon imitate Coors State and stop pretending academics and athletics were equals. The piece went on to say the sale of a university's naming rights wasn't the shocker that fussy academics claimed it was—football had long ago taken over at plenty of American universities.

Braverman looked up from the magazine. "California, Arizona, and Wisconsin all cut faculty salaries and forced furloughs. While the coaches made millions, they closed entire departments," he added, as if this was all Mooney's fault. One school president in the Midwest had been fired for suggesting downsizing athletics. He began reading again even as Mooney shushed him, and when he finished, he flung the magazine at the trash barrel. He missed badly. That's when Mooney realized the current issue of *Business Week* was on every table in the café, and probably all over campus.

Braverman picked up another *Business Week* and lofted that one, too. This one banked in off the back counter, and he raised both arms to signal a three-pointer. "We're going to need to jumpstart this thing," he said. "I've been thinking. You tell me, Eugene. What sparked our important political change in this country?"

"A police beatdown," Mooney said, "in the case of Rodney King in Los Angeles. More recently, there's George Floyd. Or else, like in 1968, an assassination? Of course, the modern American labor movement began with speeches at Haymarket Square in Chicago. That might be the best example for us to examine because my father used to say—"

"Okay, now what followed each of your aforementioned events?"

"An ugly riot," Mooney said, "and now you're scaring me. A riot? Certainly Martin Luther King wouldn't have condoned the unrest after his death. Even Rodney King appealed for calm. And regardless of my views on nonviolence, I hardly think our campus is the kind of place that could foment a riot, if that's what you have in mind. Unless they closed that new pub, that might really upset people."

"I'll come up with something," Braverman said.

Chapter 8

The farther Trevor Knighton got from the president's office, the more confused he felt. Yes, he'd named the next coach, a ten-million-dollar-a-year position. But he also got the feeling he could have ordered President Cardly to stand on one leg or bark like a dog. Cardly had chameleoned from receptionist to a balding president to a cowering magic genie granting wishes in a matter of minutes—all because Trevor asked him to.

"You're the reason why the History Department even exists," Maniscalco said, moments after Trevor had returned. Maniscalco had been furious with English over the "C" Sasha had received in Intro to Composition, which led to the department's closing. Sasha had been so stressed by the bad grade he'd lost twenty pounds the previous April, and that was worse than a "C" because he was an important part of their so-called Great Wall that protected the quarterback.

Maniscalco must have sensed his confusion. "We had to punish English, show them who was in charge," he said. He explained how Football took the concession stands away, had them pegged to clean toilets. They refused, English was sacked, except for Poetry. "Can you imagine the nerve, giving an all-conference lineman anything less than a top grade?"

Trevor said, "But what does Sasha's 'C' have to do with me and History?"

"Who do you think is selling refreshments at our games?"

Trevor looked at him blankly. How would he know? It wasn't like he was strolling the concourse for Cokes between quarters.

"The History Department," the coach said, "because of the kindness one professor showed you."

"You know Mooney?"

"Not formally, but you gave me good reports about him, and I awarded him and his department popcorn duties. And it's pretty good popcorn, too. You've got a lot more stroke around here than you think, son."

Trevor realized his mouth was open. He closed it.

"I remember saying to you," the coach continued, "don't take Mexican history. We had better choices, sure things."

"So, because of Mooney—?"

"The truth is, I can never remember his name. I think of him as Professor Walrus, with that mustache."

"Oh," Trevor said. "But does Mooney know why?"

"Nobody told him," Maniscalco said, "that's not our style. But he'd be a bit of a dreamer if he didn't understand."

"He's a nice guy," Trevor said.

"His buddy needs his ass kicked," Maniscalco said, "that long-haired loudmouth. Stay away from him."

That ended their talk. Trevor had wondered about taking another Mooney class, maybe even majoring in History. Unlike Sasha, he wasn't in a hurry to decide.

But wait. Had Mooney set him up?

Had Mooney been nice to him only because he was the quarterback, thinking there'd be a payoff? Suddenly Trevor felt paranoid, like the four times he had smoked bud. He wasn't yet a star when Mooney took an interest. Maybe his professor thought Trevor was headed for greatness. Maybe Mooney had spoken to a football coach. How else would a history teacher know which players had the most potential? The coaches probably initiated the call to Mooney because of school rules. A coach could call a professor, harangue him for a better grade, but professors could no longer call coaches because too many of them groveled for tickets.

What bugged Trevor was maybe, just maybe, Mooney had not been sincere, had been plotting to steal the concession stand from English if that was even possible. Maybe Mooney was just a crafty opportunist. In sports you took advantage of weakness, but should a history teacher use a young quarterback? Countless campus co-eds were attracted to Trevor because he played football. Maybe that had been happening with his teachers, too.

Trevor dropped onto a bench. His new Silverado pickup truck was back at the apartment because he never saw the point of driving a half mile, although most of the players did exactly that. He wasn't even sure any more why the coaches felt he needed a brand-new one. Besides, he liked his own truck better, which his father had bought for him when he turned sixteen. He didn't have to worry about spilling ketchup inside that one, which was sitting in their garage back in Dallas. While leaning back on the bench, Trevor saw some players leave the Football cafeteria, and he fell into line with them, cutting up and laughing, looking around for Sasha.

In the middle of their clowning, he noticed Mooney with another guy near those tent city nutjobs. "Ain't that your boy?" one of the players said, nudging Trevor, and it was obvious he meant Mooney. With all the stuff Maniscalco said spinning around in his brain, Trevor needed time to sort things out, so he pretended not to see Mooney as they bounced past. He could talk to the old guy later. Or avoid him again. Mooney was, he guessed, still his favorite professor.

* * *

Trevor arrived home to a quiet apartment and took steaks out from the fridge, figuring he'd prepare them tampiqueña, like he'd learned from his mother. He couldn't devour two pounds of meat, but he had to cook it before Hospitality and Tourism delivered more. Sasha could eat when he got home. Trevor heated the iron skillet, chopped up an onion and a jalapeño, tossed in the steaks, sliced the cheese. He cut off the flame when somebody knocked on the door.

Trevor welcomed his neighbors, Gerald and Jerome, with fist bumps. They were the kind of nerdy outliers Trevor's teammates might have mocked, but he had grown fond of the pair. Gerald and Jerome dressed like twins, or at least as though they were on the same team. They were unrelated, but their team was the scruffy skateboard crowd at Coors State, not an insignificant population. Both boys were computer geeks, too, majoring in Online Studies, and they occasionally helped Trevor with his technical glitches. Trevor knew why his football teammates had chosen Coors State without even asking. According to Gerald and Jerome, most students chose to enroll because they knew schooling would be easy and fun. "A degree is a degree," Gerald had said once.

Gerald and Jerome were also members of the marching band and pep band, and they never missed a game. Today they were wearing their uniforms—they'd just returned from a group photo shoot—and were pissed off because everyone was stuck wearing old marching band outfits as a cost-saving measure. Even at basketball games, when there'd be no marching. As if Football couldn't afford new band uniforms.

"You guys hungry?" Trevor asked, because he didn't care about band uniforms.

Gerald and Jerome were nearly big enough for football, although they were both doughy. The duo moved in tandem the way they did when skateboarding, and they walked together to the skillet. Gerald lifted the lid. "It's not vegetarian," Jerome said.

From his fridge full of organic fruits and veggies, Trevor built a care package. They had four guys living in their apartment, standard for university housing for students who were not athletes, and they could definitely use the surplus. Trevor tossed in a twelve-pack of Coors. Gerald and Jerome split the take into their ever-present backpacks before wishing Trevor good luck in the next game. He pulled back the drapes and watched them skate away, twenty yards back to their apartment, in their silly band uniforms. Just then he heard an anguished cry upstairs. He bounded up two-at-a-time and found Sasha in bed, bawling, an open book on his chest.

"I didn't realize you were home," Trevor said. "What's wrong?"

"I am so sad," Sasha sniffled. He showed Trevor the book, and then dropped it to the floor as if he could not bear to hold it any longer. He covered his face with a forearm.

Trevor picked it up. *Hell No! We Won't Go!*

Sasha said he was learning about Vietnam, America's involvement, the swelling of the anti-war movement, and how it had changed the course of American history.

Trevor recognized the author's photo on the back, the same long-haired guy standing with Mooney by the tent city earlier—and maybe the man Maniscalco had warned him about. "Is there a lot of death and destruction?"

"Interviews with people who didn't go to Vietnam."

"Why did that make you so upset?"

It was nearly as bad, Sasha said, for the folks who stayed home in protest, who burned their draft cards instead. "Such heartbreaking," he cried. "One guy lose his devoted girlfriend when he refused to go fight. Another gets a venereal disease at a free antiwar concert. One poor man lost a fortune of moneys when he burned the draft card."

"Did he burn his wallet, too?"

"Father disowned him, removed his name from the last will. Then? Incredible. Father dies the next day. The very next day. Son has no money and evil stepmother gets everything."

"Jesus."

"They were powerless in the face of very bad war. I met this man, the author," he said, taking the book back. "Friend of Professor Mooney's and also friend of lady who will soon be my poetry teacher. He was very interested in war in my country. Now I am interested in Mr. Braverman's war."

Trevor flopped down into a chair draped with Sasha's clothes. He'd never seen Sasha weep, never even saw him sad or homesick.

"Oh, to be powerless." Sasha sighed.

Maybe, Trevor thought, he'd hide Braverman's book. With the football team dominating, the last thing he wanted was a distracted center snapping him the ball.

Once in class, a student said to Mooney how meaningless modern American politics felt, and that was why the Mexican Revolution was interesting to her, because the peasants and field workers made an impact. A lot of them got killed, and Trevor had learned that Pancho Villa was no saint. Not like Zapata. But the peasants had a voice in their own future. And Trevor agreed, that was dope.

Now Trevor had a voice in his own future, since he'd accidentally saved History and handpicked the next football coach, although he wasn't yet old enough to buy a beer. Not that he needed to: Hospitality and Tourism delivered cases of Coors. He felt the way he did when his uncle, a Dallas cop, took him to the shooting range for the first (and last) time. Tío

Miguel shot his service revolver, as he did every month to keep sharp. But when it was Trevor's turn, he took just one shot. The power of that pistol was astonishing. He thrust the gun back at his uncle, which startled Miguel. Trevor never again held a gun. He found that kind of harnessed force terrifying. It was the same reason he didn't like motorcycles.

"Now I have made you sad, too," Sasha said. He smiled, his face still wet.

Trevor said, "I'm just thinking."

"About not fighting in the Vietnam war?"

"Other stuff."

"You are feeling powerless, too?"

"I dunno what I'm feeling." Trevor recounted the story of his morning with Maniscalco, of meeting President Cardly.

"Wow," Sasha said. "You met Mr. President. A great honor for you. I hope you took souvenir photo."

"President Cardly took a picture of me," Trevor said.

"Star quarterback is number one popular on campus."

Trevor paused, then said, "Honestly, I don't want to think about this stuff."

"Let's turn frowns upside down," Sasha said, and he made a silly face. When Trevor didn't respond, Sasha kept on. "No eye in team. My bad for making you sad. Let's cheer up."

"I just want to play football and get a nice girlfriend."

"Nice American girlfriend. Not slut dog."

Trevor laughed. "Slut dog? Where'd you hear that?"

"From teammates. Slut dogs are bad. Maybe give you disease, like poor man in Peter Braverman's book. But don't worry. You are like a spider man."

"Spider-Man?"

"You use your superpower for good. You help our coach, a nice guy. And you help our friend, Mr. Mooney. Nice guy, too."

"But I did all that by accident," Trevor said. "Was it the right thing?"

"Time will tell," Sasha said. "Time flies. Time to make the donuts."

"All true."

"Let's play," Sasha said. He took a Nerf basketball off his desk, flipped it to Trevor, and lifted his wastebasket onto the dresser. "Shoot free throws up to ten."

"Hey, I forgot. I made steaks downstairs. The way you like them."

Sasha snuffled. "We make contest to cheer up. Then we eat and we're more happy."

Chapter 9

The old library had feral cats. Most afternoons, Layla Sillimon would visit the herd of tabbies that lived in the drainage pipes near the campus food court. The cats were people-friendly if they got to know you. She'd bring a handful of Half & Half creamers, which she regularly dropped into her purse when the cashier turned to bag her burrito. Once, a creamer broke in her bag and the cats went wacko, a major drag. She'd eat among the five cats, and they would circle slowly, waiting for her to whip out the treats. They could get quite aggressive, but who could blame them? She named them Catman and Robin, Catatonic, Catastrophe, and Doggie.

The discovery of feral cats made her curious about other neglected corners of campus. She enjoyed puttering around, examining back stairs and pockets between buildings. That's how she discovered The Hamlet.

The Hamlet—that's what the protesting professors who never left had named it—rattled Layla. These professors, camped out next to the administration building, were the very people who had hired her. Layla felt a stab of guilt every time she saw their tents, but she couldn't bring herself to meet them again face-to-face.

It wasn't until late September that Layla began to walk by the three colorful tents from a safe distance, like a mother who had given up a child for adoption, then hung around the playground to observe the child incognito. She needed to help them however she could. She owed them that much.

One day, the cats trailed her until she sat across from the tents with her burrito. An old-time string band played in the autumn sunshine. Modern dance students flitted about, and others lolled around on the lawn. Next, a live lecture series unfolded, performed by the banished English profs who had remained. She recognized the first speaker, one of four professors, as the Shakespeare scholar who had driven her back to the airport after her interview. She was the one who had confided to Layla, just as they arrived at her terminal, that she'd push to get Layla hired based on their faith Layla might save them.

Layla still had an hour to kill before class. Most students wandered past as if The Hamlet didn't exist. The adults—profs, instructors, or athletics workers at Coors State—hustled by, picked up their pace as they approached, then slowed after they passed. The students were in a haze, you could forgive them for being kids, but the adults were deliberately scurrying by. In fact, the only time anyone paused to take notice was when they had no choice—a campus bus stopped right across from The Hamlet. The bus would groan to a halt and the students on board gawked, the engine drowning out the musicians.

Doggie, the one cat that loved to climb trees, was perched on a branch, whining, although she was certain he'd been fed.

For the first time, the English profs were calling attention to their situation by rocking sweatshirts with nearly extinct animals emblazoned across their chests. Not spotted owls, sadly, who needed the love, too.

Wolf was one man.

The other male prof's said Dodo.

Layla couldn't help but snort a laugh at the large-breasted woman whose sweatshirt read Humpback Whale.

The fourth, Buffalo, was a woman with a bowl-cut hairdo.

During a break in the festivities, Layla took a deep breath and went to reintroduce herself to the four professors.

The Humpback Whale woman stepped into Layla's path, smiling, welcoming her back to campus. She said her name again, but Layla instantly forgot it.

"What you're doing is so rad," Layla said. "But what *are* you doing?"

"Do you remember the last thing I told you at the airport?" Whale asked. "To thine own self, be true. Have you been?"

"Have I been what?" Layla asked.

"True to yourself."

"So far, so good," Layla said. Now she recalled this was the Shakespeare scholar.

"That's why we chose the name The Hamlet. We're fighting to be true to ourselves and to shame the university so English will get resurrected." She said most of her old colleagues were long gone, but the three other profs who lived in The Hamlet were determined to soldier on publicly for a cause, if not a paycheck.

Layla was silent.

"Do you go to football games?" Humpback Whale asked.

"They're kind of awesome," Layla said, but she instantly knew she'd said the wrong thing.

After taking a deep breath, Whale said, "The English Department absolutely does not think Football is awesome. We think it's *awful*. If President Cardly ever showed his face here, I'm afraid I'd kill him with my bare hands. You should be aware, by the way, Journalism used to have your job selling programs. Before Journalism became obsolete."

The Hamlet, Layla decided, was a bomb-ass cool social protest. "So, how can I help?" Layla finally asked. "In a practical sense. I wish I could pay you back for helping me get hired. I don't hate football, but I hate injustice, and I feel like I need to show my gratitude."

"Just off the top of my head? We're out of cheese and crackers," Whale said. "We live on the stuff. And we prefer good quality cheese. Or wine, but you'd have to put it in an unmarked container."

Layla said, "Is there something more influential that I could, like, do?"

"You could write a memo to the rest of your little Poetry Department, asking if they'd pledge support with a proclamation. You'd email the proclamation to your faculty and poetry majors, but you'd have to get clearance from the Dean, and that might mean another department meeting. Maybe you already have an Email Committee. Do you know? Better yet, you could volunteer to chair a new committee to support English."

"But then what?"

Whale sighed, as if Layla were a four-year-old. "You'd have elections within the committee. Naturally, since it was your idea to support us, you'd probably stay on as chairperson. Or you'd hold elections and require a simple majority. After that you'd elect a secretary. Since it's just you and Wilson Keats, you'll have to serve in two capacities on any committee."

"And then?"

"You'd pick a day, once a month, when everyone could meet, just like any committee." Whale was talking slower now. "You could break out into focus groups and discuss the challenges."

"But what would we actually do at these meetings?"

"I just told you, break out into focus groups."

Layla thought maybe she should just buy the cheese.

"Your committee would have to decide on the wording of the committee's goals," Whale said. "That usually takes a few months. You poets can never agree on the exact language. So, figure six months."

It was true, Layla thought, if she and Keats spoke again, they'd likely argue about everything. They'd only had one faculty meeting, and it seemed ridiculous to Layla as she listened to Wilson Keats go over the agenda. Thank God for haiku, which she was doing while pretending to take notes. At least that kept her busy composing, while he was decomposing.

"I still serve on six committees across the campus," Whale boasted. "I love being on committees. It was the part of the job I knew I'd miss the most, and I refuse to give it up. All my recent publications are about committee work. Most people don't realize William Shakespeare practically lived for committees."

"But you guys aren't officially employed here anymore," Layla said, then felt embarrassed for pointing it out.

"We're often divided about how to proceed." Whale pointed at the Buffalo woman and Dodo, sitting next to the tent and poring over notebooks. "We three agree," she whispered. "Fair is foul, and foul is fair, but we're perfectly willing to stay within the paradigm of the Coors State system."

"What's she reading?"

Whale leaned closer to Layla. "She knows the bylaws better than anyone on campus. She studies them constantly and thinks there might be a loophole that would prevent Football from closing down English. Even if it's just a technicality, we might be able to use it to reopen."

"Far out."

"And most of her publications have been on university bylaws. You should get her book. *Call to Order: Literature's Influence on the Bylaws at American Universities.*"

"Sounds interesting."

"But him?" Whale nodded at the man in the Wolf sweatshirt. "He's fed up with committees and bylaws. Not me. I still have an impact on campus through my committee work. I'm our Library Rep for English, which empowers me to order four new library books every year. That's one change I spearheaded, because it used to be a limit of two new books. Also, I'm on an Advisory Committee, the university-wide Committee for Academic Enrichment, Sophomore Studies, and the Diversity in the Cafeterias Committee. And I'm our rep for Faculty Senate. Wait, was that six?"

"Probably," Layla said.

"My dream is to one day serve on enough committees that I'd be relieved of all teaching duties."

"I guess I don't understand," Layla admitted, stopping herself from saying *Isn't that your situation now, no teaching?*

Whale gave Layla a you-will-when-you-grow-up smile. They paused while another bus groaned and hissed to a stop. Whale added, "Everyone has a part to play in this. By the way, we all love feta if you decide to go shopping."

Layla was not going on any cheese runs, but she had a sinking feeling a request, one worse than shopping for cheese, was at hand: Whale was about to suggest forming a committee together. Layla had to come up with an alternative, pronto.

"I'll write a couple poems about your struggle," Layla said. "I could do a poetry reading right here to support English. I'd get such a totally big crowd, I promise. I mean, if I didn't understand what The Hamlet was, and I'm a poet, I'll bet most other people don't either." She could even get her own students involved, have them read poems, too, and they could bring their friends.

"Perhaps in a month or two we could set that all up," Whale said, "to give you time to write the poems."

"Sister, I'll whip up two poems tonight," Layla said, "and we'll have the reading tomorrow. How about at three o'clock?"

"You're moving too fast," Whale said. "We'd have to convene a meeting with our policy committee."

Layla's brain was grinding in frustration, and her new friend seemed to sense that.

"Oh, just wait a moment," Whale said.

Whale gathered her colleagues into a huddle behind the tents, then returned minutes later. "Come back tomorrow," she said. "We're going to convene the emergency meeting right now."

The next day, Layla Sillimon returned to The Hamlet and sat in the lotus position on the hill, doing her circular breathing as English carried on their meetings. Occasionally she'd open her eyes to find a different configuration, likely another committee in full swing. They'd move their chairs around or reconvene at their picnic table. She rolled up her yoga mat after a while, ready to return to her office when Whale walked across to Layla's little hill to offer an invitation. "My colleagues need to hear you describe how poetry might raise awareness of the plight of English," Whale said.

A minute later, Layla took her seat at their table and said, "I honestly don't know how to discuss this."

Whale said, "As your Poetry colleague can attest, you should have the academic language skills to communicate on a university-wide basis. You'll see. We speak the same language as the rest of the faculty at Coors State."

Layla warmed her hands on the teacup she'd been handed. Her initial department meeting with Wilson Keats had left her befuddled.

"Basically," Whale said, "you have to keep talking the talk. It's a language, just like poetry. Or music. It's like a song, and we all have to keep the song going."

"Do you have a written proposal we can see?" Wolf asked.

"I just want to read a couple of poems, get a crowd to The Hamlet, and make everyone, like, totally conscious of what had happened to English."

"Is that goal-oriented enough for us?" Dodo asked the group. "If English is going to reestablish itself, we need to revolutionize our process-based curriculum compacting."

Buffalo raised a finger to make a counterpoint. "Certainly," she said. "But not without optimizing the competency-based units and leveraging the mission-critical outcomes. That's precisely what a poetry reading could do for us."

Whale smiled at Layla—see how easy?—and waited for her to contribute. After a moment, Whale turned to her colleagues. "However, for English to implement the multidisciplinary outcomes, using curriculum from an auxiliary department as Professor Sillimon is proposing, we'll have to extend our standards-based pedagogy." She shrugged and added, "Not to mention evolving our cross-curricular objectives."

The four English profs looked to Layla. She was about to say "Whatever," but Buffalo jumped in. "How might poetry work within our paradigm? For instance, can you assess performance-based articulation and unpack hands-on scaffolding?"

"Possibly," Layla said. She hadn't had the guts to even approach them her first weeks on campus, and now she didn't have the heart to tell them she was lost. "What exactly are you talking about?" she finally said. "It sounds totally abstract."

Dodo said, "Maybe your goal as a poet is the best place to start. In English, we try to unleash thematic lifelong learning through critical-driven pedagogy. What is the ultimate goal of poetry?"

"You just have to get used to thinking like this, Layla," Whale interjected, "if you're going to survive in academia."

Layla wanted to say, *But you guys are not surviving.* Instead, she gave it a try. "As a poetry teacher," she stammered, "my goal might be, I guess—I'd like to, you know, synergize high quality instruction."

"Terrific," Buffalo said. "That's a great place to start."

"I just thought in this case, well, I mean, what the fuck, my goal? I'd get a bunch of people to sit on the grass and listen to poems, and I figured they couldn't help but notice your beautiful tents and raise everyone's level of consciousness."

"It sounds like what you're proposing," Whale said slowly, "is for this poetry reading to repurpose skills-based infrastructures and integrate competency-based manipulatives all in a safe space. Any teacher should do that, in fact, poet or not."

"Okay," Layla said. "What do you say we do the reading at three tomorrow?"

"Let's be clear," Buffalo added. "For The Hamlet to make this work, your poets will have to mesh interdisciplinary dialogue even without tracking project-based decision-making..."

Layla thought she might start weeping.

"Why don't we vote," Buffalo said just in time. "Layla, we'll ask you to leave, then vote on your reading your book about poetry tomorrow."

"Sorry," Layla said. "I would just read two poems. I mean they're actual poems, not a book about poems."

"Of course," Whale said.

They thanked Layla for coming. "We'll get back to you soon," one of them added.

"This has been so cool," she said and handed back her teacup. She was being blown off. She'd heard Braverman talk about "death by committee," and now she understood. That's what she got for being generous. But she realized a moment later Whale was walking behind her.

"I'll escort you past the musicians," Whale said softly, her distinct change in tone a signal it was fine to talk normally. "We think Criminal Justice is keeping tabs on us. We wouldn't want you to get in trouble since you're new. Also, next time, we don't allow cats at our meetings."

By the time she made it back to her office, Layla had an email saying The Hamlet would host a poetry reading the next afternoon at three.

That evening, bored with grading student work, Layla wrote two poems in support of The Hamlet. She knew what she wanted to convey, without being inflammatory. She thought about Shakespeare, but also Oscar Wilde, who'd been ostracized. And the archetypal Hero's Journey her new English friends were on. And then 50 Cent, which led to her thinking about the rapper Drake. She was going "First thought, best thought," and she'd hardly have time to revise, but she never revised much. Art didn't work like that. Not her art, anyway.

At her noon class the next day, Layla began by asking her poetry students to send texts and messages to their friends to get them to the reading: Support English—Dig Poetry. She told her class it'd be cool if each student would read one poem, although it wasn't mandatory, and she passed around a sign-up sheet. Half the kids got on board.

At 2:40 p.m., she hurried to The Hamlet to preview her plan. She would read one poem to start, followed by the student readers. Layla would finish up with a final poem, a warm and positive one.

The four English professors sat at their table nursing cups of tea. They exchanged looks after Layla told them to prepare for a good crowd. Finally, the professor with Dodo on his sweatshirt said, "We don't have enough snacks for everyone."

Buffalo said, "Did you clear this with Campus Events?"

Wolf tossed his tea onto the grass and grumbled.

"Of course," Layla lied. "Campus Events said no problemo."

"You printed the permit?" Buffalo asked.

Layla patted her backpack in affirmation.

One minute, the area was vacant. The next, it was as though a Labor Day picnic had dropped out of the sky. By 3:10 p.m., every blade of grass around The Hamlet was covered with kids. But even then Layla had a pang of regret. She should have invited Sasha and had him bring the team, although she wondered if the coach would have let them skip rehearsal for poetry. Maybe, she thought. A mass of students slowly gravitated toward the tents. Quite a few kids stretched out on blankets and one group hooked up a slackline between trees to tightrope on. Others flung Frisbees in the distance. Students chattered away, and Layla could feel a sense of urgency.

They had no microphone, but she'd been slamming poems long enough. Her barroom voice would carry. She preferred to recite her poems from memory, so she closed her eyes and went through the first one a few times, stopping when she felt a hand on her shoulder.

"Amazing you're doing this," Braverman said.

She gave him a perfunctory sideways hug.

"And you picked an ass-kicker of a name for the event," he said "Take Back Our School. Very cool. By any means necessary, right?"

"You bet," Layla said, but it came out more like a question. She hadn't given the event a name, but someone had. Braverman showed her his notebook full of email addresses he'd collected from the throng in the last fifteen minutes. He claimed it could be used to ignite the revolution. A poetry revolution, she guessed. She started a head count, but it was impossible. A few hundred, a great crowd for poetry. She'd have to make do without a stage or podium.

"What about you sitting on a branch of that tree to read?" Braverman said. "I can help you get up there, give you a boost."

She'd broken her wrist falling out of a tree at age eleven, and the memory still spooked her. "What about me sitting on your shoulders?" she said. "That'd be plenty high."

"My shoulders?"

"It'd be fucking dramatic," she said, "with the Army jacket you have on. Like, Poetry Over the Military. Literal and symbolic."

"I could try," Braverman said.

"It's not a long poem. And you don't have to lift up every poet."

Humpback Whale appeared, offered Layla and Braverman a small plate of cheese and crackers.

"Oooh, feta," Braverman said. "Don't mind if I do."

"It's past three," Layla said, declining the cheese. "Let's get this party started." She cleared her throat and waved her hands. She coughed loudly. Nothing but more chatter.

"Shut the fuck—!" Braverman started to yell, but she put her palm over his mouth. What in the world was he trying to do? She didn't want that authoritarian vibe. She found her Tibetan meditation bell in her backpack, and her colorful tie-died hoodie, too. She pulled on the hoodie, thinking it would make her more identifiable to the crowd. "Okay, scrunch down and I'll climb up," she said.

Braverman squatted. She circled him and lifted a leg as if he were a boy's bicycle. She had the two poems in her hoodie's pouch, and the meditation bell in one hand. Braverman lifted her. She pinged the bell at five-second intervals.

The crowd began shushing. Peaceful silence spread like melting butter until everyone had eased themselves into total quiet. Braverman staggered a little under Layla's weight, and in that instant she flopped forward until her forehead, inverted, nearly touched his. They almost toppled, but he caught his balance and straightened. When he did, Layla whipped her head and dreadlocks back and people broke into a light applause, as if that had been her planned entrance. A few students let out whoops, and the crowd fell silent again. Layla reached for her first poem, accidentally dropping the bell, which clanged off of Braverman's noggin. He gasped an obscenity and wobbled again.

"Sorry," she said. "Try to keep still."

She held the poem in her fist, fearing her memory might fail her. When she waved both hands up and down, the kids in front sat down, and like dominos, the rest of the crowd followed suit. This was a long way from the San Francisco poetry slam scene, where you might never be granted total silence. She wondered what her mother would think of her daughter holding court in front of hundreds of students.

"Right on," she said. Soon, everyone was seated except for Braverman, who continued to stagger beneath her unpredictably. He grunted when she grasped a fistful of his hair for balance.

Just before she spoke, she noticed one other person still standing, Eugene Mooney, near the back. He would have been a much more stable perch, but it would be too disruptive to call him up to the front now.

"Welcome, fellow travelers," Layla began. With brick buildings on two sides, and a light wind at her back, her voice projected well. People were spread out for fifty yards onto the small hills. From her vantage point, this was a natural theater setting. "We're going to have a lot of poets throwing poems at you today. Just remember we're here to support The Hamlet. I'll go ahead and kick things off by reading a poem I wrote, unless somebody can first explain why we're here and why this tent city exists." She didn't expect anyone to take her up on that, she was just fumbling through an introduction.

"I can explain," Braverman called out below her. She felt herself lift an inch or two up toward the branches as he straightened. "We're here," he yelled, his voice gaining strength, "because this is the beginning of the revolution! We're here as comrades and brothers to save English and take our fucking university back."

The crowd applauded politely while the four English profs to Layla's side, looking confused and sheepish, took bows. Layla hadn't wanted to deliver any heavy-duty messages, and she knew college students could be counted on to cheer if anyone yelled "fuck." She'd wanted poetry to be front and center at this gathering, but now it was too late; Braverman was trying to steal the show. She should have acted on her first thought when he arrived: Lose this loudmouth.

In her view, the changes in the school's mindset, their support for English, would settle into the collective consciousness of the people and would evolve organically. But Braverman continued to shout about revolution, so she had no choice but to squeeze her thighs around his neck to cut him off. "Okay, I'll just read my poem," Layla shouted, and she tugged hard at his hair again so he would know to keep quiet.

The applause died down, but a few boos seeped through. She wondered if the jeers were for her or Braverman. He tried to look up at her. The crowd was murmuring now. A student handed up her Tibetan bell, and she pinged it again.

"Here's a poem I wrote," Layla yelled. "It's called 'The Passionate Pilgrims.'"

'The Passionate Pilgrims'
Who's in the mood for an Elizabethan feud?
We blindly pass these fly folks each day,
while English, cast adrift by football's merchants of
menace, shifts and fades
away. Alas! Shakespeare knew despite much ado,
and he left his mark on this tented park.
O! Let us grow The Hamlet, and face the haters
   down,
and the sound of the clowns
when they hit the ground,
will be sweet, and yes, a few greenbacks
might mean all's well that ends well.
Bring English back
to life and end this strife!

The crowd erupted in cheers. Anything she recited on the Coors State campus elicited cheers. Thank you, Taylor Swift, she thought.

"Uh oh," Braverman gasped. At the top of the hill, four Criminal Justice cops in bright yellow vests were stepping over students and moving through the crowd. So that's what the booing was about. A couple cops raised clubs, and the kids parted, making a clear path straight for Layla.

One of the cops tripped, causing his partner behind him to tumble. Maybe a student had stuck a leg out and caused this, but it happened quickly. That led another cop to stop and pepper spray a student. Layla screamed. A bunch of kids jumped to their feet. Layla's view of the security guards was obscured a moment later when Braverman tripped and toppled forward, face-first. She landed on her feet, like an Olympic gymnast nailing her dismount. But Braverman's face broke his fall because his arms had been pinned behind her knees. Students fled in every direction.

Layla yanked Braverman by the collar back onto his feet, then pulled his hand from his face. Blood spurted out of his nose and onto her hoodie.

"Let's get out of here," she shouted, "and stop bleeding on me." The guards were closing in, but in the scramble, she kept losing sight of them.

Braverman wiped at his nose with his Army jacket sleeve. Blood streamed over his lips, drenched the front of his coat. He looked like he'd had a bad lesson at Karate Camp, and she laughed despite herself. He pinched his nose with one hand; with the other he pulled a pair of wrap-around sunglasses out of his pocket and jammed them onto Layla's face. It was a way smart idea. "Let's beat it," she said.

He took her by the arm, and they ran, just as two Criminal Justice cops in yellow vests emerged from the crowd. Braverman yanked at a door of the Sociology building, but it was locked. They had nowhere to go.

"We don't need to run," Layla gasped. "Not yet. We just need to chill for a minute until we can find an escape route. Help me get out of this sweatshirt, I'll be too easy to spot." She leaned forward and raised her arms. Braverman pulled at it, and he nearly took her T-shirt off, too. She yanked it back down over her sports bra. From her jeans, she took a scrunchie and bunched her dreads into a sort of Jamaican ponytail, and in that instant, Layla thought using poetry for political change might be great—if it was always this exciting, this powerful.

"Shit, they see us," Braverman said. He was standing close, his arms around her in a loose hug to hide her from the cops.

Just then, a campus bus wheezed to a halt.

"Our ride," Braverman said, and they were off running again, hand-in-hand this time. A horde of students, no doubt in fear of a police beatdown, stormed the bus before Layla and Braverman got there. They cut into line, but the driver reached to close the door just as Layla got her foot on the first step.

"We're at capacity," the bus driver yelled.

Braverman shoved Layla inside. She made it halfway before the door closed on her sternum, splitting her in half with her head still outside. She reached for Braverman, wild with fear. He dug his hand in between the doors and tried to pry her free. She closed her eyes, leaned her head back, and strained against the crush, pushed desperately with her hips. She was about to pass out when she was able to jerk loose. She stumbled inside the bus, just before the doors whammed shut again. Braverman's face, a mess of blood and mucus, pressed against the glass, inches from hers, as if he had been about to kiss her.

Layla staggered to catch her balance as she fell up the steps. Two students recognized her and slid to the back of the bus so she could sit just behind the driver.

"This bus is not moving until everyone is seated," the driver called and pointed to the rules above his mirror.

"But we don't have enough seats for everyone," Layla said.

By this time, the bus was surrounded by panicked students coughing from the tear gas or pepper spray, or whatever it was. Even in their misery, Layla thought, they wanted to clamber on the bus and join a celebrity poet.

She stood and yanked open a window. "Get out of the way!" she cried to the crowd, but it was no use. Braverman, the fool, was trying to climb on board again, and she stepped down as he got the doors open a crack to palm him in the nose. The blood started gushing again just as the Criminal Justice cops surrounded the front of the bus. A shot of pepper spray here, a shove there, a kick in the knee, and the crowd fled until the cops were at the door with Braverman. They led him away, probably figuring him to be a victim, due to his age and his bloody face. A few of the students on board popped open an emergency exit window. As the cops ascended the steps, all the kids scurried to the rear to climb out.

Only Layla kept her seat. She took off the sunglasses, yanked off the scrunchie, and shook out her dreadlocks. A brief moment of panic washed over her—what would happen to her teaching career? Could she get fired? She couldn't very well move in with her mother in Belfast. The possibility of being broke again didn't rattle her so much as her fear of being left alone.

She'd ignore the fucking cops, she decided. What were they going to do, arrest her for reading a poem? She gazed out her window as if on a sightseeing tour. A bunch of students who the guards had pummeled were sprawled in the grass, and a few were knuckling their eyes. Some kids looked up at the bus hopefully, like churchgoers waiting to be dismissed. Others were on their knees, perhaps praying for the bus to magically levitate. A voice outside cut through the silence. Braverman was lecturing a Criminal Justice cop about constitutional rights. He waved his arms wildly, ignoring his nosebleed. Next to Braverman was Mooney, sweating profusely and trying to calm the cop and his friend. Next to Mooney was Wilson Keats. Well, Keats had witnessed quite a poetry reading, not the usual yawner where the audience wept tears of boredom.

One cop knocked Braverman's arm down to move toward the door of the bus, leaving the three old professors behind. This cop was dressed differently, and Layla realized he was in charge, maybe even the department head for Criminal Justice. Time seemed to get mushy, yet all the crazy sights and sounds had been so vivid, like she was tripping on mushrooms. All because of her poetry. Or was it because of that inflammatory stuff Braverman had said? Or both?

Two security cops were at their leader's side now. Others must have gotten in through the emergency exit window because they now stood directly behind Layla, as if she were a dangerous feline escaped from the zoo.

"Layla Sillimon?" the leader said.

"Duh," she said, and raised her hand. "Present, I mean."

"Do you have a TransCard?"

"A what?"

The driver said, "None of her hippie friends paid, either."

"You're under arrest for subversively entering a university bus," the cop said, "and for breaking that man's nose." He pointed back at Braverman.

"Can I cuff her?" another cop asked.

"Hey, I called dibs on the handcuffing," another said, and they elbowed each other trying to get to Layla. She offered up her hands like a prayer and both men cuffed her. The boss cop led her down the bus steps.

As her feet hit the pavement, a dark object flashed through her field of vision, and a howl pierced the afternoon. One of the handcuffers let out an agonized cry. A feral tabby, the one she called Doggie, dove down from an overhanging branch and clawed the cheek of one of her abductors. The man flailed, and the tabby ripped a hunk of flesh the size of a serving of sashimi from his face. Another guard sprayed the animal, or tried to, but the cat darted away, and the spray hit his partner in the face. The catted cop fell to the ground, cursing.

"Good, Doggie," Layla called as the cat scampered away.

Braverman, Mooney, and Wilson Keats were nowhere in sight, the cowards. The cops marched Layla to their car, and

one guy opened the back door—it wasn't a squad car at all—
and he pushed down on her head so she wouldn't bang it as she
climbed in, although there was no need for that with an SUV.
The door slammed, and she realized the two History professors
hadn't gone away at all, they'd just moved to the other side of
the makeshift police car. Only Wilson Keats had run away.

The SUV windows were tinted dark. Layla could see the old
professors, but they surely could not see her. She was already
making excuses in her mind, practicing for when the cops
interrogated her. It was her first violation, she'd say, she was
a newbie who didn't know anyone would be against football.
She'd sold hundreds of game programs outside the stadium.
Didn't that count?

Braverman and Mooney had their arms slung over each
other's shoulders and looked ecstatic, as if they'd won a hard-
fought game. The vehicle pulled away, and both professors gave
Layla raised-fist salutes of solidarity.

Chapter 10

Eugene Mooney and Peter Braverman were back on concession-stand duty that weekend, the end of the fall quarter. Braverman's role in the campus newspaper—"Poetry Riot"—had somehow been overlooked by Football and Criminal Justice, due to the chaos and the bloody nose that had obscured his face.

Mooney was having trouble focusing on popcorn preparation, realizing too late that he'd accidentally dumped in the artificial butter twice. He thought he might gag. Mooney was distracted and invigorated by what he'd witnessed at The Hamlet, where he'd arrived just in time to hear Braverman's rant and Layla's revolutionary poem. The Poetry Riot was inspirational—clearly she'd hit a nerve, and the campus was ripe for change—but since then she'd gone into seclusion. Who wouldn't have? She'd canceled classes all week, adding to the mystery. Mooney figured she would reach out when things quieted down. He couldn't get the images out of his mind—Layla, the bus, the handcuffs. As they drove Layla away, he and Braverman said it in unison: "Rosa Parks."

"Exactly," Braverman added.

"Precisely," Mooney answered. In that instant, he'd made the decision to get off the sidelines, quit being so cautious, and actively join the fight with Braverman.

Minutes after Layla's arrest, Braverman, still smeared with blood, had insisted on a trip back to his office, where he found a photo of Rosa Parks online. He lifted a new Instagram photo of Layla and Photoshopped the two great women together, so Rosa Parks looked solemnly out her bus window at Layla.

It was a bit of a stretch for Mooney, but even he had to admit there were some parallels. The red-faced driver challenging Layla's right to be on the bus. The cops hauling Layla off as if she were a dangerous threat.

Maybe she actually was a dangerous threat—to the sports factory at Coors State. Braverman believed she would now be a campus revolutionary, a spokesman. Spokesperson, Mooney reminded himself. She'd reemerge when she was rested and ready, and a wave of change would spread across their campus, then the nation. The American civil rights movements had been influenced by Gandhi and had spawned copycats—in Northern Ireland, Mexico, France, so many places. Now Layla Sillimon's poem and its impact would resonate across American university campuses. Mooney knew they were stuck with the new name, but they'd get the school to at least go back to the pre-rebranding days when academics were more than a footnote. He would be on the right side of history—and connected to the gutsy woman who threw the first peaceful punch. When Layla resurfaced, they'd calculate their next move, and he'd ask her for the original draft of her poem and get it framed.

The professors had posted bail for Layla in the lobby of the Criminal Justice Department. Layla's next legal step was unclear. Mooney wondered if there even was a next step. She was free to go, a secretary said, and the bottom line seemed to be that Mooney was five-hundred dollars lighter. Strangely, Layla must have exited through a side door. It was just as well she'd secretly slipped out since a student journalist stood waiting at the main entrance. They had shown no interest in two old history profs.

* * *

Minutes before kickoff, their concession stand buzzing with customers, Mooney confessed in a whisper he still had Layla's poem on his mind. Mentioning her was a sort of olive branch offering to Braverman, who had chafed at the idea of going back to the concession stand after the Poetry Riot. Mooney thought it was too risky to walk away yet; they'd have a better chance for change if they kept up a façade of cooperation. He sensed that mentioning Layla would soften Braverman's hard edges. "Taylor Swift was right. Her poems are transformative."

"It's like being in love," Braverman said agreeably. He wore tinted glasses to hide the black eye his broken nose brought on. "She's not a distraction though, she's an inspiration. Can you imagine being in Alabama in the weeks after Rosa Parks was arrested? You'd have hope for the first time. That's how I feel."

Mooney collected money and shoved popcorn boxes across the counter. "Look, Peter," he said, "I'll admit I was a little slow to join the revolution. But the Poetry Riot made me realize it's difficult to make changes from within our system. I'm admitting that. But I want to say two things. First, we have a job to do tonight. And after tonight, let's focus on the change we're going to bring about, not on Layla. I wonder if you're getting a little too fond of her."

Many a revolution had been screwed up by leaders with ill-advised love interests, and many a modern movement had lost its credibility by dissing their women. Also he knew Braverman was more likely to get a sexual harassment charge than reciprocation of romantic interest from Layla.

Now, Mooney believed, was the time to focus on the bigger picture. A photo of Layla reading to the crowd, with Braverman straining to hold her up, was plastered across the front page of *Rocky Mountain High*. "Campus Revolt!" the headline said. Inside, there was a smaller photo of the scuffle, which included Braverman, although he was unidentifiable due to the blood smeared across his face. The event's message was hard to identify, too, evidently. The accompanying article mentioned the plight of the English Department, but nothing about Football's place on campus since the rebranding. Clearly the revolution's message was still a work in progress.

But the newspaper also spoke to some other hopeful developments—a tangled web of campus complications that just might rattle the absolute power of Football.

Biochemistry had spent three years developing an anabolic steroid difficult to detect by NCAA drug testing. Now they were demanding compensation from Football for the years they had spent in research. They'd even compiled some pretty convincing stats proving how their steroid had reduced the Silver Bullets' time lost to injuries.

Another troubling contract labor issue had emerged. The Photography faculty of the dying Journalism Department had begun selling football action shots from their lobby—after the star players autographed the photos to jack up the prices. Photography wanted to have it count as contract labor, but Football now wanted a cut of their earnings.

Another article claimed that Football was angry with Hospitality and Tourism, who had the easiest gig on campus, cooking for the training table. Football now wanted them to add laundry duties. The laundry assignment for Hospitality and Tourism would carry over into basketball season. That would mean much less work with only a dozen hoopers. But the hypersensitive Hospitality profs had balked, cutting their own funding in half. Everything had been at an impasse since, and it seemed Football might eliminate Hospitality and Tourism mid-year. But then who would feed the team? Hospitality could wind up like English, in tents outside the administration building. On a positive note, they would probably bring a tasty selection of cheeses.

But *Rocky Mountain High* also had features on other departments that were thriving under the new regime. Engineering was starting a new project, expanding seating in the football stadium and basketball arena. They were the busiest and most secure of all the departments, due to the increasing demand for tickets.

Finally, there was a feature on Business, who, in the last few years, had their teaching loads practically eliminated so they could concentrate on managing investments for the coaching staff. The revolution was unlikely to find support from that quarter. Unless Business profs missed teaching? Mooney thought of all the group work they made their students do. Unlikely.

Mooney could sense dark clouds ahead. Coach Maniscalco had stopped by well before game time to pilfer their popcorn again, and his comment gave Mooney the chills. "How's the nose?" Maniscalco had asked Braverman, which left Braverman speechless for once. But minutes later, when Maniscalco had walked away, Braverman began muttering to himself about the next steps. Braverman was beginning to sound like a broken record: academics had to take the university back. Back from Football, back from Basketball, back to sanity. But how? Their next move had to be well considered and completely planned, more than a chanted slogan or a haphazard poetry reading.

Once the second half of the game had commenced and the lines diminished, Braverman unveiled his plan—a march. The march would begin at The Hamlet, he said, and circle President Cardly's office in a human chain-of-protest. The four English professors would join them, with Layla leading the way. They'd sing a few protest songs, Layla could read a poem, and they'd march to the stadium. There, they'd briefly disrupt football practice by parading through the stands, a safe distance from the field, but clearly visible.

"Do we have to talk about this now?" Mooney asked, thinking about the popcorn and their chores. "And doesn't Football use the practice field, not the stadium?"

"Yes. And no," Braverman said. "Football practices every Thursday in the stadium. You've never respected my research."

Coors State was already a shoo-in for a bowl game. They were undefeated and only two road games remained. They'd be off to the Fiesta Bowl, one of the biggest games in the country, sponsored by Doritos, of course. Coors beer and corn chips; it was a match made in corporate heaven. This all meant another couple dozen practices.

The way Braverman figured it, they would have three marches before the Doritos Fiesta Bowl. Each Thursday, Braverman would lead the marchers through the ritual. The Movement would mushroom as word spread. They'd walk through a new department each week to swell their ranks, and they'd always finish at the football stadium.

"I'm not agreeing to this yet," Mooney said, looking around to make sure no customers were within earshot. "For one thing, the football season is nearly over. What then?"

"We'll change the destination to basketball practice," Braverman said. "Maybe we should continue the protest in Tempe? Take to the streets on a national stage, right at the Fiesta Bowl site?"

"We'll have to ask Layla," Mooney said. "That might be too much for her. She might have plans over Christmas."

"Or she might like it." Braverman took off his Fidel-style cap and rubbed his head. The welt from Layla's meditation bell had sprouted up through his long hair like a clown's nose. He'd scooped up the Tibetan bell as the melee began. He kept it in the pocket of his tracksuit pants as a sort of good luck charm. The Fidel cap, running shoes, sunglasses, and bizarre bulge in the side of his pants all made him look like an aging communist fitness buff.

Mooney was happy to let Layla have the lead. Together, they could form a kind of Revolutionary Board of Directors. He'd explained their roles to Braverman like this:

"We're going to be Claudette Colvin. Layla can be Rosa Parks."

As a teenager, Mooney explained, Miss Colvin did exactly what Parks did in Montgomery. Colvin did it almost a year earlier, but when she turned up pregnant, she got moved to the background, social norms of the 1950s being what they were. Rosa Parks got all the credit, but Claudette Colvin sparked the movement. The men didn't need the credit; they only wanted their college back.

And Layla already had star power. Maybe she could phone Stephen Colbert, Trevor Noah, all the folks who'd loved her book. They'd also have to be certain they didn't get fractured, split into two or three movements. One enthusiastic student in a *Rocky Mountain High* editorial had suggested Football and Basketball could share revenue with the minor sports like field hockey. But that would return Coors State to the 1990s business model. Mooney wanted the university eventually to be transported back to the 1960s, when professors made the same salaries as head coaches.

"We also have to be careful not to jeopardize your push for tenure," Mooney cautioned Braverman. "LBJ was president when you started delaying that process."

"I'm glad Layla wasn't afraid to speak up," Braverman huffed, then raised his voice. "We're on the verge of change because of her, and that coward Cardly knows it. Layla has shamed us all with her courage."

"Keep your voice down," Mooney said, looking around for customers.

"I'm writing poetry of my own now," Braverman said.

It sounded like a threat and Mooney sighed. He'd be forced to read Braverman's poetry soon enough. "We'll get Layla front and center," Mooney said, "but can't you be patient for once? Things are shifting on campus; we can both feel it."

During the halftime rush, Mooney felt Braverman peering over his shoulder at one of the flat screen TVs in the concourse. The halftime special was about Sasha Dimitrievic. It was too noisy to hear, but there he was in his trademark horn-rimmed glasses. The fact that his neck was wider than his head made him appear a bit cartoonish. Mooney could imagine Sasha speaking of his love for his new American university, how comfortable he'd felt in America. Then the screen flashed to images of Croatia. The stunning beaches interspersed with shots of the destruction from the war. Then an image of Sasha's cousin's book of poetry. Mooney was elated. This meant Sasha had deftly kept poetry front and center without mentioning the Poetry Riot. The higher the esteem for poetry on campus, the better chance they'd have to move forward with Layla in the lead.

After the game, Environmental Sciences swept through the stadium, recycling what they could. Two of them gave Mooney a wave from down the concourse, where they sifted through trash to separate paper from plastic. One brought over a perfectly good, discarded case of Coors, and he plopped it on their counter. "Extras, I guess," he said. "Enjoy."

The two history professors rolled down the steel door for privacy and settled into folding chairs with the still-cold cans.

Braverman had the tip jar in his lap. It was stuffed. He organized the cash and counted out loud. The total in tips alone was close to two thousand bucks.

"Quite a margin of profit," Mooney said, taking a long gulp. "And this beer isn't bad when you're tired and thirsty."

"Like drinking fascist blood," Braverman said. They clinked cans as a toast. "To Layla."

"We'll see her Monday, I bet," Mooney said. "Forget the emails. She's swamped. Let's just stop by."

"She'd rather see us in person anyway. Should I bring roses?"

"Peter, I'm serious. Please don't sabotage our quest for an impossible romantic interest."

"Carnations then."

"I mean it," Mooney said.

"What about a house plant?"

They popped open two more cans. Although they had not seen a minute of the game, they'd heard the Silver Bullets won easily. Mooney dumped the remaining cans into their ice maker. "Let's drink all the leftovers," he said. This could be a benefit of running concessions, he realized, a mellow postgame drunk.

"What's gotten into you?" Braverman asked. "You finally cutting loose?" Mooney cocked his head, almost smiling. They jammed two cans each into their pockets and went out to find seats in the nearly empty stands. Agriculture profs worked on their hands and knees, patching up rough parts of the sod at midfield. The Music Department profs brought their instruments down to the sideline. They no longer played in the parking lots postgame because one cellist had nearly been run over by a pickup truck. Instead, they now gathered on the sideline to play the school fight song, normally a march, as a waltz. Mooney wasn't sure if this rendition was supposed to be ironic or genuine. The musicians started in, and he and

Braverman leaned back in their seats. The sound was gorgeous and the arc and sweep of violin bows gave Mooney a peaceful feeling.

Down on the field, Sasha and Trevor appeared near the musicians. For a moment Mooney thought he was imagining it or hallucinating out of exhaustion. But no—the young men were taking selfies, standing before the string section.

Mooney could feel the beer, his fourth, lulling him, and he imagined the waltz floating up into the heavens, way beyond the top row of the stadium. He was relaxing in the heart of athletic territory, but he felt surprisingly secure, dismissing his thoughts about the insurgents who had been enticed or bribed to switch sides.

Braverman must have been feeling the same luxurious contentment because he was smiling with his eyes closed. That was okay. Mooney figured even uncompromising radical revolutionaries needed to rest. He shut his eyes too and let himself drift off for a minute.

Chapter 11

Layla Sillimon arrived at her classroom fifteen minutes early to reconfigure the desks. This had to be done since every professor before her, and presumably after, kept them in rigid, militaristic rows. She knew a circle was the very best way to learn, but her enrollment totals for the new winter quarter had already created a problem. This room, the largest in the English building, would still be a tight fit to make a circle for a hundred poets. That was the enrollment for the class going into the weekend. She'd printed the enrollment sheet to call roll.

She had to admit she did like one thing about that crazy Peter Braverman. No matter how pissed off she was at him, he was about the only man she'd met on campus who didn't talk about her blouse or try to tell how to run her class. The old bear, Mooney, he was nice enough. But Braverman was the rebel, the kindred spirit, the peculiar and charming stoner uncle.

She could sense a strange vibe from him, and it was cool, in a way, because it revealed the power of his commitment. And it was exhilarating to get caught in the riot, even if Braverman was old enough to be a founding member of, like, her mom's favorite band, The Jefferson Airplane.

Layla had learned how erotic a riot could be in 1999, when she was a teenager at the Battle in Seattle. N30, they'd called it back then, although nobody used that term anymore. But the World Trade Organization still existed, the bastards. When things went nuts that day and the pepper spray got sprayed, people took off at a sprint, a screaming panic. It was a thrill, the sense of anarchy, a feeling the world was unraveling.

She'd run into a doorway to hide, but another guy, who she'd never seen before, ran up there, too. They ducked into the foyer of a swanky high-rise condominium. He coaxed her into a janitor's closet.

She fought to catch her breath, and he was laughing as he gasped. He had a leaf in his hair, and she reached up to brush it away, but he must have misunderstood, because the next thing she knew they were going at it like crazed weasels, tongues all the way down to each other's pancreases. She started to laugh between gasps, and things almost got out of control between them.

When he admitted he was undercover FBI, she was furious. But, of course, he was, in retrospect, with that Kmart haircut, stiff collar, and enticing blue eyes. She still felt fondly about the lead-up and the sprint into the safe space, and how politics and lust could mix and get crazy. It could end up in a poem someday.

But classroom seating was her task at hand. No use getting all misty-eyed about an undercover Fed. The point was Braverman was not a love interest. Or a lust interest. Or an undercover cop, or a double agent. She had dozens of emails from him since the Poetry Riot, but she hadn't responded. Although she thought about the event constantly, she just needed time to sort it all out.

"You're early," she said when Sasha Dimitrievic walked in.

"First come, first serve," he said.

She gave him a hug like she gave all her arriving or departing students. Last week she was mid-hug in the hallway when Wilson Keats hurried past. She couldn't help herself; she'd winked at him. When he frowned back at her, she'd given

Wilson Keats the finger. So much for Whale's suggestion of using the language of academia.

"Best hug I have in America," Sasha said when she let go. "I am ready for poetry." He rolled his neck and it cracked loudly.

"Right on," she said. "I see you brought a journal."

He raised his notebook. "I have been writing poems since the day we meet," he said. "I am full of inspiration." He thumbed the notebook open, and she could see he *had* been writing poems. A huge number of them.

"That's cool, Sasha," she said. "Wanna read me one?"

"But poems are in Croatian. You don't mind?"

He read one and it sounded gorgeous. He perspired lightly as he read, droplets forming where his nose met his glasses. He said the poem was about his lonely journey to America, or something like that.

Sasha asked to hear one of her poems, which she could have easily recited. But she still needed more seating, and he could handle the physical work. They went to the classrooms next door to swipe the chairs. Normally that might annoy the next professor, but with just two poets in the entire building, it made no difference, and like Sasha said, first come, first serve.

Sasha carried six stacked chairs in each arm. Within a few minutes they were squared away—nearly a hundred chairs in a circle. They'd cleaned out the classroom next door as though they were on a garage sale spree. If more students showed, they could stand. But she couldn't find the printout of her enrolled students anywhere in her backpack, so she hustled upstairs to her office and printed another copy.

On the new printed sheet, only six students were enrolled. Total.

Layla was stunned. Six. She'd had ninety a few days ago. With the old list gone, she'd never know who was supposed to be enrolled, who'd dumped her at the last minute. Did Football do this to her after learning she was pals with Mooney and Braverman? Sasha was still listed, of course. And five others, all boys, it appeared. She sulked for a minute, in a bewildered WTF kind of way. She liked being the popular teacher, and now she was like a dot-com stock after the crash.

According to the course catalog, Wilson Keats was teaching at the exact same time—Modern American Poetry. Yeah, right. Modern like MySpace was modern. Like microwaves and typewriters and rotary phones. It might kill her if Keats attracted more students.

Outside her classroom a crowd of kids mingled. Maybe she didn't need to worry, after all. She recognized a few of her poets from last quarter. She asked one young man what the deal was.

"We're just waiting to get in," he said. But he pointed at the wrong room.

"Whose classroom?"

His reply was a dagger. "Wilson Keats," he said. "But there's not enough chairs." A few students hugged Layla, insisted they'd enrolled in her class, but had gotten an email over the weekend from the registrar saying her class was closed. "We're not the only ones," another boy said. "A bunch of us got bounced."

Wilson Keats appeared, beaming broadly, welcoming the students into his chair-less room. He closed the door in her face.

Layla shuffled back across the hall. Sasha Dimitrievic was sitting alone, head down, scribbling away. She shouldn't cancel class, but it sure was tempting. She'd have to go in there and do her best to teach him, despite her embarrassment. She couldn't deprive Sasha of his right to learn. He sat up when she approached and thumbed his glasses back up the bridge of his nose.

This was totally unfair. Maybe this was karmic payback for the hateful way she thought about her colleague. Could that be it?

"Very small class," he said in a kindly tone. "Maybe we have too many chairs?"

"Maybe," she said.

"Wrap them up, I will eat them later," he said.

She gave him a sad smile. They were both quiet for a minute. She shuffled through her ridiculous printed stack of one hundred syllabi. After a minute she checked her phone and her enrollment printout again. Class should have started. She had five absences the first day, and eighty-something percent were missing. She didn't recognize the names of the absent kids—DeShawn. DeMarco. Lyndon. LaCroy. And Todd.

Moments later five tall guys burst into Layla's classroom, arguing and laughing. They were well over six feet, with different dark skin tones. Except Todd. Layla guessed the white guy was Todd. He was the tallest. And whitest.

Layla motioned them into her circle. One by one they collapsed into their seats and slid down, necks perched on chairbacks and legs extended as if they were on chaise lounges at a swimming pool.

"What do you call a white dude," one kid said, pointing at Todd, "who hangs with five brothers?"

Layla was delighted. She loved jokes, which, like poetry, used surprise and misdirection. With only four Black men in front of her, the joke was not entirely accurate, but she was willing to play ball. "Let me think," she said. "A white guy—hmmmm." Layla scratched her head theatrically while the tall white kid squirmed. "How about Eminem?"

Sasha sat up straight and raised his hand. When the fellow who posed the question shrugged at him, Sasha said, "Josip Conrad."

"Who?"

"Famous novelist who—"

"No," the kid said, and gave Sasha a disdainful look. "You call the white guy Coach. Get it?"

Everyone laughed except Sasha, although he was smiling politely, trying to tabulate the humor.

The jokester clarified by adding, "Todd isn't our coach, but that is still some funny shit for real."

Layla thanked him for sharing.

"See," he explained, "there's five brothers make up a basketball team."

Layla reminded everyone this was Intro to Poetry Workshop, and she asked them to introduce themselves. "Unless you're not comfortable sharing. If that's the case, you could totally share that fact. But let's all give a couple interesting details about ourselves, then add a few words about your thoughts on poetry or this class."

A couple of the basketballers grumbled.

"I'll start. I'm Layla Sillimon and poetry means everything to me. I read it every night, and I try to write a poem each day. My dreadlocks are twenty years old, if you were wondering. This is my first year at Coors State, but my second quarter. I make my own yogurt. My preferred pronouns are she and her."

"My name is Sasha Dimitrievic," Sasha said without even being prompted. Layla could tell he was going to be the anchor of the class, a leader, the one the others admired as a role model. "I am from Croatia. My uncle was famous poet. I am center for football team and I need two-hundred grams of protein each day, so I love yogurt, too."

"Dude looks like Shrek, am I right?" said the guy next to Sasha, and a couple of them howled. "He's Shrek! Check out Shrek. All you need is Miss Piggy to go on a quest with you."

"Let's keep things respectful," Layla said.

"I didn't mean you're Miss Piggy," the guy explained. "But what's with them dreadlocks? You trying to be Black? Because that shit ain't working."

"Let's stay focused," Layla said. The last comment stung, but she forced herself to be more concerned about Sasha. She wanted to be sure he wasn't wounded. He was smiling pleasantly.

"My name is Lyndon," the guy next to Sasha continued. "My favorite movie is *Shrek II*. My coach said this would be an easy class. I got mad skills with a basketball. That's what's up."

"My name is Lyndon, too," said the next guy. The others shouted him down. "No, I'm DeShawn. I wouldn't even want to be this bum, on the real. But," he added, pointing at Sasha, "*Shrek II* is also my favorite movie. Me and Lyndon watch it together every night."

Layla realized this group might prove challenging.

"I'm DeMarco," the third basketball player said. "These chumps here are stupid. Don't pay them no nevermind. I love poetry, like Amiri Baraka and Quincy Troupe, but I can't get into Langston Hughes or any so-called Negro poetry. But I read a lot and I'm looking forward to this class."

"My name is LaCroy," the next guy said, "and I've never seen the whole movie, but *Shrek* would be a good topic for a poem. Not this gentleman here," he added, pointing his pen at Sasha, "but the real Shrek, because of the way he's ostracized and disenfranchised due to his green skin and his disability."

Todd must have been shy, because he mumbled his name and confessed his love of Froot Loops. Layla moved on, introducing her in-class writing prompt to get them putting pen to paper. She explained metaphor and simile and said she wanted all of them to create five similes.

"What, you mean right now?" DeShawn asked.

"Just remember a simile needs a *like* or *as*," Layla said.

"Dumb as Shrek," one of them said. "That works, right? Now I just need four more."

"Stupid as Shrek," another said. "Ugly as Shrek."

"Those don't count," said the first kid. "Think of your own shit."

"I said ugly as Shrek."

"How about," Layla interrupted, "we can't use the name Shrek, okay? Let's focus in another direction."

After class, Layla went to her office, fell into Sasha's recliner, and bawled.

She'd done nothing wrong. Yet it seemed as though her happy world had collapsed. The job had seemed so cool early in the school year, but things hadn't been right since the Poetry Riot and the onslaught of suck-up messages from Braverman. A dean had emailed her to say while her freedom of speech was protected, she'd have to use better judgment about attaching her name to lost causes, like trying to overturn the decisions of the administration.

Mooney had introduced her to Sasha in the first place. Did Mooney want to help or hurt Football? She hadn't completely understood before the Poetry Riot that Braverman, and probably Mooney and the Hamlet professors, were actually trying to take down athletics. The tent city professors hadn't said a word to her about eliminating Football, but that was the subtext.

And now, at the start of a new quarter, her class had nearly vanished in the span of forty-eight hours. And Wilson Keats was more popular than she? The best way to put it was *what the fucking fuck?*

Also, near the end of class, she'd accidentally called Sasha "Shrek." The basketball players whooped it up, and although he handled it gracefully, she felt horrible.

She opened her own web page, because it always made her feel good to reread her accolades. Next she opened her emails. Just hearing from a teenage fan could lift her mood.

"A Warning," was the subject line of the second email.

It was from Tom Maniscalco, who identified himself as the next football coach. He said she was being punished by Football for instigating a riot. Football had decided (could a football decide anything? she snickered) she was negatively influencing too many students. She was now on Athletic Probation, and Football had allowed her just one player from their team, as well as a few basketball players. "We'll make our decisions based on how the semester and your Pottery Workshop unfolds. This is your chance to prove yourself."

Pottery? That was a typo, she hoped, but it was infuriating. Fucking pottery? According to this coach, she was going to have to prove herself by being—what? Patient? Lenient? Every single student of hers had gotten an "A" last quarter. Wasn't that good enough for Football?

She tried to return the email to this Coach Maniscalco with questions, but her query got bounced back—"Due to the high volume of fan mail directed to the coaches, please be patient in awaiting your response. Don't forget Coors State Football memorabilia is available in every building on campus."

Chapter 12

Rosa Parks: My Story.

Eugene Mooney held the book at arm's length. "A simple title was the best choice for a powerful woman, I suppose," he said. "Layla will appreciate this, presuming she reads outside of her field."

"Any poet worth his salt does," Peter Braverman said.

"Her salt. Layla is a her," Mooney said.

"You're kidding."

"And other poets are women as well. I just think we need to tread lightly to keep her on our side."

Braverman said, "We're doing much more than keeping Layla on our side. We've lifted her to the next level. She was famous before," and he paused thoughtfully. "But that's not the same as being a living legend. She's the woman who sparked a change on a college campus just before the Movement went national." Braverman muttered to himself, "Spark, Parks, change, game, shame."

"What are you saying?"

Braverman said, "I told you, I'm writing poetry again, and I'm interested in word play. Sparked rhymes with Parks, I just noticed." He waved a notebook at Mooney. "I thought I'd show my new poems to Layla today."

Mooney sighed. No teacher wanted to read drafts they weren't getting paid to read, and as unique as Layla was, he doubted she'd be different in that regard. You don't open your mouth wide at a cocktail party just because some guy mentions that he's a dentist. "Let's just give Layla the book and tell her our plan," he said.

"It's been years since I wrote poetry," Braverman said. He gazed out the window, as if his own past might appear there. "Not since my Berkeley days. The Free Speech Movement. Did I tell you about meeting one of the Weather Underground leaders in the Seventies?"

"Absolutely," Mooney said curtly, but he immediately felt bad for his snippy tone, and he apologized. He told Braverman he was agitated because of Football's latest decision. Each game, a student's name would be drawn at random. The lucky student—provided he or she was in attendance—would win a thousand dollars. To Mooney, it felt crass, but Braverman seemed less bothered by it. Mooney packed up his papers, shut down his computer, and approached the campus map pinned to his bulletin board.

"I got high with Mark Rudd in 1976," Braverman said, as though he were longing to go back in time.

Mooney admired Mark Rudd, the old radical Weathermen leader, but they needed to stay on task. "You tried to talk about the New York Yankees with him because he was from New York," Mooney said.

Braverman came back from the window.

"And Rudd had never seen a Yankees game," Mooney continued, "and all he wanted to talk about was Vietnam."

"So, I did tell you."

About a dozen times, Mooney thought, but he said, "Explain your strategy for the march."

The first protest since the Poetry Riot, Braverman said, would take place in two days. December 2 was getting close to the Winter Break, but neither man wanted to wait until after Christmas. Besides, after the Silver Bullets' bowl game, the opportunity to march to football practice would be over, at least until spring football practice.

"We're in agreement," Mooney said, "that Layla will lead the march originating in The Hamlet. But another poetry reading could be too risky. For her, I mean."

"Too risky at this time," Braverman added. "I'd like to read a few of my own poems the next time it's appropriate."

"For now, let's be sure we agree on our marching route." Mooney unpinned the campus map and spread it on his desk.

Braverman used a yellow Hi-Liter to mark their planned path. He was clearly hyper-prepared; he even slapped on a small photo of Shakespeare to designate their place of origin—The Hamlet. From there, they'd march to the stadium. The team would be practicing, and that was precisely the point—to tweak peacefully the nose of the football program, get noticed, but not derail the Movement by doing anything loco.

Mooney said, "We'd bypass the Student Union that way."

"Is that good or bad?"

"I don't know. We might drum up more spontaneous support there."

"Or we could create more problems for ourselves," Braverman said, as if creating problems for himself was something he'd never done.

"We'd have to cross the pond," Mooney said, "and the bridge is pretty narrow."

Braverman underlined Velma's Pond on the map. Velma had been the name of the college president's daughter in the 1920s.

Mooney added, "We'd have to march in tandem at that point."

"Velma's Pond," Braverman said. Then he said it again.

"I heard you, yes." Mooney said.

"So, it's Velma Bridge."

"I've never heard it called that," Mooney said. "But I suppose so." His friend seemed ready for yet another argument, and Mooney didn't have the energy.

Braverman grabbed Mooney's hand and forced him into the classic 1960s soul shake. "Velma Bridge rhymes with Selma Bridge. This is our Selma Bridge."

Mooney didn't think everything was an omen, but it was an odd coincidence. "Rosa Parks didn't march at Selma Bridge," he pointed out. "Martin Luther King did, but it wasn't until the third time they crossed. I'm pretty sure, but we can research it later."

Braverman pondered this. "Our Rosa Parks will cross Velma Bridge." He didn't, however, say the obvious—they had not seen Layla since the Poetry Riot.

There was one key aspect they disagreed on. Braverman had proposed the protestors march literally onto the football field to disrupt practice. That was a terrible idea, far too confrontational, and Mooney insisted they merely march around the walkway that looped the stadium at Row 40, the midpoint. Five laps to signify their five demands. Everyone, including the TV cameras and reporters near the field, would be witnesses, and the marchers would get plenty of notice.

To Mooney's relief, Braverman agreed to stay completely off the field.

Mooney raised his hand to knock on Layla's door, then paused for a moment. "She's crying," Mooney said. "Let's come back later."

"Nonsense," Braverman said. "Our Layla's in distress." He didn't even knock—he simply twisted the doorknob open.

Layla sat in her Swedish recliner, feet pointed to the ceiling, dreadlocks covering the floor like an old mop. Although she was upside down, it was easy to see she was upset. She balled a fist and pounded on her own thigh. "I'm having a terrible day," she wailed.

"What happened?" Mooney said.

"I'll tell you in reverse chronological order," Layla said. "Sasha's chair broke again a minute ago. And my enrollment for poetry workshop dropped in one weekend from ninety-six to six." She waved a class printout at them like a flag of surrender. "And instead of ninety-six poets, I got five jerks from the basketball team. And Sasha, who I love." She sobbed again.

"Whom I love?" Braverman suggested. He righted the recliner so she could stand.

"And now his chair is broke," Layla said. "I'm not saying all the basketball players are bad," she went on. "I don't mean that."

"You could use a hug," Braverman said.

"I could use a drink. Or a joint."

Braverman dug deep into his pants pocket, but Mooney slapped his arm.

"And," Layla continued, "I got a very threatening email from this football coach, an Italian guy. Everything was going great in my life, but I've been cursed ever since I read one fucking poem at The Hamlet. And I keep getting the hairy eyeball from my colleague."

"We want you to lead us on a march," Braverman blurted out.

"What march?"

"Let's give her a moment," Mooney said. "In fact, Layla, why don't we come back at a better time?"

"You're our Rosa Parks," Braverman said. He thrust the biography into Layla's face. Still inverted, she reached for the book, but when she gave up her grip on the armrests, she slid down, rammed her head into the carpet like a pile driver. She groaned a curse.

"I still say you need a hug." Braverman bent to embrace her. Layla jumped to her feet and socked him right in the kisser.

"Owww," Braverman said. "You bitch." His lip was split and instantly swelled up.

"Both of you stop," Mooney said, stepping between them, facing Braverman like a boxing referee giving a standing eight count. "We all know violence isn't the answer."

Layla examined the book's cover, flipped it over and read the back. "First of all, I'm white and Rosa was not," she said. "And it's weird you guys equate the civil rights movement with college football. Weird in a bad way."

"Please," said Braverman. "We need you. Sorry I called you a bitch, by the way."

"That's okay. Sorry I punched your fucking face. I'm not Rosa Parks, but today I am indeed a bitch. And a poet, I hope. You're good guys, but my life has become a hot mess. I have nightmares about the cops and being trapped on a bus with a bunch of radicals. Our cheerleaders send me hate mail."

Braverman started to speak, but Mooney raised a hand to allow Layla time to finish.

"I was supporting the English professors who'd hired me," she said. "Taking down Football wasn't my goal. And now, Criminal Justice professors are staking out my apartment, and this threatening email comes from the coach. I've gone from the most popular teacher at Coors State to a social pariah. Thank God for Sasha. He's the only good thing you two have brought into my life."

"What about my book?" Braverman said.

"I couldn't finish it," she sighed.

"No rush," Braverman said. "Take your time."

Mooney scowled at Braverman, then turned to Layla. "It's not the right time for this, but we might as well tell you our plan. We had this idea you could be the face of the Movement, the push to reclaim our school. It's only getting worse. You know. Football forced those ninety students to drop your class over the weekend. So, we're asking you. Formally. Won't you stand with us, in a leadership role, to take back Coors State?"

"No."

"You wouldn't even have to think," Braverman said. "We'd tell you everything to say and do."

"Fuck you, Peter," Layla said.

"It will make the world a better place," Braverman said, but it came out in a whimper.

"Not my world," she said. "My world was awesome until I met you two. No offense, but I am not Rosa Parks. And for the record, I think she was super cool. You? Not so much."

The professors trudged back across campus in a pathetic line, Mooney trailing, until they got to the parking lot where Braverman usually parked his Volvo. Mooney realized his friend was so upset that he hadn't remembered that the car had been towed and he had never reclaimed it. Mooney led him away from the parking lot. They needed to prepare their menu for concessions at the first basketball games later in the week, but Braverman was clearly not interested. There was a fifth Coors-themed pub being constructed close to the history building. Mooney deliberately steered Braverman away from the site.

A minute later, Braverman stopped at a bench and practically fell onto it. Mooney could tell he was devastated, but he was utterly unprepared for Braverman's cloudburst of tears. He'd never seen Braverman cry before. He waited until his colleague was reduced to sniffles to pat his back. "Come on," he said. "This isn't the end. She was a pretty face, but if we have to talk her into being an activist, she's clearly not the leader we'd imagined."

"Neither am I," Braverman said.

"What do you mean?"

Braverman sat up straight, took a deep breath and faced Mooney. "I'm not who you think I am, Eugene," he said.

"You're not a complete pain in the ass? I disagree."

"I'm serious. I have demons. Things I've never told anyone. Do you want to hear? Because I'm ready to confess. I have to or else I can't move forward with our plan."

"Shoot," Mooney said. "I can handle the truth."

"I never met Patty Hearst. I wasn't her driver. But there's more. I worked late nights at Mister Pizza in Berkeley. That's the only place I met the people involved in the Movement, sliding free slices across the counter to campus radicals. But I was too scared to join them."

"That's not so bad," Mooney said. "Pretty short confession. What about Mark Rudd? You smoked weed with the leader of the Weather Underground, right?"

"Oh, God help me," Braverman gasped.

"Let it out now," Mooney said. "Go on, you'll feel better."

Braverman took a deep breath. His voice was weak. "Mark Rudd came to Berkeley when he was underground in the mid-1970s, I guess, and he was there to speak privately to the local organizers. It was all very hush-hush, no publicity. One night at Mister Pizza, I went to take a leak. He was in the john, getting high, and he offered me a hit. I had a terrible coughing fit. I thanked him and went back to the counter to work."

"You didn't discuss—"

"I didn't even know it was Mark Rudd until he left. Anyway,

I quit Cal without withdrawing, flunked everything, then took two years off and finished up at San Jose State."

"That's okay. San Jose was where you led those marches, right?"

Braverman was silent.

"Peter?" Mooney put his hand on his comrade's shoulder.

"I wasn't a radical," Braverman said. "I never marched on campus. Never carried a sign. I didn't drop out, but I nearly flunked out at San Jose State, too. I never took LSD. I didn't even smoke pot much until I was forty. And I didn't realize how bad the Vietnam War was until it was over. What could I do with my life? I couldn't protest Vietnam in 1980. I never did a single thing in protest of anything. Other than the bumper stickers on my Volvo, I mean. Yet, I read a helluva lot, and I realized over the next few years how horrible the war had been, how awful Black people had been treated in America, how disgraceful it was only three percent of women had the chance to play sports in high school. I devoured all the old issues of *Ramparts*, read *Soul on Ice*, and two Angela Davis books. But by the time I had a grip on the 1960s, it was all history." Braverman paused. "History," he repeated.

"And that's when you decided to pursue History as your field."

"And to specialize in Vietnam. But up until the Poetry Riot, my life was a laughable lie. I was a phony until the day I carried Layla Sillimon on my shoulders. That's why I'm telling you—I couldn't live with the utter falseness of my life any longer. Not with my best friend thinking I'd been a heroic campus radical."

Like a drowning man, Braverman reached for Mooney's hand. "My role in the Poetry Riot was the high point of my campus activism," he continued. "The only point, really. That's the reason I don't want to lose that feeling now. I felt proud of what we did. You and me and Layla are the only sane ones on this campus." Braverman paused and put his other hand on Mooney's now. "You're an honest guy, Eugene. And you know me better than anyone. You see how I am. I know I overreact, I push too hard, and yes, I'm annoying. I know it. I know it. Not to get too Freudian, but I'm certain it's my reaction to doing nothing when I was younger. I just don't want to do nothing forever. I want to make a difference, do something important now. And I knew I could tell you the truth about myself without you judging me for living this lie for so many years."

Braverman released his grip. "What's the matter, Eugene?" he said. "You look like you're going to be sick."

Mooney turned his face away and stifled a sudden urge to jump to his feet and run. This was the perfect time to tell Braverman about his own imperfect past. But Mooney couldn't do it. Not yet.

"What's wrong?" Braverman asked. "You're angry I let you down."

"Not at all," Mooney said, and he stood. "It doesn't matter. Let's go back to your office and finalize our plans."

Chapter 13

"What if some jerk punches me first?" the biggest student asked.

Eugene Mooney said, "You still react peacefully. You possess a deep faith in our future. Isn't that right, Professor Braverman? The forces in the universe bend toward the long arc of justice. That's a direct quote from Martin Luther King, pretty much."

"Dope," the young man said.

Mooney and Braverman were managing the final preparations in their department conference room with a dozen diverse students, handpicked for their leadership potential. March Away from Madness, Braverman had tagged it.

Mooney figured the longer their plans were kept quiet, the better chance they'd have to pull it off. That morning they'd unleashed the student-leaders to use social media and message their friends. Each leader had promised to bring a dozen students, meaning there'd be more than a hundred marchers. Mooney didn't realize until just before the meeting that Braverman had recruited the student-leaders mostly from the beaten-down ranks of women's volleyball and softball, formerly successful programs that had been left behind after the rebranding.

The two professors had made a conscious decision not to include their fellow teachers. Just like in the 1960s, it'd be the students against an unjust system, showing older folks the new way. Professors, instructors, adjuncts, secretaries—everyone else would follow eventually. Even if Layla Sillimon was not destined to be the face of the Movement, students would take back their education—and, when the Movement went nationwide, the future of American universities, too.

"We're not seeking to defeat or humiliate President Cardly or Football," Mooney said, "but to win their friendship and understanding." The students nodded along to the gentle rhythm of Mooney's voice. "And," he added, his voice rising like Dr. King's, "nonviolence means willingness to accept suffering without retaliation."

"Where is Layla Sillimon?" a curly-haired young woman asked. "She started this whole thingy."

"She was invited," Mooney said quietly. "Her role is still being discussed."

"Whatever happens," Braverman said as he put his palm on the cheek of the biggest kid, "don't lose your cool."

Mooney studied Braverman. He never thought he'd hear his friend publicly proclaim any such thing. And the tactful way Braverman just sidestepped the mention of Layla's name, at this time of heightened emotions? Nothing less than remarkable. Maybe Braverman's confession about his college days had helped him finally to mature. Mooney hoped so.

Mooney had had a sleepless night, reliving the foolish blunders he committed as a high school senior. Not just in quitting football. He'd tried to do the right thing and wound up hurting a group of students, a shameful mistake from long ago that he could never erase. He'd finally settled into a fragile realization at 4:00 a.m.: leading this campus Movement would have to serve as atonement for the harm he had caused all those years ago. Only then could he fall asleep. Braverman need never know. It was traumatic enough to confess to himself.

Braverman said, "Professor Mooney will help me demonstrate a nonviolent response. Lie down on the floor here, Eugene, the way you will if the cops arrive."

"Real cops?" one young woman asked, "or those jerks from Criminal Justice."

Mooney dropped down on his belly, head turned to one side.

"On your back," Braverman said.

"That hurts my neck. Unless you have a pillow."

"What are you going to do, carry pillows on the march?" Braverman snapped.

Mooney rolled onto his side, and hoped his look was enough: nonviolence must be practiced in the tone of voice as well as in actions. He suddenly realized he might prefer a nap to a march. He'd skipped breakfast because he thought being hungry might be a motivator. Also because he imagined Gandhi or Dr. King wouldn't have been devouring huge meals before their showdowns with history. But they hadn't weighed in at 240 pounds, and they didn't lift weights at a fitness center twice a week.

"Watch how easy it is," Braverman continued, "to lift someone who is struggling and rigid." He motioned for three of the young women to help take hold of Mooney. "Just four of us, and we aren't very strong. Eugene, you get rigid and angry."

Mooney made himself stiff and forced out a half-hearted growl.

"One, two, three," Braverman shouted.

The students grunted and Braverman staggered. They got Mooney a foot off the ground, but Braverman lost his grip, and Mooney slammed back down on the carpet, ribs first. The fall knocked the wind out of him.

"Well," Braverman said, "the police will be a lot stronger than three college gals."

"That's a shitty thing to say," one tall young woman named Tonya said. "Gals?" She was the captain of the volleyball team and seemed every bit as angry as Braverman usually was.

"She's right, Peter," Mooney said, sitting up. "But let me go limp here and you'll see what Professor Braverman is getting at. Okay. I'm a wet noodle. Try again."

The women pulled, and so did Braverman, but this time they couldn't move him an inch.

"See?" said Mooney. "The power of nonviolence is astonishing."

Just then, one woman—the offended one—grabbed a fistful of Mooney's hair, squatted over him, yanked hard, and yelled, "You're under arrest, you sonuvabitch."

Mooney bolted into a sitting position and stifled a yelp. It felt like he'd been scalped. He staggered to his feet, rubbing his head. The young woman pulled away from Mooney and exchanged fist bumps with her former teammates.

"There's no call for that," Mooney said.

"Sorry," Tonya said with a grin. "Doctor Braverman here got me a little riled up." She gave the men a sarcastic curtsy.

Mooney accepted her apology, ignored the pain, and led the group to a large table.

"We hate Football," Braverman said, "but again, we don't hate the football players. We've got no beef with them. They are very much our allies, although they don't know it yet."

"One last time, where are we stopping in the stadium?" Mooney said, his voice rising.

"Row 40," the student-leaders shouted back, not entirely in unison.

Mooney led his student-leaders to the window to see marchers already assembled near The Hamlet. Was that President Cardly standing at the window above the tents? The shadow in the window swiftly disappeared. The call to action had spread in the past hour and the students were stirred up, relatively speaking. Mooney did a rough headcount and figured about a hundred kids. One student leader wondered aloud if the march was too close to Christmas break. A lot of kids in his dorm had already hightailed it home. Those who remained seemed to be the fringe students, fringe-looking, the kind who would have never followed football, but might not miss a campus reggae concert.

The volleyball captain who'd grabbed him by the hair had convinced her friend on the school newspaper to stream the march online in real time. There'd be no lengthy speeches to kick things off. Speed and timing would be imperative in mobilizing the marchers. They had released the five demands that very morning, emailed them to the school paper and local media. Braverman wanted to be involved with the final demand: to lead the new oversight board. Mooney figured if his buddy had interest in an administrative role—and he'd gotten tenure by then—that was his business.

It was perfect football weather. Crisp, no wind, sunny. Just before they arrived at The Hamlet, Mooney's knee began to ache, but he knew better than to complain to Braverman. Shoulder-to-shoulder they strode, the students behind them. When Mooney turned back, one young man was rehearsing Kung Fu moves. Mooney frowned and the kid stopped.

At The Hamlet, the smell of garlic and roasting meat floated up like a dream, serenading Mooney. English had gone all-out for once with food prep. This wasn't cheese and crackers. The profs were serving tapas in ceramic dishes to the marchers. Ham croquettes, sausages, and fried calamari. He forced himself not to look around for Layla.

The student leaders gathered their cells to issue last-minute instructions. This was part of Braverman's idea, adapted from his research into Vietcong covert actions. Keep members of each cell ignorant of the names of the leaders of other cells. That way, even if the Criminal Justice profs tortured them, their Movement might be halfway protected. Mooney wondered if that system could be trusted. It seemed each cell leader was a deposed and humiliated team member from various women's sports. He went to inspect the makeshift kitchen and thank their friends. The two men, in their Dodo and Wolf sweatshirts, were slicing up a Spanish tortilla-style potato omelet.

Dodo said, "You'll need your strength today, Eugene. This is what the Spanish Armada ate before battle, according to my research. Although admittedly it's not my field." He held a plate under Mooney's nose.

Mooney inhaled deeply and felt his eyes well up. The Spanish Armada had failed miserably, he knew, and divers were still pulling the wreckage out of the Irish Sea to this day. It might have all been worth it, though, if the Spanish navy ate like this. He wondered what part tapas played in the Spanish Civil War, and if Franco's troops ate them. Or the Lincoln Brigade and the leftists. He could look that up later. The chorizo was amazing. The bravas potatoes had a bit too much garlic—meaning they were perfect. He laughed to himself. Maybe the garlic would keep the Criminal Justice thugs at bay. When he bit into the ham croquette, he sighed.

"Let them cool," Dodo warned.

"It's not that," Mooney said. "They're a culinary miracle."

Braverman burst into the tent. "Eugene, what the fuck? We've got a revolution to jump start."

"You're not going to eat?"

Braverman shook a doggie bag at him. He'd already gotten his to go.

"What about our student-leaders?"

"They ate before the meeting."

"I'll just be a minute," he said, jamming a chorizo into his mouth. Dodo offered him a bag, and Mooney filled it, not with the food on his plate, but from the spread of bowls on the table.

"I'll be outside," Braverman said. "You're not going to feel like marching if you keep eating like that."

A minute later, Mooney found him at the exact spot where he'd once propped up Layla on his shoulders. Braverman said he wanted to start the march there to prove you could kill the revolutionary—Layla was dead in the metaphorical sense, as an insurgent—but you couldn't kill the revolution.

Braverman rang Layla's meditation bell, gently motioned for the students to sit. "After we enter the stadium, we'll walk five laps around Row 40," he reminded them for the fourth time.

Mooney did another quick headcount. They didn't look so imposing seated cross-legged.

"Do you have anything to add, Professor Mooney?" Braverman said, as though they were team-teaching a class.

Mooney had pored over Gandhi's landmark book, *Non-Violent Resistance*, and considered a dozen quotes. He pulled back his shoulders and stood tall now to do justice to Gandhi's memory.

"A small body of determined spirits," Mooney announced, "fired by an unquenchable faith in their mission can alter the course of—"

"We can't hear you!" a student in the back hollered.

More shouts followed.

"Dude said he had an unquenchable thirst for spirits."

"Let's rock and roll."

"Please say the quote again," a woman yelled.

"Gandhi was a communist."

"So what?"

"What about a poem from Layla Sillimon?" somebody else called.

Mooney repeated the Gandhi quote, louder this time, and a few students clapped. Braverman raised a clenched fist and every student followed suit—not exactly the kind of gesture Gandhi usually inspired, but Mooney pretended not to be bothered.

The Hamlet profs waved and shouted thank you to the marchers. The woman in the Buffalo sweatshirt was sobbing. "We love you, Eugene," she yelled.

Mooney felt a lump in his throat. They walked out from under the aspens that surrounded the red brick administration building. His doggie bag bounced against his leg.

The marchers stopped at Velma Bridge. Mooney was last, and he couldn't be certain from fifty yards back, but he hoped the Criminal Justice thugs were not lying in wait. To his relief, it was just curious kids. Still, he felt his palms get sweaty. He wanted to race up to the front and say to Braverman, Keep marching, Brother, we're almost to the Promised Land.

The marchers crossed the pond and Velma Bridge without incident, although Mooney felt an odd emotional tug. For the first time he wished Layla was along. Even from outside the stadium, Mooney could hear the whistles and shouts. His knee was throbbing now, and he squatted to loosen it up, or at least have it stop hurting so much. To his surprise, it felt better.

Up ahead, Braverman entered the stadium and disappeared down the steps toward the field. At Row 40 they'd reconvene, then hang a left and circle the field. The marchers would be close enough to the turf to get everyone's attention, but not so near anyone could honestly accuse them of ruining practice. Security would be called, and they might arrest the marchers, but the instant Criminal Justice got near, that would be the key moment. The marchers would go limp and lie down on the cement. By the time Mooney got to the entrance, Braverman had already led the marchers down to the agreed-upon meeting place.

But Braverman didn't turn left at Row 40. And he didn't turn right.

A white woman marcher with a flaming-red Afro and big sunglasses had jumped the line, passed Braverman, and he was pursuing her down to the field. Every few steps he shouted at the students behind him to stay put. Had they forgotten the route? The marchers began to chant and move toward the grass, too, but Mooney couldn't quite decipher what they were saying.

"Wait, Peter!" Mooney cried out. "Wrong turn."

Practice stopped. The players turned to face the marchers. A few took off their helmets and yelled insults, but most of them just stared in wonder. Mooney could make out Trevor's number 10. He was standing next to Tom Maniscalco.

When Braverman got to the end of the stairs he regained the lead, right at the very edge of the field. He seemed to be addressing the students, whose line stretched out to the top of the stadium. Mooney was stuck at the back.

Mooney skirted the aisle and made it halfway down by slowly hurdling seats, then stepped off to the side. From there he could clearly take in everything, from Braverman at the cusp of the gridiron, all the way up to the stragglers at the top of the stadium. Mooney pitched his empty tapas bag below the seats and burped.

Braverman raised his hands to quiet the group. Mooney couldn't hear all of Braverman's instructions, but he heard "nonviolence" and "Doctor King." Braverman was keeping to their plan in that regard, but why the hell was he so close to the field?

In the next moment an argument broke out, and Braverman spread his arms like a school crossing guard at a dangerous intersection. Mooney saw who had jumped the line—the white woman with the red Afro and huge mirrored sunglasses. She pointed a finger in Braverman's face. They seemed to be in a heated debate until Braverman eased her arm down and directed her back up the stairs.

The red Afro woman retreated for a moment, but she suddenly ducked past him, jumped onto the field, and took off at a sprint.

Five other students quickly followed suit, as if blowing past security at a Bruce Springsteen concert. The line moved down the stairs quickly now, as marcher after marcher jumped onto the field in a burst of anarchy. Mooney skipped down the steps to help Braverman halt the remaining marchers.

"Please stop," Braverman hollered, politely for once, but it was no use. Mooney got to his side as the last of the students flooded the field. The professors were the only ones left in the stands. Braverman dropped his arms in frustration and bounded onto the field, too.

Mooney saw the first hit. As the marchers scurried around the field aimlessly, a player, number 68, took out the red-headed-Afro woman at the ankles with a perfectly executed tackle. One player gave a war whoop. The redhead rolled onto her back, as if playing dead in a children's game. Probably a smart strategy under the circumstances.

That broke something open in the psyche of the other players, and an orgy of tackles followed. Within thirty seconds, most of the protesters were flat on their backs, grasping their ankles or ribs in agony. The field looked and sounded like the aftermath of the Battle of Zacatecas in the Mexican Revolution—more casualties than Mooney could count. He felt the tapas push up in his throat. A thick lineman clotheslined a longhaired student, laying him out. A couple of the coaches ran over and chest-bumped the lineman.

That's when Mooney lost his shit and leapt onto the field.

He bent down into a three-point stance to go after one of the cheering coaches, the cocksucker. Just before he got to his target, Mooney lowered his shoulder into the coach's spine. They crumpled to the ground in a heap, but Mooney was on top. The coach grunted like a pig. Mooney dug in a short, sharp kidney punch, then rose to his feet, his head on a swivel, hunting for his next victim. He vomited violently onto the artificial turf.

Two coaches at midfield directed players to keep tackling the marchers. Mooney wiped the vomit from his chin and ran at them, rolling into the pair with a perfect cross-body block and taking both coaches out at the knees with a sickening crunch.

When he rose again, he was face to face with Trevor.

"Professor, that was a heckuva block."

"Thanks, Trevor." Mooney bent over, hands on his thighs, struggling to catch his breath.

"Illegal as hell, though," the quarterback continued. "Let's get you out of here, too." Trevor grabbed him by the shirt to lead him toward the sideline.

Mooney thanked him, but he felt adrenaline racing through his veins. And anger. Or passion. "Wow!" he said. "Look." He pointed at the stands and Trevor took the bait. Mooney karate-chopped the quarterback's arm and raced back into the fray.

Every marcher was prone on the grass, and their cries of pain mixing with the triumphant whoops and trash-talking of the coaches and players. Although the three coaches Mooney had flattened remained prone in this grotesque mismatch, they were the only scores for the marchers.

Braverman stood alone at the opposite sideline, both arms in the air, flashing the Victory sign like Richard Nixon. Or the peace sign. Was he laughing? Mooney found Tom Maniscalco in his sights, pounding on the backs of two muscled-up brutes. The players then took off in tandem, straight for Braverman.

Mooney knew he didn't have the speed to save his friend. Instead, he tackled the coach, twisted Maniscalco's ear and moved swiftly away to avoid retaliation.

"Watch out, Peter!" he yelled. Braverman broke into a sprint along the sideline away from the approaching pair, as if he could step out of bounds for safety at any moment. Just as Braverman was nearing the end zone—where there'd be no reward or respite—a helmetless Sasha, in his square glasses, appeared out of nowhere. The giant Croatian blasted the lead player chasing Braverman off his feet and into his teammate, saving the skinny professor.

Crossing the goal line transformed Braverman back to his aggressively opinionated self. There were no peace signs now. Despite the gruesome body count, he broke into a jerky end zone dance until he clutched at his hamstring, which must have cramped up. Braverman was a dedicated distance runner, but unprepared for a sideline sprint.

Mooney trudged over to his friend, wheezing and stepping over marchers who rolled around the grass begging for help. Many of the students, Mooney was certain, were just fine, but simply too scared to stand. Several sharp whistles sounded. He tasted vomit from earlier and sweat was pouring down his face.

"What's with the celebration dance, Peter?" he asked. "We just got our asses kicked."

"Fifteen-yard penalty," Sasha said when he appeared next to

Mooney. "Not allowed to celebrate a touchdown. We take time-out now, discuss survival strategy quickly, yes?"

The coaches and players plodded like zombies past the wounded marchers toward their two ringleaders in the end zone.

"This reminds of American history," Sasha said, gesturing at the field.

"The Cal-Stanford game of 1982," Braverman said.

"No. Like American General Custer."

A fine historical reference, Mooney thought, but before he could congratulate the Croatian, Braverman pleaded his case. "I didn't want things to explode like this, Eugene, but that redhead is crazy. She's the one who got everybody riled up. You gotta believe me. I would never let you down." He bent to his right leg and moaned in agony.

Coach Maniscalco was near the end zone now, the team at his heels. Mooney realized one of the coaches he had leveled was Bill Anderson, the head coach who was retiring soon. Maniscalco blew his whistle and motioned the team to form a semi-circle around him.

"You two are better suited for selling popcorn than playing football," the coach said. "Get away from those losers, Sasha. I'm trying to decide their fate."

"Holding still, please," Sasha said, and he gathered Braverman by the waist, squatting to hoist the professor onto his shoulder in one motion. Then he did the same with Mooney. Sasha staggered a little under the uneven weight but quickly righted himself and walked to the steps leading into the stands. Mooney held onto Sasha's head, bumping his glasses by mistake, then righting them.

"Wait just a minute, Dimitrievic," the coach hollered, but Sasha kept climbing. "You bring those men back here right this minute."

Nobody on his team moved, likely stupefied into passivity by Sasha's raw strength. Sasha was sweating profusely from his head, and Mooney struggled not to let his grip slip.

"This is the way to travel," Braverman said.

Mooney felt his chest tighten. He was still struggling to breathe. A crew of Criminal Justice cops with pepper spray entered the stadium above the opposite end zone, where the marchers had arrived earlier. The few students on the field who could move limped toward the sideline, looking to escape, including the woman with the red Afro. Moments later the redhead hitchhiked a piggyback ride from Trevor, the lone player not at his coach's side. Mooney hoped nobody else noticed the quarterback aiding and abetting a rebel, whose red Afro blurred next to Trevor's red helmet. Although the hair didn't have a beer can logo on the side.

"We'll never escape this way, Sasha," Mooney said. "Let us down and we'll make a run for it."

At a passageway that led into the concourse, Sasha slid the professors off his shoulder pads. "See you later, crocodile," he said.

The men ducked into the bowels of the stadium. Mooney ignored an exit sign and staggered into the dark.

"We don't have time to use the toilet, Eugene," Braverman called, hobbling along behind. "We need to hide."

"Follow me," Mooney said. "I have a plan."

Chapter 14

Trevor Knighton's wrist had been aching again since that—what would you call it? The practice protest, he guessed. It was a different ache than the one brought on by over-signing autographs, but once more his throwing arm hurt. He'd gotten an email of apology from Mooney, but nobody seemed to know where the heck he was hiding. With school out for Christmas break, a professor could be anywhere. Maybe even Mexico. Mooney and Braverman, according to their online postings, claimed to be underground and directing the revolution from a secret place.

Trevor wasn't the only one looking for his old teacher. He'd seen Criminal Justice professors staking out Mooney's office, where Trevor had to answer pointed questions. One had threatened Trevor with a Taser gun until he recognized the school's quarterback.

"Be careful," the Taser man warned Trevor. "Mooney is an animal. He's dangerous and can't be trusted."

Mooney *had* turned into an animal, Trevor thought. The football team was supposed to be focused on the Fiesta Bowl showdown with USC, but the players' mindset at practice that week had been dominated by the odd events. It pained Trevor to admit, but he blamed the team's obsession not on Mooney but on Coach Maniscalco. All college practices were filmed, so naturally the march into the stadium and ensuing free-for-all was captured for review. The team's four film coordinators had edited down the video, using slow motion, splicing in music to turn it into a bizarre highlight reel, and they screened it at their regular film session. The players guffawed, while coaches treated it like a normal breakdown tape—the highlights repeated as Maniscalco praised individuals who had leveled the marchers. The protestors were passive if you could call running for your life "passive."

Even the disposing of the injured students, many of whom were too frightened to move, was captured on film. The players dragged them off the field by their ankles. The marchers didn't struggle, which must have been a planned strategy.

Only one marcher fought back, Professor Mooney. His blocks and well-executed tackles passed without comment during the film session. He was a beast on an insane search-and-destroy suicide mission.

The end of the film revealed the team could have gang-tackled Sasha, with both professors on his shoulders, but they had been momentarily dumbfounded. By the time the chase began, the professors had disappeared.

Trevor recognized himself at one point, standing off to the side on the bottom left corner of the screen. While the camera focused on the brutal tackles, he was conversing with Mooney like they were formulating a plan during a time-out. To Trevor's relief, this part of the film passed without comment—as did his piggybacked rescue—since there was plenty of positive violence to focus on. Strangely, seeing Mooney whack his arm on screen gave Trevor a sharp pain again. His forearm had swollen up that evening, but rather than tell the athletic trainer, he iced it on his own again. He didn't want the coaches wondering about their quarterback's health before the final game, their shot at going undefeated.

The players had been mostly praised amid the laughter. That's why the knives from Maniscalco stood out at the end. "Now watch our dumbass Croatian, fellas," the coach said. "Sasha, can't you tell who is on your side after being in this country for a year? Do we need to find you a fucking translator again?"

The team busted up, hooting as the play unfolded—Sasha's perfectly efficient block allowed Braverman safe passage into the end zone. One player said Sasha was a dumb Polack. A few others jeered and threw towels at him. It was the only malice within team ranks that Trevor had heard in a year. He wondered if the coaches were looking at him differently when the lights came back on. He had crossed a line in helping a wounded protestor, but had they noticed?

When the players were dismissed from the meeting, Sasha was called to a private conference with Maniscalco. Trevor waited for him outside, but when Sasha appeared five minutes later, he refused to reveal much.

Neither of them had tackled a marcher, and Trevor's aiding the protestor seemed to have gone unnoticed. But not Sasha's blocking for Braverman. Trevor wasn't proud of his reaction—he had mostly stood by and watched in awe until a rabid Professor Mooney appeared, then took off, and Trevor was reduced to spectator again, a spectator with a throbbing throwing arm.

"I thought what you did was fantastic," Trevor said to Sasha on the walk home, "but I bet the coaches are not happy with you."

"I follow my instinct. I help under the dog."

"The underdog."

"Bad idea for marchers to march in field," Sasha said. "Maybe we get helmets for our professor friends for next march. I make funny joke."

"I haven't been on the underdog team since eighth grade." Trevor sighed.

Two weeks later, Trevor was suiting up for the Fiesta Bowl in Arizona. This would be Bill Anderson's final game as head coach. He'd already faded into a sort of figurehead in the last few weeks, with Coach Maniscalco taking charge before the games and at halftime.

Each player had his own routine and superstitions. iPods, undressing, and dressing. Stretching, pooping, praying, and puking. A manager announced five minutes until the team meeting, and moments later Sasha appeared at Trevor's locker, presenting his roll of white tape in one hand, his helmet in the other. Trevor always wondered why Sasha didn't get athletic goggles or a simple elastic strap, but he'd long ago stopped asking. Their ritual had been done in silence for two seasons—no "please tape my glasses" or "is that too tight?" Just the exchange of tape and the securing of Sasha's square spectacles.

Just as Trevor was about to start their taping routine, one team manager tapped him on the shoulder. "Coach Maniscalco wants to see you in the hallway," the manager said. The timing was odd, but the request wasn't unusual. There were always last-minute strategy changes and anxious reminders.

Maniscalco was waiting in the hallway. "I've decided not to start Sasha today," he said, "due to his insubordination at practice. He's going to be on the bench."

The news should have been a shock to Trevor, but like every player, he'd been trained to put everything out of his mind except the task at hand—in this case, winning a nationally televised bowl game. He nodded at the coach, but before he could go back to the locker room, Maniscalco added, "You go tell Sasha."

Trevor ducked into a corner of the locker room to think, but also to give himself a pep talk. This wasn't the time to get caught up in a team feud or disciplinary measures. He had to be focused to perform well, and he had to put any and all distractions out of his head. He took several deep breaths to calm himself.

Back at their lockers, Sasha was sitting patiently, facing away from his quarterback. Trevor whispered the bad news into his roommate's ear. Sasha twisted around to face Trevor, looking at him quizzically, as if he'd forgotten all the English he'd learned since arriving in America. Trevor was about to repeat the awful news when Sasha turned back around without speaking. Trevor took up the athletic tape and made several strips, putting each one on the back of Sasha's jersey, where they'd hang until he was ready to use them. He quietly secured his roommate's glasses strip-by-strip, like a paper-mache project in kindergarten. Sasha's hairless head still had that sandy roughness from months of practices and games. Trevor fastened the last strip of tape and added his usual final touch, a gently bongoed drum-roll on Sasha's skull.

Sasha was supposed to respond with, "I'm ready like Freddy." But today he did not. Trevor tugged on Sasha's shoulder pads to jolt him into remembering his line, then he leaned over to catch the Croatian's eye. "Sasha," he said, "are you crying?"

"Very smoky in here," Sasha said through a forced smile.

Trevor quickly wiped at the single tear with a towel. "I bet coach sticks you in the game after the first series. You wanna talk about this?" He didn't wait for an answer, just pulled his friend toward the toilets. But there was no privacy there with three lines of anxious teammates. Trevor led him out of the locker room, back into the quiet and empty hallway. Only a few minutes remained before Maniscalco's pregame talk.

"The coach told me I am embarrassed," Sasha said, holding back tears.

"You mean today? Oh, at your private meeting."

Sasha nodded.

"No, Coach must have said you were an embarrassment."

"Oh," Sasha said, and he stopped crying. "Which one is worse? Embarrassed or embarrassment?"

Trevor thought for a moment. "Being an embarrassment is a lot worse."

"I have disgraced the Silver Bullets."

"Briefly. Just once if you think about it. Today we have a chance at redemption."

"Very sad to be yelled at by coach. I block my own teammate, a great national tragedy. Now the coach punish me."

"We'll talk about all this after the game," he said, "after we kick their asses. Just be ready, I know he'll put you in there." Inside the locker room somebody blew a whistle. It was time for Maniscalco's speech, so he tugged at Sasha's uniform, led him back inside.

The coach demanded quiet and said they had a special guest who was going to say a few words. "Let's hear it, you guys, for our President, Martin Cardly. Marty?"

Patches of applause bounced off the cinderblock walls, and a couple players hollered. But nobody appeared.

"Where did he go?"

"He's in the john," somebody said. The locker room remained respectfully quiet until a flushed toilet roused them back into a cheer. President Cardly emerged, looking sheepish.

"Sorry, guys," President Cardly said. "It's not just players who get nervous bowels before the Fiesta Bowl. I'm here today to tell you how proud everyone at Coors State is to have our name associated with a fine football program like yours. All of us, every teacher and administrator, want to thank you for allowing us to continue as part of this university. But most of all, we want to tell you that no matter what happens today, win or lose, we'll continue working for you guys to make Coors State a better place to play football."

Before the players could applaud, Coach Maniscalco stepped to the front and held up a hand. "Let's get this straight, Martin," he said. "No matter what happens? Are you suggesting it's fine for these young men to lose today?"

"In the context of what I said—"

"Because that is not okay."

"Yes, sir."

"Finish," Maniscalco said, "but hurry up about it."

"If you could just allow me—"

But the players had already taken their cue from the coach and returned to the clatter of last-minute game prep. Sasha tried to hush the guys by banging on a locker for effect, but that caught on in the wrong way. Soon dozens of players banged on lockers, and in the deafening din, Trevor and Sasha guided Cardly by the elbows until they were out the door, and their president could hurry down the hallway. By the time Trevor and Sasha were back inside, the coach had already called the team together for prayer. The quarterback and the Croatian froze, bowed their heads, but they were far away from the rest of the team.

When Trevor took the field for the first series, he failed to consider what should have been at the top of his mind—having a new center hiking the ball to him every play would disrupt his timing. As if his sore throwing arm wasn't distraction enough.

Trevor fumbled on the initial Coors State possession, and USC marched to a touchdown minutes later. From then on,

Trevor was extra careful with every snap, but being cautious meant he wasn't his usual swaggering self and it showed—the team couldn't generate any offense. Midway through the second quarter, he couldn't help himself—he sat next to Sasha when the defense was on the field, hoping that Maniscalco might see them together, that the visual might spark a change in the game plan. It didn't work. Trevor tossed four interceptions, more than he'd thrown all year, and in the end Coors State lost badly. By the time Sasha got his chance, Trevor had already been yanked, so they didn't play a single down together. With two minutes left in the game, and the Silver Bullets hopelessly behind, his own role in Sasha's punishment began to sink in. He should have stood up to the coach, argued on behalf of his roommate. Instead, he'd betrayed him. He vowed he'd make it up to Sasha somehow.

The team was dead quiet afterward, except for the occasional slamming of a locker. The players wandered around with icepacks and dazed looks. Trevor hadn't been in a losing locker room in over a year. Sasha didn't even bother to shower, boarding the bus before anyone else. Trevor followed suit, skipping the shower, but before he made it to the bus, he got cornered by three African American guys from their offensive unit, all key players.

"Look, Trevor," one of them said, "we know your daddy's got money, but we need our free rides here. You keep messing up like today, we could all get blamed. You'd cost us our scholarships. We can't pay for school on our own."

Trevor began to say something cliché about doing his best, but another player pointed a finger in his face and added, "I hear you spending more time with that crazy old professor than with the Coach."

Trevor mumbled an apology and slid away, but the truth was the game's result hadn't sunk in yet, nor had the comments about his father's wealth or the fact that he'd be fine financially without his full ride. He was thinking about something else. He found his roommate in the rear of the bus, alone. Now it was Trevor's turn to weep, but it wasn't for the loss. Rather, it was because he didn't defend Sasha, hadn't pushed back before the game when he learned of his roommate being benched.

"I let you down," Trevor said. "I'll never do that again."

"We are embarrassment," Sasha finally said.

With school out for Christmas break and the bad loss, no throngs greeted the Silver Bullets on their return to campus. And there was no hope of Sasha going home to Croatia, although Trevor could have easily traveled back to Dallas and invited his roommate along. They admitted to each other that they'd rather mope around their apartment than travel in public. While they didn't have homework, they still had four weeks remaining in the winter quarter. Sasha had become obsessed with his writing and kept busy by revising his poems.

Trevor's holiday misery alternated between two emotions: feeling guilty about what happened to Sasha at the Fiesta Bowl and being so bored he read and reread Sasha's latest poems. The poems were pretty depressing and confusing. Sasha even loaned him a book on the Serbo-Croatian war, although it had nothing to do with his classes. They spent New Year's Eve dateless, together, and alone, watching *Die Hard* and, at Sasha's suggestion, the first two *Shrek* movies. They also downed a case of Pabst Blue Ribbon beer in rebellion against everything.

On an unusually warm January afternoon just before classes were to start, they got up the nerve to show their faces, to meander around campus. When they passed the tent city of The Hamlet, Trevor, on impulse, waved at the four professors lounging in the winter sun.

The women, in their buffalo and whale sweatshirts, booed. That hurt.

"Football doesn't contribute to the mission of a university," Humpback Whale shouted.

Neither does camping, Trevor thought, although he knew it would be a shitty thing to say. These folks were down on their luck, too. But Wolf waved the athletes over and unfolded two chairs, a nice gesture. The men knew who Trevor and Sasha were—not from television or the newspapers but because Mooney had told them about the duo.

Wolf surprised Trevor by saying, "Tough loss."

Rather than spew the usual clichés, Trevor confessed he'd lost his motivation before the game even began. He quickly changed the subject to Mooney and Braverman's disappearance. Mooney had been an important influence in his schooling, Trevor said, and he wondered how two professors could vanish. Did the Criminal Justice Department simply "disappear" them, the way a dictator might? Wolf, however, kept returning to the game, and why Trevor had lost his focus.

"Very bad game," Sasha added.

"In more ways than one." Dodo nodded.

"Afterwards the coach give me the old tomato," Sasha added, just as the women professors sat down.

"Is that so?" Wolf said and raised an eyebrow. "An old tomato. How interesting."

"A motivational tool, no doubt," Dodo added. "Sports psychology." The four professors leaned in their chairs toward the Croatian.

"The coach must be thinking in metaphor," Whale added warmly, as if she had forgotten about her hissing at the players.

"Wait," Trevor said. "Coach gave you an old tomato? You didn't tell me that."

"Because I help the professors escape," Sasha said and shrugged.

Wolf said, "You tossed it in the trash, I suppose?"

Trevor mouthed the words "old tomato," trying to sort out what Sasha meant.

"The old tomato is my ass on a boat to Croatia if I try stunt like this one again."

Trevor could practically hear the wheels turning in the English professors' heads. Tomato tomato tomato. Old tomato.

"Ultimatum!" Trevor shouted.

"Damn," Buffalo said. "I shoulda had that."

"He gave you an ultimatum, Sasha," Trevor said. "That means it's your last chance."

"A fat chance?"

"No," they all said in unison.

"It derives from the medieval Latin word ultimatus," Dodo said.

"It just means you can't screw up again," Whale said kindly.

Wolf said English finally had something in common with Football—both had suffered a stinging loss. "Although Football might have a better shot at bouncing back," he added. Wolf passed a bowl of peanuts to the players. They each grabbed huge handfuls.

"We did watch the game," Humpback Whale said. "I'm sorry to say we were hoping you would not win."

"That's all right," Trevor said. "I'm sorry they cut your department."

"How nice of you to say," Whale said. "Now I wish I could take back my wish that you'd lose every game."

Sasha said, "We cannot turn back the clock."

"Speaking of which," Dodo said, "I don't know if it's good news or bad news, but President Cardly was fired this morning.

Criminal Justice professors dragged him out of his office in handcuffs. We saw the whole thing from here."

"Who will be our new president?" Sasha asked.

"That'll be up to Coach Maniscalco," Dodo said. "He won't take it to committee like we would."

"Or elect a chairman," Wolf said.

"Or chairwoman," Buffalo chided.

"Or start an ad hoc committee to foster new ideas," Humpback Whale said, "with the Step Ladder approach to brainstorming. And the coach won't empower compelling facilitators to deploy cross-curricular articulation, either. You can bet on that."

Buffalo said, "You can also be certain that Maniscalco won't adhere to the bylaws or governing practices clearly stated in our policy manual. Or even accept subsidiary motions to convene a vote."

Dodo shook his head, disgusted.

Trevor had no clue what they were talking about. "Do you guys know where Professor Mooney really is?" This was the second week that Mooney had tweeted about his underground existence. The Hamlet profs claimed ignorance.

Sasha said, "He posts it on the innertube."

The professors stared at him blankly.

"That's what Sasha likes to call the internet," Trevor said. "He's joking."

"Tweet, tweet," Sasha said.

Dodo handed Trevor his phone to show Mooney's latest tweet.

All Power to the Professors!
Peter Braverman and I remain committed to the ideal of a university for educational purposes and not to showcase a sports team.

Next was this:

We are battered and bruised after being abused by Football, but we refuse to give in. You can tackle the revolutionary, but not the revolution!

And then:

We also remain committed to the ideals of nonviolence but understand we may lose our lives in the struggle, especially if we march onto the football field again.

And finally:

We welcome our team's Fiesta Bowl loss as progress. We will now turn our attention to the overemphasis of basketball. We will be making a public statement at a basketball game soon.

Mooney welcomed their loss in the bowl game? That hurt Trevor a little.

Dodo said, "I don't mean to ruin your school year, but Football also decided to take the basketball concession stands away from History. I think our professors Mooney and Braverman are in trouble. Something radical is going to have to happen if History is going to survive." There'd been a few home basketball games this season, but their conference games were coming up soon. History was being punished, their very existence was in doubt. With Professor Mooney AWOL, Trevor figured they'd better visit Layla Sillimon for guidance as soon as the break was over.

The next morning, Trevor was surprised to get a phone call from Tom Maniscalco. "I hope your roommate isn't going all radical anti-war communist," he said.

"He's not, sir."

"See that he doesn't. You hear from that crazy professor?"

"Which one, sir?" Trevor asked.

"Mooney." Maniscalco swore to straighten Mooney out if the professor ever came out of hiding. Trevor wanted Mooney safe from harm and wished the annihilation of the marchers had never taken place. Might Mooney have deliberately intended that as a distraction to cause a Coors State loss? Trevor hoped not.

"I've already figured out how to get the little guy, his buddy Braverman," the coach said, as if they were discussing a new game plan. "I'll make sure he gets denied tenure, which he's up for in February."

Trevor was pondering this info when he heard a click. His coach had hung up. He flopped down on his couch. With the season's sad conclusion so close in the rearview mirror, he'd been feeling a sense of aimlessness. He had no schedule. No weightlifting, no study hall, no practice, no film, no press conference.

Trevor and Sasha spent their remaining vacation days wandering the campus, bored. They'd stop by The Hamlet with snacks, hoping for a chat. "The campus might have undergone a radical shift," Buffalo told Trevor one day, "if only Mooney's timing had been different." In her opinion, witnessing peaceful marchers used as tackling dummies could have mobilized the entire student body, but because it went down so close to the holidays, nobody paid attention.

Professor Mooney had never mentioned to Trevor that he believed the lofty status of Football was a problem. Neither had Braverman. Why hadn't they approached the players? It was confusing. "What can we do to help?" Trevor wondered aloud to Buffalo. He and Sasha leaned forward in their seats.

"Lose games on purpose," she suggested.

"Kick a touchdown for the other team," Whale added.

"We will be on the bench in a minute in New York," Sasha sighed.

"In a New York minute," Buffalo said. "I'm from New York, by the way. You can probably tell from the way I say 'New York.' Also, you might quit football and join our protest. During our next committee meeting, I could propose putting up another tent."

Trevor said another player would gladly step up and fill his coveted quarterback position. Quitting would be futile.

"I make a metaphor," Sasha said. "We are prawns in the chess game of life."

Everyone laughed.

One cold afternoon, just a few days before classes were to start up again, Sasha elbowed Trevor and pointed out Layla Sillimon, across campus, limping into the English building. Off they went at a trot. Trevor fell in behind, but then he picked up the pace and passed Sasha. The race was on.

"We are racing to poetry." Sasha laughed. They ended in an all-out sprint. At the entrance, they doubled over to catch their breath.

"Man, it's funny how fast we got out of shape," Trevor said. "Four weeks, and I feel like I haven't played football in four years."

Layla was overjoyed to see them and invited the guys up to her office. She knew they'd lost their bowl game, although it became obvious that she hadn't tuned in. That was all right. Trevor asked about the history professors as soon as her door closed.

"It's a mystery," she said. "But I reread his tweet. Totally cool."

"They are in dangerous position," Sasha said. "We should find them to make sure they get enough of the protein."

Trevor said they'd been bringing food to The Hamlet, and they'd be willing to help feed Mooney and Braverman.

"I love The Hamlet," Layla said.

"And do you love also the professor Peter Braverman?" Sasha asked.

"Where'd you get that notion?" she said.

"Because I am thinking maybe he loves you," Sasha said.

"I don't want either Professor Braverman or Mooney to get in trouble," she said, "but no, I don't love Braverman. He's too old for me. Among other issues."

"What Dr. Mooney did was crazy," Trevor said. "Marching right onto the football field in the middle of an important practice? That was too confrontational. They were asking to get their asses kicked."

"I did not hear them ask," Sasha said.

Layla was silent. Trevor continued: "Professor Mooney said they were copying Gandhi and Martin Luther King, but I can't imagine Gandhi zigzagging across the field."

"I think Martin Luther King would have punted," Sasha said. "Do you get my jokes?"

"I guess not," Layla said. "But I disagree, Trevor. I think the march needed to bring things to a head for everyone concerned."

"Water beneath a bridge," Sasha said.

Layla hesitated for a moment, as if she had something important to reveal. She said finally, "I'm so glad to see you guys. There's always next year, right? Sorry if I sound like a coach or your mother. I just don't want you two dragging your asses around like your dog died."

Trevor sighed. "It doesn't sound like Mooney is going to be making any concessions."

"No more popcorn?" Sasha asked.

"Not like that," Trevor said. "Concessions as in giving up on their quest."

Layla squinted at the players. "Mooney makes concessions," she said slowly, as if it might be a good title for a new poem.

Chapter 15

Layla leaned back in Sasha's recliner and rotated slowly until she was almost upside down, her new chill-out pose. She was feeling major pressure. She'd poked around all over town in search of Braverman and Mooney. Nothing. Neither professor was responding to her emails or phone calls. Being underground, they were no doubt in fear of having their accounts monitored. Well, maybe this was her karmic payback since she'd avoided them for weeks after the Poetry Riot.

Today—a cold enough Monday for her scruffy black leather motorcycle jacket—she'd planted herself in Sasha's recliner to think. They had to be somewhere. She retraced everything she knew about them, their habits, Braverman's impulsiveness. And how Mooney would double-check the lock on his office door and use sanitized wipes before eating or take a deep breath before answering the simplest question. They were quite the pair, the reckless Peter Braverman and the cautious Eugene Mooney. And yes, she liked them both a lot, in small doses. Mooney was less annoying. Yet, Braverman seemed younger, livelier.

With blood rushing to her head, Layla felt a strange twitch in her gut. The twitch told her that Peter Braverman was a good man. Or at least a decent human. Some men truly needed a woman. He was not, like, bump uglies material, but she decided she could indeed be a real friend to him. Although it would be far less complicated to be friends with Mooney. Then again, she couldn't be close with one and not the other. She would have to set boundaries with Braverman, explain that he was old enough to be her father, and they were not going to have a physical relationship.

For the last two months, Layla had been thinking of her own father. Or to be more specific, wondering what the hell he was like. That couldn't be directly attributed to Braverman, could it? Not that Braverman reminded her of her dad, just that—well, it was complicated. She missed her dad, but could you miss a person you didn't remember? Maybe this would inspire a poem later. Thinking about her father, in turn, made her rethink her mom. Meaning, she was beginning to admire how her mother sold and sacrificed everything in San Francisco to work for social progress. Layla didn't want her own life to make a mockery of her mother's values, so she had made the decision, before their big march. She'd help Mooney and Braverman.

What she couldn't be for them? Rosa Parks. She wouldn't mind the publicity of being Rosa Parks, but cops creeped her out, and handcuffs terrified her. Layla knew what men truly wanted, wanted more than sex. Or power. They wanted inspiration, motivation, a muse.

A quest.

So she'd tried her best to help the professors when they'd paraded into the stadium. Braverman had been talking all that trash to the marchers about Gandhi and nonviolent resistance and going limp, but his eyes were saying something else entirely. An anonymous gesture to kick-start their revolution? She was down with that, but she wasn't about to publicly risk her job over a possibly Sisyphean task.

Reclining now, she had a revelation. Snap! She knew exactly where Braverman and Mooney were, right this very minute. She somersaulted out of Sasha's recliner and stood quickly. Way too quickly. She swooned as the blood rushed out of her brains, reaching for a bookshelf to balance. "Go easy, sister." She laughed, then yanked open her bottom file cabinet drawer and stuffed a hemp handbag full of granola bars, a carton of organic almond milk, and the wig.

"Beware of Guard Dog" signs were posted all around the stadium. Layla didn't hear any dogs, but to be safe she squatted near a side entrance to entice them. She was upwind, but after five minutes there wasn't a sniff. Or a bark. She whistled a few times to make sure. Nothing. Maybe attack dogs wouldn't bother vegetarians.

Classes would start up again in three days, but nobody was coming back to campus before they were required to—especially the football team. Not a single car sat in the parking lot. But Layla smelled something familiar in the air besides her patchouli. What was that?

She paced back and forth in front of the chain-link fence, counted steps, and retraced them. The fence was topped with star-like clusters of barbed wire and was at least twelve feet high. Still, she thought she could make it up and over. She peeled off her motorcycle jacket and held it in her teeth. It was heavy, but she'd need it when she got to the top of the fence. She shifted her handbag's strap across her chest to keep her hands free, like a bandolero on a Mexican revolutionary. She counted steps, then rocked back and forth to prepare for a running start. Through clenched teeth she said, "Build that wall!" and sprinted at the fence as best she could on her tender ankle.

She got about two-thirds of the way up before she stalled and struggled to get her footing. Her Doc Martin boots were better than her usual Birkenstocks, no doubt, but the wide toes weren't helping. And the goddamn leather jacket kept getting in the way. She bit down harder, clawing to the top where she slung the jacket up over the barbed wire. With the jacket as a rough cushion, she moved quickly, leading with her hips like a high jumper.

As she swung over, she lost her grip, then her balance. She grabbed for the leather jacket with both hands just as she began a free-fall, catching one sleeve and finding herself suspended midair, like a Rastafarian Tarzan. Should she jump? Climb back up? Or just hang there until—until what? Until the fucking season started again next September? Suspended four feet off the ground, suddenly her jacket tore loose, and she fell, landing on her feet like she'd done at the riot when Braverman toppled. But she jammed the fuck out of the same bad ankle. She yelped. The leather jacket lay at her feet, the lining badly torn.

Layla limped through the concourse, trying to get her bearings. The signs for the West Exit looked familiar, and a minute later she stopped at the counter. She sniffed and finally identified the familiar smell. Fake butter and popcorn. She'd guessed correctly.

She rapped on the counter. "A popcorn and a large Coke please," she said into the small gap at the base of the steel roll-up.

A moment later the window clattered up, as if the concession stand was open for business. "We have a special today," a bearded Peter Braverman announced without missing a beat. "A popcorn and Karl Marx's *Das Kapital* for fifteen rubles."

"Quit with the wisecracks, Peter," Mooney said. He had a scraggly beard going, too. "Get her in here." He tapped his palm on the counter, as if to say *Up you go*.

"I can't," she said. "I just screwed up my ankle. The same one."

"The same one as what?" Braverman slid over the top to the customers' side. "I'll give you a boost, comrade sister," he said. But Mooney unlatched the door at the side of the counter. Braverman hustled her in and said, "We heard a horrible scream."

"Yours truly," Layla said.

"Sounded like a monster limping down the hallway."

"Me again."

"What was with all the whistling before that?" Braverman asked.

"The Beware of Guard Dogs sign," she said. "The sign was all bark and no bite." She pulled her jeans over her left knee.

"You're all bruised," Braverman said. "You need ice."

"An old football injury," she said.

The men looked confused. Mooney shrugged and filled a plastic shopping bag with ice and knotted it. With great care he gently raised her leg onto his own knee. When he tried to unlace the boot, Layla waved him off.

"How can we ice it with your boot on?" Mooney asked.

"Get me that bucket. I've got to submerge it. If you take the boot off first, it'll swell up worse."

"You're a poet, not a sports therapist," Braverman said.

"I learned this from Sasha," she said. "Basic ankle injury stuff."

"Why would you talk to him about—?"

"I should be doing the interrogating," she said. "You guys have been hiding out here this whole time?" What a place to live—folding chairs, collapsed cardboard boxes for makeshift beds in opposite corners, plastic bags of popcorn for pillows, but no blankets other than their jackets.

"How are you guys spending your time here," Layla asked, "besides tweeting?"

Braverman said they were bored. The light of the Coke machine wasn't enough to read, not that they had any books. They were nearly out of charge on their phones, which they'd tried to limit to using five minutes a day. Layla happened to have a charger in her bag, so they immediately made use of that. Mooney, cautious as always, added that they didn't want to turn on any lights once it got dark. A leftover space heater from the last football game proved handy. The men had been surviving on chocolate and popcorn. Diet Cokes took the place of morning coffee. (Regular Coke had run out quickly, but that was probably just as well.) They'd go on bathroom reconnaissance missions before sunrise, use the toilets, wash up. Then again at bedtime. They hadn't brushed their teeth in a week. There were no janitors or coaches or players around. "Today was the first time we've popped corn since we made our pillows," Mooney said. "Our food supply was running low."

"You gotta cool it on the popcorn," Layla scolded. "I could smell it out in the parking lot. How'd you even get in here?"

"Never give up your keys," Mooney said.

"Speaking of giving up," Braverman said sadly, "we thought you'd given up. On us."

"Not on us so much," Mooney added, "but we figured you'd walked away from the revolution."

"You figured wrong, fam." She dug down into her hemp purse and tossed them a couple granola bars. They tore into them.

"My goodness," Mooney gasped. "Who knew these could taste so good?"

"Too bad we can't set up a gourmet kitchen like The Hamlet," Braverman said. "Eugene here is the only man in America to lose weight eating chocolate."

Mooney chewed thoughtfully. "In the Mexican Revolution," he said between bites, "many women had bullets strapped across the chests, not purses."

"No kidding?" Layla said.

Mooney said, "Women did a lot more than feed Pancho Villa's troops. They were called soldaderas."

Layla reached into her hemp bag again for the red Afro wig. She quickly stuffed her dreadlocks up the back and pulled the wig down tight. She put on the sunglasses and set her jaw, trying for her fiercest look. "Recognize me now, amigos?" she said and tucked one of the popcorn pillows under her arm like a football, jumping into the classic stiff-arm pose.

"It was you," Braverman gasped.

She smiled.

"You started the chaos," Mooney said. "You were the crazy redhead, the first one onto the field."

"And the first one tackled," Braverman said, a sense of wonder in his voice.

"You guys are smart. You should be college professors," she said. "That's exactly right, a woman led you into battle. Don't lecture me about the soldaderas. Action was what you truly wanted—'Got a revolution, got to revolution.' Jefferson Airplane rocked that song in 1969. Right?"

The men nodded, their mouths agape.

"I ignored all your silliness about nonviolence. You didn't really mean it."

"But we're trying not to alienate the people," Braverman stammered, "who might consider me—us, I mean—too radical." He turned to Mooney. "Honest, I was quoting Dr. King's 'Been to the Mountaintop' verbatim when this crazy redhead leapt past me."

"You guys needed me," she said, dismissively.

"But why the red wig?" Mooney said.

"No blonde ones." She yanked it off and shook out her dreads.

"I mean why not just be Layla Sillimon, revolutionary poet?"

"Without tenure?" she asked, as if that were the most obvious thing in the world.

The men groaned.

"Fuck tenure," Braverman said. "We can't change the world if we're worried about job security."

That's when Layla told them the football coaches were going to block Braverman's bid for tenure. The men went quiet. Layla knew she'd ruined the mood. It was hard to be a revolutionary when you're worried about tenure. Or eating. Layla said she'd come back at midnight to slide tangerines, sandwiches, and magazines under the fence.

When she was gone, Mooney said, "Peter, we may have to compromise because of your bid for tenure."

Braverman spit in disgust and said, "You can forget about me ever compromising."

A few days later, the quarter resumed. Layla's two Intro to American Poetry classes were a groove, but her third class, the Workshop, was an energy suck, even with just six students. She'd had plenty of time over the holiday to analyze the poems they'd submitted. Sasha's was pretty lively, blending Croatian with English, sometimes within the same line. She didn't have the time to translate, but it felt powerful.

DeMarco's poem was the most bad-ass, a narrative imagining Amiri Baraka borrowing a pair of shoes from Langston Hughes and shining them—"pimping them up," DeMarco wrote—but not returning them to the older poet until he'd walked from New York to Georgia and back, wearing holes in them.

LaCroy's poem wasn't bad, although it was an obvious rant about injustice against the lower classes and about as sharp as a marble.

Todd, the tall white guy, wrote a poem called "Why Todd Lancaster Rocks Your World." It was a list of things, things that were apparently his best assets. He had a really hot car with a state-of-the-art sound system. His poem rhymed and used iambic pentameter. The narrator of the poem referred to himself as "Hot Toddy."

Lyndon's poem? So annoying. He titled it, "Fuck This Shit," and typed Fuck This Shit over and over again, one line after the other for, wow, a whole page. He didn't even experiment with his line breaks—clearly he was not listening in class. It kept ending in the same place and it wasn't, to be honest, so interesting, even with the last few stanzas in bold font. And this was his best poem of the quarter. She was already pretty tired of Lyndon because he was a human fun-sponge, soaking up all positive vibes.

DeShawn's was the worst, though. The Worst. He was absolutely lunching. He'd typed the letter "D" over and over again. They'd had a long discussion about how experimental poetry worked, and Layla's own poems were often experimental, but come on, the letter D wasn't a poem no matter how many times you typed it. Another case of a young poet not listening to his mentor. Why even take the class with that attitude? What was she going to suggest for revision? Try another letter, like "F"?

It was going to be another weird class. Layla went downstairs fifteen minutes before the start time to drag the seats into a circle. The swelling in her ankle had nearly subsided and she'd lost most of her limp. On her way to teach, she peered into Wilson Keats's classroom. She knew he liked to lump his three classes in a row, just a fifteen-minute break between, and why wouldn't he? When you were dumping the same drivel on students, century after century, why not put up an assembly line?

There he was between classes, alone, sitting at a table—asleep. What a joke, Layla thought. What a metaphor, even, the old white guy poet dead to the world. In a way, he'd been asleep for a lifetime, ruining the minds of young poets.

Layla had a mischievous idea, but she'd have to work fast before any students showed up. She set her book bag down in the hallway, slipped off her sandals, and tiptoed up to Keats. Man, he was out cold. She grabbed a colored pen at the white board behind him. In huge red letters, just above him, she wrote:

SILENCE!
Write a poem about a time when you were surprised. I will continue to sit in meditation here. Place your finished poem on my desk and exit quietly. No talking, no questions.

Keats hadn't moved. She drew a crude cartoon angel above the assignment and slipped out. Students would arrive soon, and when he woke up, they would have a good laugh at his expense.

Lyndon came into workshop with his headphones on, mumbling, "Fuck this shit." Maybe it was a rap song he was digging and perhaps the only line, like his poem. Had he been plagiarizing his own CDs? Today she'd try to get the class to discuss how Lyndon might revise. They'd move on to Sasha, DeMarco, Todd, and LaCroy. She'd save DeShawn and his "D" poem for last.

Once the basketball season started in early December, the players had become less obnoxious. Layla had been to a couple games, and yes, she enjoyed basketball more, although she couldn't tell Sasha that. It was more interesting to see ten guys running around practically in their underwear. Football players looked like clones, while in basketball, the athletes' personalities were apparent. The tsunami of aggression from the Silver Bullets on the court was startling, the way they jumped and dunked and made faces at the referees. It was closer to jazz, so freeform. Football was like the fucking army.

Braverman and Mooney had actually worked the first two basketball games, before their march. Had both men been smart enough to request professional leave without pay for the rest of the quarter before going underground? She'd forgotten to ask.

Lyndon plopped down across from her with his headphones on. A minute later the other basketball players appeared in a cluster, arguing about what happened in a recent game. Sasha arrived just behind them.

Layla welcomed everyone back and said they'd start by considering Lyndon's poem.

"Man," DeMarco said, "that's not a poem. What is wrong with you, fool?"

"Let's not get personal," Layla said. "But tell us, DeMarco, why isn't it a poem?" She was relieved she wouldn't have to shoot down Lyndon's submission by herself.

"Because it's not even trying to be art." DeMarco leaned over, jerked out Lyndon's earbuds, and said, "We're analyzing your poem. Give us some respect."

"I liked it," DeShawn said. "My mom says fuck this shit a lot."

"I was thinking of your mom when I wrote it," Lyndon said. "I think about your mom all the time."

Layla reminded them that the author was to remain quiet and take notes.

LaCroy said, "I appreciated the angry edge of the poem, but it's not doing enough. I guess I mean it's not doing as much as it could."

"Maybe," Sasha said, "the poem should not trap the anger behind same dull language like bad rap music."

"Fuck you, Shrek," Lyndon said. "No such thing as bad rap."

Layla held a finger to her lips to quiet him again.

Todd said the poem made him feel alienated, that he had trouble connecting to it. Then DeMarco stressed again that any poem should strive to be art, and the class had a compelling discussion about what truly constituted art. Layla was happy about that, until she realized Lyndon had put his earbuds back in and probably missed the entire lively back-and-forth.

DeMarco's and LaCroy's poems were well received by the group. The class bashed Todd's poem because it rhymed, but Layla defended the musicality of it.

Sasha's poem riled up some of the group yet again.

"Talk English," DeShawn said. "You in America."

"Yeah, Shrek," Lyndon said, yanking out his earbuds. "English not good enough?"

Layla had saved DeShawn's poem for last.

"Dude," Todd said, "Don't you have any other letters on your keyboard besides D?"

Lyndon said, "DeShawn's poem is the bomb. This is the livest shit I've ever read."

Layla asked him what he liked best.

"I like the rhythm of it, the way it builds and builds," Lyndon said. "I read it out loud to myself and by page three, man, this thing grew wings and really sang to me."

"You're a fool," DeMarco said.

"No personal attacks," Layla said.

DeMarco took a deep breath. "The poem feels foolish to me. And it seems to be mocking the reader and possibly even mocking the instructor and the entire class."

"Fascinating, DeMarco," Layla said. "Go on."

"Check it," DeMarco said, exasperated, "I don't see how this poem sheds light on the human condition."

"It means being a human is boring," DeShawn said. "Like this class."

"Shut up," LaCroy said. "You're the author, you have the right to remain silent. This," he shook the poem at DeShawn, "only sheds light on your sorry ass."

Layla deliberately let her class out early, but DeShawn didn't budge. He kept shaking his head disdainfully, as though he'd been whistled for a foul he didn't deserve. Layla feared he'd get profanely aggressive after a rough-and-tumble workshop where his "Fuck This Shit" had come under intense criticism.

Instead, DeShawn said he wanted to tell Layla something. He admitted he had major anger issues, rooted in his father's absence. Apparently, his father only came around on birthdays. "You don't know what it's like," he said, "growing up without a dad. That shit can make you do erratic stuff."

Layla didn't correct him, didn't interrupt, she just listened and nodded. DeShawn claimed LaCroy was the only player on the team who had a father at home, and she should make a point to be empathetic about that fact with all the basketball players. He said he was sorry for the poem he turned in, but it reflected his true feelings. Hearing DeShawn's confession and background, she did feel more compassion, and there was no need to tell him her personal story yet, that she'd been discarded by her own dad. Instead, she'd dig out some father-related poems by Robert Hayden and William Carlos Williams to share, and she'd poke around for more contemporary writers.

And then? She noticed Lyndon had left his earbuds underneath his chair. She'd return them next week, but when she pulled at the cord they were plugged into his iPhone. It wasn't the right thing to do, but she turned the phone on just to see what rapper he was so obsessed with, who was it that he'd prefer to listen to instead of his own poetry workshop. That's when she had the biggest shock of the workshop so far: Lyndon had been listening to Ralph Ellison's *Invisible Man*, and the book was nearly finished.

So, what was the deal with his fitful behavior, acting that way? Or wait—what was the deal with her own negative judgment of Lyndon for these last few weeks? She left the room feeling far better about the workshop, despite her exhaustion.

Most of the students in Wilson Keats's class had already left, Layla noticed, when she'd finished with DeShawn. Two poets remained, scribbling away—and Keats was sitting still as a stone. One remaining poet checked her watch and bent to the ear of the other to whisper. They stood in unison, marched their papers up, placed them on a stack, and made for the exit.

"Good class?" Layla whispered to them.

"Bizarro," the young woman said.

"Great class," the other said as they breezed past. "Keats didn't say a word for once."

Layla kicked her sandals off again and glided slowly to the front of the classroom. She wanted to swipe a couple of the student poems just for laughs. She kept her eyes fixed on Keats in case he should stir. He was the unhealthiest looking dude on the planet—pale and gray, clearly in need of some organic greens. Should she erase her writing prompt? Would he know her handwriting? She crept along until she was parallel with him.

His mouth was open, and he'd been drooling. A cold front of air hit her, and she hugged herself against the chill. Her breath caught in her throat. No wonder he was so still. Wilson Keats was dead.

Chapter 16

Sasha was hysterical and couldn't catch his breath. Trevor guided him to their couch and fetched a glass of water. Sasha pushed it away as if it were poison. "I can't understand you," Trevor said. "Take another deep breath and let it out slow."

"We must act," Sasha said.

"Act in what?"

"Oh, evil place is football training room."

"They gave you more steroids?" Trevor asked.

"He is choking."

"Somebody choked?"

"Come, I will show this terror." Sasha's English was getting worse by the minute.

Trevor grabbed a sweatshirt, and they hustled out the door, Sasha leading the way in a brisk jog. Despite Sasha's frantic desperation, it felt comfortable, natural, to be following his best blocker again. Occasionally he'd feint to one side and tuck back in behind Sasha. He didn't have time to yank on his sweatshirt. Instead, he balled it up and clutched it to his forearm. He could feel tremors in the earth emanating from Sasha's sneakers, as though trailing a freight train. Students stepped back to clear a path for them as they rambled across campus.

"Go for it, Trevor," one student yelled.

"Season's over, dude," said another.

Sasha shouldered the front door of the athletic training building, and it flew open, burst off at the bottom hinge, and dangled like a broken drapery rod. They pattered down the steps when Sasha halted as if an imaginary ref had tooted his whistle. Doubled over and struggling for breath, Trevor finally said, "What the hell?" and whacked Sasha on the back.

Sasha was shaking. "Very bad inside," he gasped and pointed at the guilty room. "I was icing my knees in other room when I hear the cries."

"What cries?"

"Very bad memories for Croatian," he said and motioned for him to put his ear near the door.

"I can't hear a thing," Trevor said. "Let's go around to the other side to get closer." He led Sasha to the student trainer offices where they let themselves in. The lights were out, but the whirlpool room down the narrow hallway was bright. The players inched toward the light, stopped short, and huddled in the dimness, among boxes of athletic tape. The whirlpool jets whirred to life.

"Tell us where Mooney is," a voice commanded, breaking the silence, "or you keep getting this bath all day."

Splash. Gurgle. Violent coughing.

Sasha got close to Trevor's ear. "Waterboarding," he said. "Our coach tortures somebody."

Trevor raised an eyebrow.

Sasha held up a finger—wait a minute. He pulled a piece of paper from his pocket, tilted it toward the light, and scrawled a quick drawing—a stickman on a board, gagged, blindfolded. He made the curvy waves of the whirlpool behind the stickman's head. Next he drew two men with sharp teeth, their hands on the long board.

Trevor nodded. He understood waterboarding.

But Sasha continued drawing. He put little teardrops just under the blindfold. He made a Coors State badge for one torturer. One got "Criminal Justice" across his shirt, a gun in one hand, a pitchfork in the other. It was becoming a very elaborate drawing.

"Never mind, I got it," Trevor said. The buzz of the whirlpool meant they could talk quietly. "But who is the victim?"

When the coughing fit stopped, a timid voice begged for mercy.

Trevor recognized him. "It's President Cardly," he said.

"Former president," Sasha corrected him. "Make very bad speeches and coach blame him for our bowl game performance was horseshit. But not his fault," he added, as if to himself. "We must save former president. Unfairly blame."

There was terrible gagging, then the president asked for a Kleenex.

Another voice boomed above the gurgling of the whirlpool. "Fuck the Kleenex. Where are Braverman and Mooney?"

"This is very bad," Sasha whispered. "I don't care about coach's old tomatoes."

Trevor thought for a moment. "I don't want the coaches to see us here."

"My friend, I am disgusted by these tortures. Coach is out of control. Are you so very disgusted, too?"

Trevor nodded a yes. He decided to take a quick peek, get the layout, before they made any foolish moves. He crept to the doorway, knelt, then jerked his head back. Sasha's drawing wasn't exactly accurate. Cardly was tied down and blindfolded and hooded, and the torturers were pouring Coors, one tallboy can at a time, into his mouth and nose. Maniscalco was overseeing it while two other men—Criminal Justice professors, Trevor thought—did the dirty work. Sasha kept working on his sketch.

"Forget the drawing," Trevor said quietly. "You can finish later."

Sasha said, "I draw a plan." He did a quick new sketch with the torturers blindfolded. Trevor didn't get it. Did Sasha want to torture them back as revenge? Trevor made a face at him. Somebody switched the whirlpool on high. Cardly screamed.

"Just tell me now," Trevor said.

"Hand me roll of tape," Sasha said, pointing at the boxes. He whispered the plan.

Trevor would cut the lights. Sasha would subdue Maniscalco, dragging him in the dark to the ground, face down. Trevor would do what he'd done before every game for Sasha with the roll of tape. "Except no glasses on the coach," Sasha murmured. "You tape over his eyes, mouth, then tape his wrists together." Sasha would already be subduing the two Criminal Justice profs.

Just then, Cardly came up for air, gagging.

"Don't speak once we get started," Trevor said. "Coach would recognize our voices. But what should we do with President Cardly?"

"Former president."

"Once a person has been president, Americans always refer to him as president," Trevor said, but he wondered why Cardly, like the four English professors, would keep hanging around after being disgraced. "Professor Mooney says it's called an honorific. Anyway, we won't have time to untie him."

"You cut lights to start. I get coach. You take your time taping; they will panic and fearful in dark. We carry Mister President like Croatian Christmas tree. Ready, yes?"

Sasha tapped Trevor's back—go! Trevor jumped into the doorway and found the light switch with his right hand. In the split second before the sudden darkness, Trevor realized their timing, by sheer luck, was perfect. Everyone had their backs to the door except President Cardly, who was about to get another can of beer dumped into his nose and mouth.

"We were like team ropers at the rodeo," Trevor said as he led the way back across campus.

"I would like to see American rodeo one day," Sasha said. "Yippee tie-yie-yes."

They had Cardly on their shoulders, wrapped under white towels as if he were a human burrito. This was for everyone's safety. Cardly wouldn't want to be recognized on campus. Trevor and Sasha didn't want to be known as the rebels who bound and gagged their coach.

Cardly was a talker and they kept up a running conversation. Trevor couldn't decide where to take him. Their apartment was not an option.

"We hide president in Professor Mooney's office?" Sasha suggested.

"It's probably being staked out," Cardly chipped in. "Can't I just stay with you fellows? I'll do the dishes."

Trevor said that was too risky. Besides, he figured if they kept him on the couch they might not be able to watch sports all weekend. "We need a place nobody will look," he said.

"Where nobody at Coors State would care about," Sasha said. "Most invisible place."

"The most insignificant place," Trevor said, continuing Sasha's train of thought.

"The History Department," Cardly suggested. "Although that's merely my opinion."

"Sorry, keep quiet for a minute," Trevor said. After passing a group of students, Trevor had an idea. He veered to the left, toward the tents of The Hamlet in the distance.

Cardly somehow figured it out. "The Hamlet? What if they torture me, too? Should I apologize to them?"

Trevor said it wasn't necessary. "They're our friends now."

Whale unwrapped the towels. Cardly was shivering and smelled like the aftermath of a frat party—understandable, since he'd been carted across campus on a chilly day in a shirt and towels drenched with beer. All the English profs, Whale said, used thermal sleeping bags good to forty below. They were actually too warm most nights, even in January. She sent Trevor to her tent to get a sleeping bag, and he returned to find Cardly perched on her lap. She was rubbing the president's chest. He no longer seemed upset. Trevor covered him with the blue down-filled bag. Cardly pulled it up to his chin and sighed.

"These folks know how to live," Trevor said, tucking Cardly in. "They'll take care of you."

The other profs prepared dinner—a simple vegetarian spread. Cardly curled up under the sleeping bag on Whale's lap, while Sasha gathered the folding chairs around the card table. Dodo took drink orders. Cardly asked for a beer. Moments later, a six-pack appeared. It wasn't Coors. He studied the label.

Buffalo set out almonds, Gouda cheese, hummus, French bread, and a cold lentil salad. Trevor almost said it'd be hard to bulk up for football on that diet, but it was, in fact, delicious.

"You'll be secure here," Wolf said to Cardly. "Nobody's checked on us since the riot. Nobody paid any attention to us even when we really existed."

"I still exist," Buffalo said instantly. She was the quickest to take offense. "That's pretty clear from our bylaws. Even the administration can't terminate your existence without putting forward a motion, and I certainly didn't hear one. It would take a referendum."

"There were times when I was teaching fifteen students total in my three classes," Dodo said. "I was barely existing."

"Maybe one day," Sasha added, "some more African American professors could also exist at the Coors State." He looked to Trevor for reassurance. "Is this possible?"

It got quiet.

"Good point," Trevor said. "It's not just you guys who are ignored."

"Anyway," Wolf said. "It all stems from the top. We were ignored because the powers that be wanted it that way."

Cardly sputtered an apology. Whale rubbed his balding head and said, "There, there." They seemed to be warming up to each other quickly.

Buffalo circled the table to comfort Cardly as well. "He meant the coaches wanted English to be invisible. Everyone knows you didn't make any important decisions."

"Not for years," Wolf said.

"That's right," Dodo said, "not since you sold our university to Coors. That wasn't such a great idea."

"Unless," Wolf said, "you only tabulate the record of the football team and their attendance. In that case, it was a terrific move. We've improved dramatically."

The others nodded and smiled at Cardly. Trevor was glad to see how tender and forgiving the professors were.

"What would you say, in retrospect, is the purpose of a university?" Dodo asked.

"Surprisingly, it's not to win football and basketball games," Cardly said. The table quieted, but he quickly broke the silence. "The main purpose of a university is to not get sued. That's our immediate short-term goal. I'd ask myself every day, *Might I get taken to court for this? Could this wind up as a lawsuit?* Yet, it's true that most presidents are measured by the success of football and basketball. And I don't like Coors. The beer, I mean." He looked admiringly at the can in his hand again. "This brown ale is pretty good, though," he said, but he wasn't looking at the bottle. He was looking at Whale the way Trevor had seen his teammates look at the cheerleaders.

Sasha pounded a fist on the table. The almonds jumped from their bowl, scattering. Everyone stiffened.

"I like Slobodan Milosevic!" Sasha cried. He covered his face with his hands.

"Okay," Cardly said. "To each his own, I say."

"Even Stalin was kind to his dogs," Wolf said. "Our friends in History could verify that." He gathered the scattered almonds and returned them to the bowl.

"There's good in everyone, Sasha," Whale agreed. "You only have to serve on university committees for five years or so to learn that. Especially the ad hoc committees, which can often be thankless jobs. We don't hold anything against you."

"Wait," Trevor said. "You told me you hated Milosevic, that all Croatians hated him."

"Yes. And now I like him."

The table was quiet, except for Dodo crunching on loose almonds. "He did have a lot of charisma, I suppose," he finally said.

Trevor replayed Sasha's statement in his mind. His English was okay until he got excited, and this had to be a mistake. Sasha admired a war criminal? I like him, he'd said. But why would he—"I got it," Trevor announced. "You mean I *am* like Slobodan Milosevic. Right?"

"No, not you," Sasha said.

"Right. You meant you are similar to Milosevic."

Sasha nodded.

"How are you like Milosevic?" Dodo asked. All the professors leaned forward, and so did Cardly, shifting to the front of Whale's lap. His sleeping bag-blanket fell to the earth, exposing his narrow frame. Whale covered him up again.

Buffalo tapped Whale and said quietly, "President Cardly seems warm enough now, dear. Why don't you put him down?"

Sasha pulled his square glasses up onto his shaved head and said, "I am on the wrong side of history. Like Milosevic." He said to Trevor, "We are on the wrong team, my so good friend. And history make judge us."

"Will judge us," Trevor said.

"It's not too late," Dodo said.

"What time it is now?" asked Sasha.

"I mean it's not too late for you to change teams. And change our school."

Trevor said to Sasha, "I thought maybe we did change teams, Sasha. Back at the whirlpools."

Cardly popped open another can. "I can't get the taste of Coors and bile out of my mouth," he said.

"We bound and gagged the head coach," Trevor confessed, "and two Criminal Justice dudes."

The English profs stared at Trevor in awe, as though he'd just tossed an eighty-yard touchdown pass left-handed. "We knew you'd helped President Cardly escape," Wolf said. "We didn't know you'd subdued his captors. You two are heroes."

"No, you English professors are heroes," Sasha said. "Fallen heroes. Yes, we save our poor president. But we not take public stand like The Hamlet. We leave battle, sneak away like Ninjas."

"Ninjas for Academia," Buffalo said. "Maybe that's a memoir for me to write."

"Or an ad hoc committee we could form," Whale said.

"A memoir won't qualify as a publication," Dodo said. "It isn't your field."

"I know the bylaws," Buffalo snapped.

Wolf ignored his colleagues. "You two," he said, pointing at the players, "can rally your whole team now. Convince them to join the Movement."

"Or just lead by example," Buffalo said.

Trevor said, "We need Professor Mooney. He'll know the next step. People are paying attention now. I even heard a student say he'd never go to another game. That's crazy."

"The rumor is that Mooney and Braverman are planning a major move," Dodo said. "Criminal Justice has the school on Orange Alert."

"A major move that will rock the school," said Buffalo. "I hope."

Cardly sat up and explained why the coaches would deny Braverman tenure soon. Braverman was more radical, more committed, he said, and Football stripping him of his job might kill the Movement. That would leave Mooney alone.

"To save the Movement, we've got to save Braverman," Wolf said. "Otherwise, Braverman will lose his cachet, be seen as disgruntled and with an axe to grind."

"Why grind an axe?" said Sasha.

Trevor waved a finger to say it wasn't important.

"I think you're right," Buffalo said. "It'll be decided right after the basketball season, and the minute Braverman doesn't get tenure he'll get a police escort off campus. That will crush poor Eugene's spirit."

"But where are they?" Whale asked. "They're sending out these passionate communiqués via Twitter. Eventually they're both going to have to lead the Movement in person."

Cardly said, "Your so-called Movement, which I have doubts about, very much depends on Braverman staying at Coors State. I'll bet you didn't know my father was a history professor." His father had taught at Ohio State for decades and was regarded as the leading scholar of the footwear worn in the

American Revolution. But he'd feuded with Football and was forced to retire early.

"Back to Braverman," Dodo said. "How can we ensure he gets tenure?"

"Form a committee," Buffalo said. "Isn't that right, President Cardly? We'll nominate a chairperson, hold elections, and break out into ad hoc committees and focus groups. If we're going to engineer student-centered problem-solving, it's imperative we streamline mission-critical staff development, and a committee is the only—"

Wolf leapt across the table and grabbed Buffalo around the collar. She squirmed like President Cardly had earlier. The other professors protested weakly, but nobody moved—as if killing off the idea of yet another committee was a brutal necessity for the revolution to move forward.

"Just a minute here," Cardly finally said.

Sasha stood, pulled Wolf's arms apart, and helped him back to his chair.

"No more fucking committees," Wolf said when he sat down. "I'll say one thing for Braverman and Mooney. They were right in storming the field that day. At least they did something."

"Apology accepted," Buffalo huffed.

The crew got quiet. Trevor could hear Sasha munching on almonds. It sounded like gears grinding. Then it stopped.

"Okay," said Sasha. "I cannot play for coach use torture. I am a radical dude and I change teams." He spread his arms to the English profs. "Can I be on your team? I work hard. I am poet, too. And team player."

The English profs shouted a hearty welcome. Cardly reached down from Whale's lap for another beer.

Sasha went on: "Trevor and me on the same revolutionary team. He is quarterback. You will join me, my so very good friend?" he asked, turning to his roommate. "We will fight this evil on our college."

Trevor felt his face get hot. Everyone was looking at him, awaiting his up-or-down vote. Sasha smiled eagerly. Trevor said, "No eye in team," and shrugged. The Hamlet profs didn't get that joke, but he didn't care—or understand what joining this new team entailed—but he hugged Sasha anyway. The profs applauded politely and most likely counted the embrace as a "yes" vote. Sasha must have, too—he raised both fists.

What the heck could he and Sasha do to make a difference? Trevor didn't know, but he had to back his friend. If this all turned out to be a dumb idea, it wasn't like anybody would die. Besides, this was a private decision, and nobody was going to hand the quarterback a microphone and ask him to make a speech or anything.

The profs clinked coffee cups. Cardly popped open a beer— was it his fourth or fifth?—but Trevor figured he deserved it after being waterboarded all afternoon.

Sasha was buoyant on the walk back to their apartment, recounting all kinds of Croatian history, comparing their quest to the 1990s struggles back home. The implication was, of course, that they would quit Football. Sasha might be ready for that, but was Trevor?

Trevor knew it made no sense to go hunting blindly for Mooney and Braverman. What if they were to find the History profs, what then? Would he and Sasha renounce their scholarships? Live in tents at The Hamlet, subsist on almonds and cheese? Turn in their playbooks? Could they still hit the football buffet for dinner each night? Might maid service continue? How public was this declaration supposed to be? Was it something they could take back, get a "do over?" And could the coaches deport Sasha if his scholarship was cut? If they didn't change their minds soon, they'd have to tell Coach Maniscalco. The ultimatum Sasha had gotten from the coach would be pointed at Trevor next.

Trevor figured if he was going to back out of his commitment he had a twenty-four-hour window to tell Sasha. It made him queasy, but he would have to try to let himself imagine his life without Football.

"We need your advice," Trevor said to Layla after he filled her in on all that had happened.

Sasha went right to his recliner, tested the levers, and settled in. "Check me out," he said, pulling on her red wig and flipping topsy-turvy in the chair. He was back to his playful self, but Trevor scowled and told him to be serious.

"I've joined the fight, too, in my own way," Layla said. She wasn't wearing her usual Amish-punk-hippie attire. Instead, she was in a black business-style pantsuit. "You know about my dash across the practice field, but I've also been taking our friends supplies at night. Don't tell anybody, okay?"

Trevor was relieved to hear Layla knew their whereabouts. "We won't tell," he assured her, "but what can Sasha and I do?"

Sasha tossed the red wig at Trevor's face. "We are on new team," he said.

"That's great," Layla said. "Congrats."

Trevor passed the wig on to Layla. "Don't put this on again," he joked, "unless you've improved your speed." He hadn't recognized Layla that day until it was time to clear the field. He'd carried her to safety, dumping her at the women's bathroom. Thank goodness the video crew hadn't caught that.

"Trevor joins me in the fight, too," Sasha said. "Time for peaceful revolution. Why," he continued, "are you wearing all black. You are Johnny Cash?" In the silence, he said to Trevor, "American singer. The Man in Black."

"Cash is cool, but I'm in mourning for the other poetry professor."

Trevor said he was sorry, they hadn't heard. "Was it in the school paper?" Trevor asked, but he realized that was a dumb question. *Rocky Mountain High* had gone to a new format—sports only. In fact, just Football and Basketball.

"I was the one who found Wilson Keats," she said. "I went to play a joke on him because I thought he was asleep. That's bad karma. And on top of that, now I have to absorb one of his classes and that's a pain."

"Pain in your ass," Sasha said as if to correct her.

Trevor got a call from Maniscalco three days later. His tone was casual, and Trevor reminded himself that there was no way his coach could have discovered his own quarterback was the guy who'd taped his mouth and eyes shut. Or helped beat up and bind those Criminal Justice cops into submission.

"Did you hear me?" his coach was saying. "I said you were named MVP of our entire league."

Trevor wasn't totally shocked, but the timing gave him an awful pang. If he quit Football, he might be throwing away more than a college career. It could amount to millions of—he took a deep breath, then another. Even the league's Most Valuable Player couldn't be 100% sure he'd play professionally. He knew that. He really did.

"And," Maniscalco continued, "we're going to honor you at halftime of the basketball game this weekend. You'll have sixty seconds to make a speech. Try to think of something to say, you can't meander around."

Trevor thanked his coach and confirmed he'd be there.

"What about Sasha?" he asked. "I'm just curious. He made All Conference, right?"

"He would have," Maniscalco admitted, "but I blackballed him. Don't tell Sasha."

Something in Trevor's head snapped like a cheap chopstick. He didn't know everything about this "Movement" that his professor friends were plotting, and he enjoyed playing football. But this was the second instance of his coach screwing over his roommate, and he'd vowed to Sasha it wouldn't happen again. And on this occasion, he had time to think. It wasn't minutes before a bowl game.

"You still with me, Trevor?" Maniscalco asked.

"What?" Trevor said. "I'm right here." The feeling in his gut was now a mule's kick. He didn't want to transfer to Knox College, but maybe he could transfer—well, anywhere. But that was it, he decided. He scribbled down the details about the ceremony, but they barely registered. Trevor should have done more the first time, and he'd always regret that. But now, Trevor decided, he was quitting football.

Back in his apartment, Trevor paced for a few minutes, then shadowboxed crudely to work off his anger. Should he tell his roommate? Or would Sasha be better off not knowing? Was Sasha, by quitting, trashing his future, a chance at an American college degree? Trevor's family could pay for his own schooling if he lost his scholarship. But he couldn't bear it if Sasha got kicked out of America. Sasha genuinely wanted a degree in English, even if the diploma had a beer corporation's logo on it.

Trevor yelled for Sasha, who came thumping downstairs. "Listen," Trevor said, thinking on his feet, calling an audible in his own head. "Coach said I won the league's MVP."

"Most Valuable Person?" Sasha said and did the raise-the-roof gesture.

"Player. They want to honor me this weekend."

"You are a big man of campus still. Party time."

"Forget all that," Trevor said. He didn't want to burden Sasha with what Maniscalco had told him. Instead, he asked his roommate to accept the award with him at the basketball game.

Sasha shook his head and said, "But you are special winner. Not me."

"I'm going to hand my award to you."

"I am the humble center. Make block. Boom. On his ass."

Trevor imagined going out to half court with Sasha, arm draped over his pal. Maniscalco would probably go ballistic. But the coach couldn't deny Trevor his award, not in front of 18,000 basketball fans. Maybe Trevor could bring along Mooney and Braverman and—no, wait, he couldn't do that, not unless he wanted to get them arrested. But what would he say to a sold-out crowd in sixty seconds? Sure, he'd talk about Sasha, give him credit, hand his roommate the trophy. Then it hit Trevor. He'd have a microphone. And a captive audience.

"I could give you the microphone," Trevor suggested. "You can say that you are switching teams, that you renounce Football."

"What about you?"

Trevor plopped onto the sofa next to his roommate.

Sasha turned on the lamp for him and said, "You are best friend. We must help the good guys here, help take back our justice." When Trevor didn't answer, Sasha told a long story about the Yugoslavian basketball team, said it was the greatest international squad ever, better than America's Dream Team. But the war had torn them apart. "They never again play together for Olympic gold. War damages the friendships.

Our cause is fix broken American university system, but also nonviolence cause."

"Agreed," Trevor said.

Sasha went on. "And we must remain as good friends after the struggle. This is for education for all and end sports dictatorship of Coors State. Maybe we play together again one day when we change the system. Friends always."

It didn't make perfect sense to Trevor—the war in Yugoslavia, education in America, their friendship? But Trevor couldn't allow his friend to be stomped on again and do nothing to defend him. Braverman had said sports had run roughshod over academics. Yet, it all felt pretty normal to Trevor, except for the Jacuzzi torture stuff. Maybe the sheer power of the gesture—the league's MVP saying enough is enough—could become an on-court pep rally for priorities and justice.

"Trevor, my so good friend," Sasha said, "this is our time. But I should not be good with microphone. You make statement, announce we retire from Football, talk about academics. I will walk out with you, arm-in-arm, but not speak. Hey, I will edit your speech like my poems. For imagery and grammar mistakes. Hah hah."

Trevor realized he'd have to mention Professor Mooney in his speech. Sure, Sasha had blocked for him, but Trevor owed this awakening, or revolt or whatever the heck it was, to Mooney. And Mooney wouldn't be where he was today (wherever that was—Layla had been vague) without his friend Braverman. It almost wouldn't be right to be making speeches without mentioning Mooney, and you hardly ever saw Mooney without Braverman.

Trevor's head was spinning. He needed time to think, and the basketball game was fast approaching.

Torture, Mooney, Braverman, Sasha, maybe Layla and academics—no way to condense all that into sixty seconds. He'd better write this whole speech down. Already four people to thank, and he didn't want to get nervous and forget. He'd also have to mention President Cardly. But, yes, he'd have to hand the Croatian the MVP trophy. They'd stand tall together at midcourt.

Trevor had already taken some big steps. He'd agreed in principle at The Hamlet to join the fight. But now? This public speech would finalize his walking away from Football for good. It felt like a kind of death, but an honorable one. He'd be making a move that couldn't be easily undone. And he needed Professor Mooney to be there.

Trevor realized Mooney could make a speech, too, and so what if the speech went over their allotted time. How the heck the professors might get safely onto the court without being arrested, though, was anybody's guess. Could Trevor get Mooney his microphone? The professors would have to devise a game plan, a serious and creative game plan. Mooney and Braverman couldn't just drop down from the sky.

Chapter 17

Despite their proximity as concession-stand room-mates, Eugene Mooney hadn't been able cough up his own confession to Peter Braverman. Pondering his big blunder in high school kept him awake on his mattress, a stack of cardboard boxes. At night, while Braverman slept peacefully, Mooney, even in the dark, could feel his face flush with shame. All this baloney he preached to his pal about judgment and planning? What a hypocrite.

Mooney had grown up in Maywood, just west of Chicago, where his father was a labor union organizer. Their family was one of the few that didn't panic as their neighborhood shifted from Anglo to African American. Mooney had been a promising football prospect at Proviso East High School—a standout linebacker, although he'd declined to ever tell Braverman that. Burned out, he'd quit football before his senior year, at exactly the same age his father had been when he gave up sports. Mooney came to regret deeply the move when five former teammates were awarded full scholarships. Instead, that year he ran for vice president of the senior class and won in a close vote. His idea was to use student government as a tool to push for the same progressive causes that had blossomed in Chicago in the late 1960s.

The Black Panthers had been prominent in Maywood because the chairman of the Chicago chapter was Fred Hampton, a Proviso East graduate who was killed by cops in 1969. Two years later, an unofficial—and unsanctioned—student chapter had sprung up at the high school. By 1976, they still hadn't registered with the principal's office and were not recognized as a school-sponsored activity, although everyone knew they had never ceased meeting on school property. As vice president of the class, Mooney had to make sure all extra-curricular groups were sanctioned, and he very much wanted to help the Black Panthers' student club become street-legal, to legitimize their organization, so they could work within the system for change. It would be easy. Mooney could assist with the paperwork, have them recognized, find them a faculty sponsor, and budget some modest funding for events. Maybe he would even help recruit white members to their cause. An ex-teammate told him the group was to meet one Friday, just after 8th period, on the steps outside the rear entrance. As a goodwill gesture, Mooney walked to Dunkin' Donuts on First Avenue for a mixed dozen. But the errand took longer than expected, and he interrupted their meeting with his pink-and-orange donut box.

In his excitement, he spoke over their leader. "I can help make you guys legit and get you an audience with the Student Council." Met by an icy silence—and without any real plan—he maneuvered through the crowd with his offering of donuts and handshakes. Nobody partook. Their silence gradually turned into obscenities, although one kid did thank him for coming. He downed half the donuts on the walk home and tossed the rest. Looking back, he could point to the incident as when he began battling his belly.

Even after the Panthers shunned him, he still hoped to get them registered. He described his efforts at Student Council, but that turned out to be a mistake. Somebody at that meeting ratted out the Panthers to the principal. Two days later, their leader—a bookish and bespectacled kid named J. Michael Thomas—got served with a two-week suspension for leading an illegitimate activity on school property. Instead of returning to Proviso East, Thomas dropped out. The student Panthers never met again, and they blamed Mooney, assumed his blundering had ruined their movement.

And they were right. He was mocked and abused by Black kids the rest of his senior year. On two occasions, in the cafeteria hallway, he was pelted with donuts. Years later, Mooney learned J. Michael Thomas served a prison term.

"Maybe you shouldn't have quit football," his father had said, except he didn't mean "maybe." What hurt the most was the way his father, an organizer by trade, had disparaged young Eugene's lack of preparation and planning. "At least when I quit boxing," he'd say, and his son knew the rest. Organize and plan.

The next year, Mooney moved out east for college, where he kept abreast of the Black Panthers' national demise in *Rolling Stone*. Huey Newton was in exile, the Panthers were fading, and Mooney couldn't get his ham-fisted fuckup out of his head. In his mind, the downfall of the student chapter of the Black Panthers had precipitated the end of the movement.

Since then, the only thing he could think of to do with his life, short of apologizing to a Black Panther Party that no longer existed, was to think, to plan, to consider his speech and actions carefully. Have a coordinated structure and be realistic. At that fateful donut meeting, he should have provided a printed handout, brought along a potential faculty sponsor, had a black football friend with him. Perhaps even have introduced himself with a cool nickname for street cred. "Moon Dog," maybe.

And now, Mooney had gotten caught without a smartly considered organizational plan for the first time since 1975, and he had made things worse by going commando, tackling coaches, and releasing mayhem. Gandhi would have sat in meditation in the bleachers. Stayed committed to nonviolence no matter what the provocation. Mooney knew he was not wrong about this monster, big-time athletics, which had hijacked higher education. Nevertheless, five years from retirement, he should have possessed the right balance of wisdom, anger, and righteousness to be productive. How could he direct the Movement if he couldn't carefully plan an event or lead by example? He would have been just as effective that day charging onto the Coors State football field wielding another box of donuts. And how could he manage Braverman if he couldn't manage himself?

Mooney sat up on his makeshift cot. Braverman was breathing softly in his bed. He sounded like a child. The red light from the exit sign crept into their concession stand, enough to illuminate his friend. Braverman didn't look like a child in that light. He looked like a tired old man. Mooney had a realization. This might be their last chance to make a difference.

Eating an all-chocolate diet, something Mooney had daydreamed about as a child, had grown old after two days. He figured he'd dropped twenty pounds, likely the only time in human history that a man had lost weight while eating Snickers and Three Musketeers. After the candy was gone, he got weary of the taste of Diet Coke and was now subsisting on water and unsalted popcorn. Eating the same food every day was a drag, and he was surprised to learn after a week that he preferred to hardly eat at all. The concession-stand diet was not at all Gandhi-esque, but he nonetheless saw it as a kind of penance for the Black Panthers Club. After Layla discovered them, her vitamins and apples and protein bars were a welcome addition and his weight stabilized.

Layla told them about Trevor's MVP award and the impending halftime speech during which he would announce that he and Sasha were quitting football.

"Far out," Braverman said.

"But what motivated him?" Mooney asked. "I'm delighted, naturally, but why now?"

Layla told them the story, and how Trevor had made his decision.

"It was more personal than political," Layla added. "The point is Trevor wants you two joining him and Sasha at midcourt to address to the crowd."

"We'll be arrested," Braverman said.

Mooney thought for a moment, then said, "Remember our last basketball game, Peter?"

"We lost in overtime," Braverman sighed.

"Why were you so upset, though?"

"How many three-pointers do we allow before changing defenses?"

Mooney shook his head. "I meant the halftime entertainment."

"Uggh. They called it Operation Show of Force."

Criminal Justice honored their top students with a military-style demo—ten kids fast-roped down from the rafters in ninja garb. "And you, Peter, insisted we walk out in protest. I had to talk you into staying."

"We saw a helluva second half," Braverman said.

"What are you getting at?" Layla said.

"I'm saying Criminal Justice repeats the ceremony a few times each season. They must leave all that rope gear up there."

"And you're, like, worried they'll rain on Trevor's parade on Saturday?" Layla asked.

"What I'm suggesting," Mooney said, "is Peter and I go ninja, fast-rope down from the rafters to midcourt."

"I don't know how to fast-rope," Braverman said. "I'm no ninja. What if I land on my head and get killed?"

"I'd worry," Layla said, "about one thing. Maybe the gear is still up there, but what about appropriating Chinese culture and stereotypes?"

"Ninja is just an expression," Mooney assured her. "We'll do the research." He tore open an empty popcorn box to sketch out the timing and logistics.

Layla said she'd check out the library for books on fast-roping.

Nobody in the national media had picked up their story of going underground, and whatever they'd accomplished in the last few weeks had been muffled. Mooney's access to his Twitter account had been blocked. He suspected Football had leaned on Computer Science to make that happen.

Nevertheless, Layla said a counter-insurgency was growing. A core of professors had banded together to defend big-time sports. They claimed they had the support of the majority of the faculty, and Mooney didn't doubt that. At their on-campus press conference, with Coors banners as a backdrop and two free kegs of beer to draw people in, they had stressed how athletics was the only measurable part of the university—academic departments didn't keep score or get compared to conference rivals. And in a free-market capitalist society, nobody would pay a nickel to hear about Chaucer, colonialism, or atomic fusion. That's what Wikipedia was for. What people really wanted— the students and town and supporters and alumni—was a damn good football team. What institution would punish its most successful program while propping up crusty and ancient ways of thinking? The right-wing professors offered to donate more tents to The Hamlet for other failing departments that resisted the call of the future. The reactionary pricks had even given Braverman and Mooney a nickname: The Lonely Dinosaur Club. On top of that, a recent campus survey showed that most undergrads thought the university's emphasis on sports was a positive development. When asked about their favorite aspect of campus life, the Coors-themed pubs and their low-cost beer and giveaways were the student body's clear winner.

These were depressing developments. The only thing that could cheer Mooney up lately was Layla, her organic meals, and magazines. Sometimes she'd read an inspirational new poem, then stick it to the wall using her chewing gum. (Mooney believed it might be dangerous evidence if they had to scram quickly. They always shredded her poems after she left, which pained both men.)

One morning, Layla recited a new haiku.

"Soldiers of learning
Popcorn box shields no comfort.
Valiant touchdown death."

"I like the image of the shield," Braverman said. "I can almost see the red and white stripes blowing around in a storm."

"It's a downer, isn't it?" Mooney asked. "I guess I don't understand great poetry."

"It's glorious," Layla said. "The soldiers score in the end."

Braverman sat up straight. "The soldiers conscript the language of the enemy in the last line. Touchdown."

"That's right," Layla said. "That's exactly right." She smiled at Braverman.

Mooney set up folding chairs and called their meeting to order. A sold-out basketball crowd would provide a better stage, they all agreed, better than football practice. And Trevor would have a microphone, but what would he say? And how would he get the microphone to Mooney?

Layla explained her understanding of how it would all go down. Total darkness, then a spotlight would shine on Trevor as he walked to midcourt. Bringing Sasha along would appear impromptu, and nobody would have the nerve to tell the league's MVP that he couldn't have an escort. Trevor would have one minute for his speech. But he'd stretch it into two.

"Why involve Sasha?" Braverman asked.

"For emotional support," Layla said. "Trevor wants to share the spotlight and the trophy with Sasha. And since Trevor is going to hand off the microphone to you, he'll need Sasha to screen for him."

"Block," Braverman said. "In basketball they screen, but in football they block."

"Whatever," Layla said. "All this is after the Silver Bullet Dancers do their routine. The second half might be delayed if we cause another riot."

"Second half?" Braverman sniffed. "I doubt there will even be one."

"We don't know what will transpire," Mooney said. "If we do make it down from the rafters, what do I say before I get arrested?" But he was already formulating the speech in his head.

"Oh, I forgot," Layla said. "President Cardly is hiding out in The Hamlet."

"Crazy," Braverman said. "You can't hide in the middle of campus."

"You can when nobody cares about English. I think it's a wicked move. Although Cardly told me he's having trouble sleeping."

"Torture victims are often haunted in their dreams," Mooney said solemnly, "to again put things in historical context. The nightmares can go on for years."

Layla said the president wasn't having nightmares. "I gave him my red wig and he sleeps in it, just in case Criminal Justice bursts into the tent. He keeps it on twenty-four seven. It gets hot and keeps him awake at night."

The men nodded.

"Also, it appears President Cardly has hooked up with one of the English profs," Layla said with a sly grin, "They've got their own tent and they're sharing a sleeping bag."

"Who?"

"The one in the Whale sweatshirt."

"I thought she was gay," Braverman said.

"So did Buffalo," Layla said. "There are broken homes in The Hamlet. Buffalo blames Cardly, insists he sold out to a beer company illegally. She's checking the bylaws to see if the entire transaction was inappropriate. But let's get back on task."

"So we'll land as close as we can to Trevor," Braverman said, "A simple handoff."

"His last," Mooney said softly. They'd have to somehow set up in the rafters and be ready to drop down. There'd be no practice run.

Braverman said, "We'll probably have only a minute before the microphone gets cut or Eugene gets tackled."

"Nobody is going to tackle me," Mooney said. "I'll have Sasha there to block."

Mooney knew this was false bravado and plenty could go wrong. Plenty. Two middle-aged professors were going to try a daring military maneuver that had to be perfectly timed. Mooney felt a wave of anxiety, and he looked to Layla. Her dreadlocks were tied back in a ponytail. She had just a trace of age in her face. Just as quickly as the anxiety swept over him, it was gone.

Remaining in their concession stand, they decided, was too risky—spring football was right around the corner, and they could hear coaches and managers in the hallway nearly every morning. But there was nowhere to sleep before Saturday's basketball game.

"You're both welcome at my apartment," Layla said, as if reading Mooney's mind.

"You're the next best thing to Rosa Parks," Mooney said.

Layla ignored that and said she'd be back in the parking lot at midnight with a ladder.

After Saturday, Mooney thought, their lives really would be up in the air. He and Braverman would likely be arrested right on the court, in front of 18,000 fans. He considered himself a progressive guy—maybe not a radical, but a progressive. But he'd never imagined being arrested, or what the impact would be. Of course, the second half would get called off, but he hoped classes would not be canceled on Monday. If his arrest sparked a national movement, it would be worth it. Mooney's anxiety washed over him again. It wasn't just about being arrested. It was the waterboarding that might follow. He knew he would crack easier than Braverman.

Chapter 18

Layla hated doors. She had taken them all down months ago, put up curtains and beads, even for the bathroom. Her digs, the whole rental house setup, made her professor pals uncomfortable, she could tell.

She'd spent the morning shopping for the men, but she couldn't find a single book on fast-roping, so instead, Mooney watched *Black Hawk Down* on Netflix. Braverman, however, refused to partake in a movie that glorified war. Instead, he sat at the side of the television with his laptop, facing his friends, and did what he always warned students not to do—he puttered around YouTube as a form of research.

Layla's place as a temporary campsite was a great joy to all of them. The second day she made a big veggie stir-fry and they downed three bottles of red wine. After that she'd figured what the fuck and brought out an ice-filled ceramic bong. They got completely toasted, turned silly, then hysterical. Layla had saved her favorite hate mail letters from the cheerleaders, and Braverman coaxed her to share one. She tried to read it aloud but couldn't get through it without busting up. The girl had addressed the letter to "Dear Bitch Face," and challenged Layla to be hoisted to the top of one of their human pyramid formations, if she "wasn't too scared." But what would that prove?

Mooney said he hadn't smoked dope in years, but Braverman still did, and he didn't have a coughing fit every hit. It was just a super-cool time, the most fun they'd had together, and it made her sad to consider what was in store—the men would get arrested and tortured and likely lose their jobs. Mooney made her feel worse, inadvertently, by examining the photos on her fridge and pressing her about her parents. She deflected the questions without revealing much, but she promised herself to talk to the men about her father someday.

The next morning, she shopped for black tights, matching long-sleeved shirts, and black skullcaps. She was driving home when Trevor phoned. Sure, the ninja costume would be great for fast-roping, but he had come up with his own excellent idea on how to get the professors into the arena unnoticed in the first place: pep band uniforms. Decked out in pep band getups, nobody at security was likely to hassle them, according to Trevor's neighbors. Gerald and Jerome had agreed to take the night off and loan out their uniforms.

On the day of the game, Layla drove to the band room at Eamon Hall to collect the uniforms. She wanted to stay, since the pep band party was totally rocking, with JELL-O shots and the whole bit. The musicians were sweet and not at all curious about why a poet needed pep band outfits.

Back home, Braverman and Mooney were cleaning her place as if their mothers were arriving for the weekend. Maybe that's what happened to divorced guys—they learned to scour and scrub to impress women. At one point, Layla walked into the kitchen to find Braverman's legs sticking out from beneath the sink. He was fixing her leaky faucet without being asked.

Layla wanted the men to shave their beards for their big night, but Trevor convinced her of a more realistic option. He loaned her his hair clippers, and the professors got their beards down to a manageable stubble. She didn't have to convince

Mooney and Braverman about donning the band uniforms, either—they thought it was a smart plan.

One of the uniforms fit Mooney pretty well—tight but workable. The other uniform was nearly as big and hung off Braverman like a gaudy drape. The hats made them look like riverboat captains, too large but in just the right way, especially when they were angled down over their eyebrows. It gave the men a spritely, younger appearance, as did the tassels on their shoulders.

A moment of panic crashed Layla's little party when she realized they had no band instruments to appear legit. She should have asked Gerald and Jerome.

"We'll be the only band members without horns," Mooney agreed. "And how are we going to get our ninja stuff inside the arena? What if Criminal Justice is checking backpacks?"

"I can put mine on underneath," Braverman said. "Easy."

"I can't," Mooney said. "I'll burst out of this thing."

But Layla had an idea. "I've got two guitars. Let me empty one case, and you guys can stuff your black outfits inside. One of you will have a music case, the other can pose as the director. You'll change in the rafters, the old switcheroo, and store the band getups in the guitar case." Layla insisted it was a cheapo case and she didn't need it returned. She removed a guitar, put in their folded ninjawear, and latched it shut. She'd promised Gerald and Jerome she would return the band uniforms, but how? Well, whatever, she'd worry about that tomorrow.

"You think security will let in band members with an acoustic guitar?" Mooney wondered. Layla reminded him that Criminal Justice students worked the pass gate, and they weren't the brightest. Mooney motioned to her for the guitar, and he examined it lovingly before handing it back.

"Do you play?" she asked. "It's in tune."

Mooney said he had taken lessons briefly in junior high, although he only remembered the fingering for one chord. Braverman dug through the case and found a harmonica. He wiped it off and blew a sad blues.

"Nice," Mooney said. "I'd forgotten you could play that thing."

Braverman wasn't bad, and he riffed while Layla got busy, just as her own mother used to, packing organic peanut butter sandwiches into their rigged and loaded case. Braverman stopped playing and offered her the harmonica.

"Keep that," she told him. "I never learned."

"Your tongue is the key," Braverman said. "It all happens inside your mouth. I could show you."

This was the kind of suggestion that would have felt creepy to Layla last semester, but now she understood Braverman better—and how to clarify that she wasn't interested. "Nice try," she said, but she laughed when she said it.

Braverman went back to their drawings and calculations on the table. "From the rafters to the floor is probably 150 feet down," he said. "We're going to have to use our imaginations here."

"That's cool," Layla said. "Really, the goal of any form of education should spark the imagination so—"

"What the hell are you talking about?" Mooney said suddenly.

His aggressive tone caught her off guard, and she instantly regretted falling into the silly academic-speak she'd learned from English. "I guess," she said slowly, as if fumbling for an answer to defuse this, "it's like John Lennon's song, 'Imagine.'"

"I'm sorry, Layla," Mooney said. "I meant what Peter said. It's not fifty yards. No way."

But Braverman had done the research, and Mooney had a problem—he was deathly afraid of heights. "I deliberately didn't want to consider how high up we'd be, I guess," he said and slumped in his chair. "What now?"

"You could hit the bong again," Layla said, "We all could. That would be good for our anxiety. That's what I do before faculty meetings."

Braverman put a hand on Mooney's knee. "Go on ahead, Eugene," he said. "I hadn't seen you so happy in years."

"Ahhhh," Mooney grumbled. "Last night was fun. But I think it might make me more paranoid."

"You don't have to go through with this," Braverman said softly. He paused, then added, "Layla and I could do it together."

"Like hell," she said.

"Just a thought," Braverman said, and he raised both palms to pacify her.

Mooney sat forward, his head in his hands. He seemed to be talking to himself. He leaned back and took a deep breath. "I can do this. I've got this. Did you know that one academic claims that Pancho Villa was actually afraid of horses? He's written a book about it."

"I've heard," Braverman added reassuringly, "that Gandhi was embarrassed about his nipples, but he walked around half-naked to get over his mental block. It had nothing to do with a life of poverty or him owning just one loin cloth."

"That's interesting," Mooney said. "Wait just a minute, that can't be true. Are you still high?"

Layla bit her lip until Braverman burst into laughter, then they all laughed, long and hard, as though they really were still stoned.

Layla drove them to the basketball arena in her mother's VW van two hours before tip-off. She had packed two pot brownies from her freezer for her own enjoyment. She wouldn't down one until just before the game. She'd drop the men off, park near the English Department, and hang out at The Hamlet until she heard from Trevor and Sasha. At a stoplight, she offered a bite to the professors, but they declined. She didn't mind. Fellow travelers had to find their own paths.

A few hundred yards from the arena she stopped, texted Trevor, and gave him the lowdown before she let the professors out of her van. She tried to imagine them floating down like angels of the apocalypse. Trevor had an extra ticket, which was cool because she didn't want to sit alone, although she realized that's exactly what she would be—alone—when her friends were on the court at halftime. She had to stop herself from blurting out that she didn't want to be by herself.

And she wouldn't be selling game programs, which she also didn't want to talk about, but the men didn't ask. Football had punished Poetry, due to her support of History. This would be their last night selling programs, and her poetry students would have to handle it alone. She had no desire to sell programs tonight. She wanted to witness the whole epic halftime revolt. She trusted her students to deliver the take on Monday.

She looked up from her phone and said, "Trevor wants a photo of you two in your band uniforms."

"I'm afraid we shouldn't be producing evidence," Mooney said. "This will be our secret memory, Layla."

"I'll never forget our wonderful time at your place," Braverman added with a paternal tone, "and I feel like for some reason we should just go back and stay there. It's like we're walking out on you now, Layla." He turned to his friend and said, "Grab that guitar case, Eugene, or we'll be stuck in these silly uniforms."

Before they got out of Layla's van, Mooney gave her his office and house keys. Braverman did the same. She sat curbside for a few minutes, her car idling. The men shuffled away in their billowy band uniforms toward the basketball arena, where their bright shining moment would culminate in being handcuffed. Maybe worse. Braverman's striped pants were sagging off his ass, just like her basketball poets'. She was surprised to find herself choking back tears.

"What kind of pep band," she said to herself, "has a fucking acoustic guitar?"

Chapter 19

Mooney had already sweated through his shirt by the time they arrived at the West Gate. A sign was posted there: Media, Cheerleaders, Pep Band. Eight cheerleaders, male and female, were presenting their IDs at a long table, and the professors fell in line. More cheerleaders appeared behind them. That was fine, but off in the distance a bunch of brass players were approaching. Mooney wanted to get through security quickly—the legit band members could blow their cover. The line inched along. A tall cheerleader turned back and eyeballed Braverman up and down with a smirk.

"Have a good game," Braverman said to her. "Cheer well."

"Fuck you, band geek," she said. "Quit staring at me."

Braverman sniffed, but before he could lash out, Mooney gripped his arm to calm him.

Mooney wondered if this was the same cheerleader who had penned the piercing hate mail to Layla. As the line moved forward, he tugged his cap down over his eyebrows, but he could still see Braverman's feet. His friend was hopping in place as he did when agitated. The cheerleader had hit a raw nerve, and Mooney—

"Next," the kid behind the table said, waving them forward.

"Pep band," Mooney said.

"Yeah, pep band," Braverman said. "The both of us."

"Names?"

"That's correct," Mooney said. Like a fool, he'd forgotten to ask Layla the band members' names. He tilted his visor up a bit. Two young men, no doubt Criminal Justice majors, were seated before him. One kid was muscled up and splotched with freckles. The other couldn't have been five feet tall.

The musclebound student said, "Maybe you're okay to go ahead. I better check." He picked up a walkie-talkie and asked for assistance.

"If it's too much trouble," Mooney began.

"Just give me a minute. And I might need your names." The walkie-talkie filled the air with static.

Mooney had an idea. They'd duck out of line, go to the back, call Layla, then return. Before he could do that, Braverman elbowed him aside.

"Who are you, the Gestapo?" Braverman said sharply. "We're band geeks. Are you blind? We're tired of giving you our names year after year and getting the goddamn third degree. I've been practicing all week, and I don't appreciate you violating our Fourth Amendment rights."

"Which one was the Fourth?" the short kid asked.

"The right to be a band geek," the freckly musclehead said. "Hey, the game is sold out and people are trying to sneak in. We're just doing our jobs."

"And furthermore," Braverman shouted, "what the heck do you think this is?" and he whipped a harmonica out of his band uniform, as if to prove that the Fourth Amendment included the right to bear harmonicas.

"A kazoo?" the kid said.

Mooney pulled at Braverman's shoulder, but it felt thick and immovable like Sasha's. Not a good sign.

"What year are you guys?" the freckled security kid asked, getting his courage up. "You look a little old for pep band."

"I'm class of 1982," Braverman said. "Didn't you get the memo about tonight's Pep Band Alumni Reunion? We used to rock this joint, and it wasn't even built then. Give me that," he said. He jerked the case-that-did-not-hold-a-guitar from Mooney, slamming it down on their table. "I suppose it doesn't say a thing on your little fascist list about the reunion, huh?"

"It might," the short kid said, and he thumbed through pages. "You guys are probably fine to go ahead."

But the stout student with the freckles wasn't such a pushover. "What's in here?" he said, tapping the guitar case.

"An iPhone 19," Braverman said. "Haven't you seen the new iPhone cases?"

The short one smiled. "Cool," he said.

"We're waiting," somebody called out. Then, "Move it, band geeks."

Mooney looked over his shoulder. Half the cheerleading squad was at their heels, and behind them must have been thirty pep band members.

"He's messing with us," the freckled one said. "Why would they make an iPod case as big as a guitar."

"You're pretty smart," Braverman said, "for a Criminal Justice major. That's right, it's a guitar case. You can open it and see. My friend here can even sing you two bozos a song."

"That's not necessary, Peter," Mooney said and pulled the case back. Braverman was about to blow their cover. Didn't he remember there was no guitar inside, just their ninja gear?

"You're being awful aggressive," the short one said. "We're not supposed to take any lip."

"Okay," the freckled one said. "I'll bite. Play us a song." He tugged the case away from Mooney.

Mooney swallowed hard. Busted. Before the game even began, too, all because of Braverman's stupid temper. How in heaven's name would they explain the all-black outfits? The boys fumbled with the latches until the short one popped the top. Mooney cringed.

"Nice," the short one said. It was a shiny guitar.

One of them had grabbed the wrong case. Not him, Mooney hoped, it must have been Layla or Braverman, although it didn't matter now. Mooney hadn't played a guitar for years, but he recognized the Gibson label, a much nicer model than the one he'd held briefly at Layla's, probably worth a few thousand bucks. Soon they were going to lose the guitar and be stuck in these silly uniforms, even if they did skate past security.

"Let's hear you play something, Mr. Summer of Love," the freckled guy said. He thrust the guitar at Braverman.

"Sing 'Mountain Cold Refreshment,'" the short one suggested. "I love the school fight song."

Mooney stopped himself from answering and faced away from the security table. "We took the wrong case," he hissed at Braverman.

Braverman turned to the guards again. "I told you, I play the harmonica," he said, flashing the instrument at them again. "This guy here is the guitar wizard." He passed the instrument back to Mooney. "Play 'Revolution' by the Beatles."

"No, the school fight song," the freckled guy said. The short one cued up his phone to record.

"I'd rather not," Mooney said. "Besides, people are waiting." He pointed the guitar at the line, but at the same time he found himself pulling on the shoulder strap. He remembered a single chord. If Layla hadn't tuned this one recently, they were screwed. E-minor was just two fingers. He'd never been a singer. He made the simple shape and strummed through with the meat of his thumb. The E-minor rang out, lonesome and pathetic like a dirge.

"You say you want a revolution," he sang, "well-el you know, we all want to change the world." The minor chord was all wrong.

People behind booed, but the security kids laughed. "You guys suck big time," the freckled one said, "so you must be in the band. Next."

Braverman pulled the guitar away from Mooney and dropped it back in the case. "Wait till you see our halftime show tonight," he said and slapped the cover shut. He handed Mooney the case and pulled him into the arena.

Braverman suggested a lap around the concourse to search for a stairway up into the rafters. Mooney said, "Before we do that, you've got to calm down."

"I could use a beer," Braverman said.

"Are you crazy? We have got to get out of these outfits."

Below them, near the court, a dozen Math professors huddled over calculators and computers at the officials' table, preparing to do the game stats. Family, Consumer and Childcare profs were giving the hardwood a good once-over, rubbing out trouble spots on hands and knees.

And sure enough, Layla's graduate poetry students were posted at their stations with stacks of programs. Mooney figured he and Braverman would have to be extra careful—he'd met a couple of Layla's poets before, but he didn't trust anyone tonight. The arena was nearly empty, although a sellout was looming. Mooney approached an older-looking student vendor he didn't recognize and asked for a game program—what did it say about honoring Trevor?

The young man checked his watch. "I'm not supposed to sell them for another seventeen minutes," he said.

"I remember when they used to be free," Mooney said. "Hey, what kind of poetry do you write?"

"The good kind," he said. Then, "Football says this is our last night."

"Ours, too," Braverman said. The student looked at him quizzically.

"This is our final issue," the student poet said, "a collector's item. We're going to wind up cleaning the locker rooms I hear. You guys are in the band?"

"In a manner of speaking," Mooney said. He waved a fiver at him. "Come on, buddy, sell me a program. We've got to get going."

The vendor said, "The arena is not even open to the public yet. Look." He pointed up. "Electrical Engineering is still adjusting the television lights."

"Oh, right," Mooney said, gazing up at the Engineering professors. He could barely see them, but thankfully he could make out remnants of roping gear dangling above.

"The coaches don't like to let the public in until the TV lights are on," the young man continued. "It's all about atmosphere."

"How'd those guys get up there?" Mooney said. "I'm just curious."

"How would I know?" the poet said. "Come back in fifteen minutes and I'll sell you a program."

Mooney pulled Braverman away. "Let's see what door they come out," he said, looking up. Braverman was fuming about Poetry—well, Layla—losing the gig, but Mooney shushed him when moments later three Electrical Engineering professors gathered their gear and made off along the railed, narrow catwalk until they were directly above. One of them launched a paper airplane. It was well constructed, and it took a long, slow, circular arc, around and around until it crash-landed.

"Geez," Braverman said, "that's quite an airplane."

Mooney grunted in agreement, but just then he lost sight of the profs. Where the heck—a door behind them flew open and bonked Braverman on the back of his head. His band hat flew off and he dropped to his knees. The trio of Engineering profs walked away. The door read "Authorized Personnel Only." Mooney put down his guitar case to help his friend to his feet, but Braverman pointed and said, "Get the door."

Mooney wedged his hand in just before it swung shut, but it was as heavy as a tuba. He stifled a howl, tugged it open, and motioned for Braverman to join him. Braverman slid past. "I fucked up my back," he gasped.

"I think I broke my pinkie," Mooney said, and waved his hand in Braverman's face. The stairway was poorly lit.

"No more guitar chords and you'll be fine," Braverman teased. "You did swell back there, by the way."

"Damn," Mooney said. "I left Layla's guitar by the program vendor." He could see instantly this didn't play well with Braverman. Still on edge after the cheerleader's insult, he was likely to be on a righteous rampage the rest of the evening. Maybe even the rest of his life.

"I can't let Layla down," Braverman said. "I'm going back." He shouldered the door open an inch and peered out.

"It's too dangerous."

"Fuck that," Braverman said. "Cover my back."

Mooney kept a toe in the door while Braverman returned to the usher. *Cover his back how?* he wondered. Braverman was chatting the guy up. He recovered the guitar, pulled cash out of his pocket, and bought a program.

"What were you thinking?" Mooney said moments later.

"You wanted a program." Braverman handed it over.

"I was just curious about Trevor's award, but I really don't need more luggage." He tucked it into his belt, anyway, just in case it had intel on the halftime show.

They crept up the stairs with the guitar. "You realize," Mooney whispered, "that now we have to fast-rope in these goddamn pep band getups."

"We'll probably lose the hats at some point," Braverman said.

"Who ever heard of a revolution started by the school band? We look like fools."

"You look more like Captain Kangaroo, to be honest," Braverman said.

"Thanks. You look like Che Guevara."

"Really?"

"No, not really, Peter."

Mooney's breath caught in his throat when they reached the top. The catwalk was wide enough, maybe three feet, but there was just a single railing on each side, and the walkway was grated, so he could see right through to the court. His impulse was to run back to the stairway. Instead, he got down on all fours and motioned for Braverman to do the same. Mooney's knees hurt instantly.

"Nobody can see us with the television lights," Braverman said. "Why don't we just walk?"

"Because I'm scared shitless."

"You've been rehearsing all morning."

"I'm not afraid of public speaking," Mooney said. "I'm afraid of heights." He knew enough not to glance down until he had to. Instead, he thrust his head back and crawled as if playing "chase the puppy" with a toddler.

"Think about it like this," Braverman said. "We're not going to get higher tonight. We're only going to get closer to the court."

Mooney looked back over his imaginary puppy-dog tail. Braverman was on his feet, smiling. Despite his low center of gravity, Mooney felt quite a bit of swaying, a noticeable wobble and drift whenever he moved. Over midcourt lay a minor miracle—a fast-roping unit was still in place. It felt solid, permanent. Criminal Justice indeed planned to fast-rope their top students down on a regular basis. Other sets of gear were spaced out across the catwalk.

"Now what?" Mooney said.

"I'll find another, unfasten it, and move it closer. Keep an eye on the guitar." Braverman sauntered off as if going for a Coke. Every few feet he bent to the base of the walkway, like a sea captain checking the rigging. Braverman came back with a thick, coiled black band in hand, very different from what Mooney was hooking up to his waist.

"Look, a bungee cord," Braverman said.

"You won't get to the court. You'll just keep bouncing up and down."

"I can't get the fast-roping gear to loosen, it's welded. This is better, I'll be a decoy. I'll bounce around until you get the microphone. I did a few bungee jumps in the 1990s."

"Not above a basketball court. What if you land on your head?"

"Layla will be impressed."

"Goddammit, Peter, we're not trying to impress her."

"We can't share a microphone anyway. We're not Simon and Garfunkel, as you just proved at the pass gate. Trust me, nobody can create a crazy distraction like me. I'll go first, security will come after me. Then you make a safe landing and it'll give you time to make your speech."

Mooney thought about it. "What about Layla's guitar?"

"That's part of the distraction. I'm taking it," Braverman said, and opened the case. "What could be more distracting than an old band geek bouncing on a bungee cord thrashing a guitar?"

"Maybe you're right," Mooney said.

"Hey, show me how to play that chord."

"Okay, but don't make a racket yet. Put two fingers here, on the second fret."

Chapter 20

Great seats, Trevor thought. Row two, behind the Coors State bench, and close enough that he could hear the trash talking, although the basketball game hadn't even begun. He wore a sport coat and tie for the occasion, but Sasha had gone casual in a Silver Bullets sweatshirt. For Trevor, the high-flying action of college basketball held great appeal and he could feel the pressure building as the opening tip-off approached. The place erupted when the starters were announced. It was hard not to stand and stomp his feet with everyone, clap in unison.

Trevor had listed Sasha Dimitrievic and "sister" as his guests for the pass list. The sister was Professor Layla Sillimon, and nobody at the pass gate seemed to mind that the quarterback's kin rocked thick blonde dreadlocks and Birkenstocks.

That morning, Trevor had considered canceling this halftime announcement, his premature retirement plan. NCAA rules, it was being reported nationally, were about to change radically, greatly altering the big-time sports landscape. A college athlete could now sell his likeness and image, do commercials for cash, or sign autographs for a stipend. The Silver Bullets already led a casually cushy lifestyle, but there would soon be big payoffs for the best athletes, a completely legal pot of gold. Trevor had never hurt for money, not with his father's lucrative business, but still, this could make him financially independent before his twenty-first birthday. That couldn't be dismissed out of hand.

Trevor had read the article aloud, hoping Sasha might suggest calling off the halftime speech, but his roommate was unmoved. "Money and poetry are not friends," Sasha said grimly. The Croatian went on to point out that the new rules would increase the status of football on campus, take things in the wrong direction. "Good news for teammates, bad news for professor friends who we love so very much," Sasha concluded.

Trevor hadn't notified his parents about his MVP ceremony because he knew they wouldn't want to witness his premature retirement. He wasn't even certain what it was he wanted. Or that it was the right thing to do. But he'd decided to go through with it. And all day he'd been too jittery to eat, so now, thirty minutes before tip-off, when he saw Layla slide some brownie squares out of her backpack, he began to salivate. On impulse, when she was talking to Sasha, he grabbed one and took a bite.

"Whoa," Layla said. "You trying to relax?"

"I guess," Trevor said, chewing ravenously.

Layla turned to him, her eyebrows raised. "That's a marijuana brownie, sweetie," she said.

Trevor gulped instinctively, which was exactly what he shouldn't have done, because he swallowed a big chunk. "Why didn't you tell me?" he said, handing the rest back.

"I'm telling you now," Layla said. "Sorry."

It tasted grainy, earthy. He reached into his pocket for a napkin to spit some out and dumped it under his seat. He felt lightheaded, but he knew it was from the shock, not the weed. How long until it took effect?

Layla said it probably wouldn't kick in until well after halftime. Trevor asked if he should go barf in the men's room. She said no, it was likely too late, and his belly would gurgle then his mind would expand, but it might not hit him for a while, and anyway it wouldn't impede his ability to address the crowd. "I mean, unless you haven't eaten recently," she added. "Then it could hit you pretty quick. I haven't eaten since breakfast myself." She offered him the rest, but he waved her off.

Just before tip-off, the team came back to their bench, glistening with sweat. One player called out, "Whassup, Shrek!"

"Look, one of our poets," Layla said, and she stood to wave. "Hi, Lyndon."

Lyndon tapped a few shoulders until the entire starting five were looking up at Trevor, Sasha, and Layla.

"We gonna fuck these dudes up, Miss Layla," one of them hollered. "We fuck 'em up for you!"

"Sounds super," she yelled.

"Why you so ugly, Shrek?" another player called, and he laughed and slapped palms with his pals.

Layla said, "They love you, Sasha."

"Bond between poets," Sasha shrugged. "Like brothers."

"And sisters," Layla added.

"And ballplayers," Sasha said.

"Not so much anymore," Trevor said.

"My roommate is a little bummed out," Sasha explained.

"He'll cheer up soon. But Sasha," Layla said, "I'm so proud of you for talking the talk."

Sasha stood, cupped his hands, and shouted, "Don't let these punks fuck up your shit." He sat back down and faced his friends. "Street slang of African Americans," he said.

Layla said, "You sounded very authentic."

Trevor had been surprised last week when three basketball players from Sasha's poetry workshop came to visit their apartment for no obvious reason. The Croatian had returned home from class disheartened on a few occasions, but the basketballers had warmed up to him as the semester wore on. It was great how Sasha kept absorbing American speech, too, although this halftime stunt might end Sasha's improvement— if Football sent them both packing.

"I practice with President Cardly. He has much free time."

"Too bad he couldn't be here tonight," Layla said.

"Cardly is here," Trevor said, "somewhere. He wanted to show his support but stay under cover." Trevor scanned the crowd.

Perhaps the former president's most popular move had been to aggressively encourage beer sales at games—Coors inside the arena, and Chemistry's craft beers outside. Even at twelve bucks a pop, the fans sucked it down. Cardly had sneaked into the game disguised as a beer vendor—a baseball cap with Layla's red wig blossoming out the sides. Cardly knew their seat numbers and said he'd stop by. He was a great leader, Trevor had decided, because of his ability to adapt. Seconds later, as if on cue, Cardly appeared, the square metal beer cooler clearly weighing heavily on his narrow frame. The wig made him look like an aging Ronald McDonald. "Cold beer here," he said, staying in character.

"I'm not twenty-one," Trevor said, "until June." A certifiable lightweight, Trevor rarely drank more than a couple. It was too soon for the pot brownie to make an impact, but maybe a beer would calm his nerves.

Cardly said, as if reading Trevor's mind, "You're leaving here in handcuffs either way."

"I'm over twenty-one," Layla said. "I'll have three beers."

"Make that a double," Sasha said.

Cardly, confused, struggled with the arithmetic.

Sasha tried again. "Beer for me and water for my horse. That is John Wayne from famous American movie."

"Okay, fine," Trevor said, not wanting to feel left out on his big night. "I guess I'll have three beers, too." He could sip one now, and if he made it back to his seat after halftime, he would pound the others.

Cardly passed over nine cans, but he waved Layla off when she reached for her purse. Tonight the beer was on him, and off he went.

Sasha said, "Do you think we can spot our professor friends?"

"Let's not all stare up at once," Trevor cautioned. "We don't want to alert anyone." Pretending to check the scoreboard, he subtly scanned the rafters. But the glare of the lights was like looking at the sun. Just stick to the game plan, he reminded himself. Give the speech, hand the trophy to Sasha, pass the microphone to Mooney. He quietly went over his speech with Sasha, and his friend nodded along, flipping a finger up for each of his talking points. 1) Overemphasis on sports. 2) Why torture was wrong. 3) What was best for American universities. 4) The old-fashioned ideal of education. 5) Thank the three professors, then thank Sasha. 6) Announce he was quitting football.

The game started with Coors State soaring for consecutive dunks, and the student section kicked up a rowdy cheer.

"You seem stressed," Layla said. She reached into her bag to offer Trevor another brownie bite. He declined. She put on a pair of sunglasses to look up. "I can see Eugene practically right above us," she said. "But I don't see Peter."

"Let's hope he didn't change his mind," Trevor said. He motioned to borrow Layla's sunglasses, whose frames featured pink and purple butterflies. Now he could see Mooney sitting cross-legged and peering down. And Braverman! Above the opposite free throw line. He told Layla, who told Sasha. Was he beginning to feel stoned? The lights in the arena were dazzling, but he wrote it off as nerves. Just past the scoreboard hung the jerseys of basketball players who'd had their numbers retired. Football had a similar display in their stadium. In that moment, Trevor realized he'd never have his own number honored. If he quit tonight, he'd never play another down, certainly not at Coors State. Not after what he was about to say to a sold-out basketball crowd. Maybe he'd be still remembered forever at the school, even across the nation, as a cult figure—the Colin Kaepernick of college sports.

"Can you feel the brownies yet?" Layla shouted. "I think I'm feeling it, and it's not even close to halftime."

Trevor swooned and again considered going up to the men's room to vomit. He could count the times he'd smoked pot on one hand.

Layla laughed, draped an arm over him, and told him it would be great. She let her arm linger. Finally, she said, "You'll be flying. The beer will wash it down, get it in your system sooner."

"Will I still be able to give a good speech?"

"Better than good," Layla said, squeezing him hard.

Sasha and Layla smiled at him, and he nearly said he loved them. Trevor understood now that he was, in fact, very high. The truth was he loved everyone in the arena, but he decided to wait until he had the microphone to say so. That would be an important talking point, too, he realized.

"I love you, too," Layla said. Trevor was pretty sure he had not said that out loud. "What a game, huh?" Layla added.

With all the media time-outs—they came every two minutes, another new NCAA rule—the game dragged on. At the 8:00 minute mark in the half, Trevor felt like a balloon was expanding slowly in his head. He got his notecards out of his sport coat pocket and reviewed his talking points. Everything still made sense, that was good. On the court, the players ricocheted back and forth and back like characters in a video game.

Trevor noticed the coach didn't have much to say when the Silver Bullets had the basketball. His main advice was focused on the defensive end, and that advice was twofold. First, to trap, to double-team the man with the ball. That occasionally resulted in a steal, but sometimes not, which led to this exclamation from the coach: Fuck! With the defensive play right in front of Trevor and his crew, that became the backbeat.

Trap. Trap! Fuck. Trap. Fuck! Trap! Fuck.

Layla didn't understand, or else she was getting silly, shouting it even when Coors State had the ball. Twice the coach turned and glared at them. Sasha tried to get her to cool it, but she seemed determined to keep up the chant. A few of the students nearby joined in, but the older fans clearly did not approve. Trevor tugged gently on Layla's blouse and motioned for her to sit. "I don't think the coach appreciates us yelling that," he said. "You might be confusing his players because they could trap or fuck at the wrong time."

The scoreboard now said six minutes until the half, although game time was different than real time, Trevor thought. It could be as much as a half hour before his speech, with all the time-outs. The coach seemed to have calmed down somewhat, no doubt because Coors State was up twenty points. Trevor referred to his program to see which player had popped in a three-pointer. He could remember the football players names, and there were a lot more of them, so why couldn't he keep the basketball team's names straight now? No wonder all the coach said was trap and fuck. He probably couldn't remember their names either.

"What's so funny?" Layla asked. "You've got the giggles, huh?"

Trevor pointed to the names and held the program up to Layla. He was short of breath, almost hysterical.

Layla studied the page. "You're pointing to Todd. What's funny about Todd?" She was laughing now, too. She hugged his neck like he'd tossed a touchdown pass.

"Not Todd," he blurted. "He's okay," and he busted up again.

Sasha bent toward them and said, "What's the joke, artichoke?"

The game swirled around as if there were two dozen players on the court—Trevor could hardly discern whose ball it was, let alone whether it was time to trap or fuck. He could literally hear the swoooosh of the twine when the ball went through the net, but how was that even possible with all the noise? The cheerleaders were bouncing up and down and next there were hundreds of them on the floor and it must have been a time-out because the music got louder although Lyndon was yelling back at the coach, just the fuck part, not the trap, and the cheerleaders were kicking their legs at Trevor and he might have recognized one from freshman year then the gals faced Trevor and one of them raised her shirt and flashed her navel ring or was he just wishing she would? Either was cool and Layla was on her feet dancing next to him swishing her hippie skirt back and forth and whooping it up and she was yelling trap and fuck again but at the cheerleaders and the horn blew to end the time-out and the noise shook him to his socks so he took his shoes off to get a better look at his feet as the game started up again and didn't the coaches understand not to use all twelve players at once and why on earth would there be two basketballs at one time, it was the funniest thing he'd ever seen but also very, very possibly the most beautiful, the way it was like a dance, an urban cultural dance his online Sociology prof might have said and that was a wonderful dance indeed, different than the cheerleaders and which one—the next thing he knew, Layla was shaking his shoulder. She was wearing that red wig again. But how did she get it? Where was President Cardly?

"Halftime," Layla said, "we gotta go." She held his notecards in her hands. He didn't remember giving them to her. When he motioned for her to give them back, she tore the cards to shreds. "You're too high to read anyway," she said. "Trust your gut."

Trevor turned to the Croatian. "Help," he said.

Chapter 21

Eugene Mooney closed his eyes, dangled his legs over the edge, and silently reviewed their plans. Fifty seconds into Trevor's talk, Braverman was to bungee jump as a distraction. Seconds later, Mooney would fast-rope down, and Trevor would hand over the microphone. Mooney hoped the quarterback's on-the-field savvy would keep him from panicking when Braverman made his plunge, as that hadn't been discussed.

Coors State was winning by thirty points when the halftime buzzer buzzed. Mooney motioned to his friend across the catwalk, pointing to his watch. The Silver Bullet Dancers had the first five minutes. Unless Trevor got wordy, they'd have plenty of leeway. The music started up and the dance routine took shape below. Its symmetry, in contrast to the chaos of the basketball game, delighted Mooney. He tapped his hand in time to the music. It was a 1960s number, a good omen, but who was it? The Zombies? The Box Tops?

"Hey, Peter," Mooney shouted, but the music made communicating impossible. He realized just then—"Good Lovin'" by The Young Rascals.

The music stopped and the crowd quieted. That's when Braverman accidentally dropped Layla's guitar.

It narrowly missed a Silver Bullet dancer, landed with a dissonant whomp, and snapped at the neck. The dancers let out a piercing scream in unison, as if they'd rehearsed the guitar's crash landing. The crowd got quiet. Below, Criminal Justice profs blinked into the lights above then started hustling toward the stairs the professors had used. They'd be at the catwalk in minutes—possibly before Trevor began his speech. The crowd was murmuring. Braverman shrugged at him, and what could Mooney say? "Be more careful next time"? He used his gloved hands to pull the rope snug. He'd be poised to drop down early if security got too close on the catwalk.

The TV lights went dark and a spotlight lit up Trevor directly below. Sasha and Layla flanked him. The PA announcer bellowed this was a special night to honor conference MVP Trevor Knighton.

Even from above, the Croatian appeared as thick as Braverman's lost Volvo. He led the others arm-in-arm out to midcourt. Trevor stumbled, maybe out of nervousness, and Sasha pulled him upright.

The trio was supposed to stop at the spotlighted half-court circle, where Coach Maniscalco appeared with a microphone and a trophy. He began by listing Trevor's accomplishments. But the trio wandered the court as if lost in a vast desert. In the burst of applause, Maniscalco caught up to Trevor, who had stopped to kneel over the broken guitar as if in mourning. It was an odd moment, and Mooney struggled to make sense of what he was seeing. The coach tapped Trevor on the back and gave him the trophy and the microphone.

This was not what they'd planned. There'd be no easy handoff after his speech if Trevor didn't get back to center court, pronto.

Three Criminal Justice profs in bright vests burst through the door into the rafters then moved cautiously along the catwalk toward Braverman. Mooney waved frantically to alert him. Just as they got to Braverman's side, he whirled, and in a fit of desperation—or courage—tried to leap over the railing, his bungee cord attached. But the security guards caught him before he went over, wrestling his arms behind his back and handcuffing him. They hadn't noticed Mooney, not yet.

Below, Trevor took the microphone and waved at the crowd. "Oh, man," he said. "Look at that guitar. That's sad. I want to say that Football is over." He handed Sasha his trophy, then fumbled around with one hand in his pocket, maybe looking for misplaced notes, and slurring his words as well, not a good sign. That wasn't nerves, Mooney thought. Layla stepped into the spotlight and whispered to Trevor before sliding back into the shadows, along with what was left of her guitar.

"I saw an incident I want to tell you about," Trevor announced. "Not that guitar. I mean I saw President Cardly get waterboarded."

The crowd erupted in cheers again, but Trevor held both hands up to quiet them, as if the noise kept the quarterback from calling his signals.

"Sasha is very upset about that," Trevor went on, "but let me start over. I couldn't have won MVP without my teammate, Sasha Dimitrievic." Layla gave Sasha a gentle push into the spotlight, where he took a modest bow.

Far above Trevor, Braverman had disappeared. The guards must not have seen Mooney, and he offered up a prayer for Peter, the stubborn SOB. Braverman would withstand any enhanced interrogation techniques his captors threw at him if it meant protecting the revolution.

Trevor waved the crowd silent again. "Does everyone know what happened in Croatia? Sasha could explain it. What I want to say is that I need a break from football. It's, like, too important and all. Know what I mean? Right, Sasha? We all need a break. But I guess I'm still deciding what, like, I'm going to do."

Almost a minute had expired, and Trevor hadn't exactly ignited the crowd. Why wasn't he sticking to his speech? Mooney hoped he wasn't wavering on his commitment to walk away. Trevor tapped the microphone—although it was obviously working—and wandered into the dark. The spotlight zigzagged to find him, picking him up in one corner, where he handed the microphone to Sasha. Trevor sat down cross-legged on the court.

"Why the hell did Trevor do that?" Mooney mumbled.

The crowd was getting restless. Sasha fidgeted, then said something in Croatian into the microphone. Now, that was nerves, Mooney thought. A couple students yelled at Sasha from the stands, and he haltingly drowned them out, switching to English to say school was more important than sports. More people hollered in protest. Layla carried her shattered guitar back into the spotlight and grabbed Sasha's wrist to pull his microphone up to her face. "Everybody chill out!" she yelled. This time a wave of boos mixed in with catcalls.

That's when Mooney began his descent.

Halfway down, Mooney nearly lost his grip and his ridiculous pep band hat fell off, but with the spotlight now on Sasha and Layla, perhaps nobody noticed. Mooney continued his descent in the dark while Sasha continued to stammer.

"We won't play football anymore," Sasha said, finally getting confidence in his voice. "Thanks to a history professor. Look, here he is now."

The television lights burst on again just as Mooney landed. He instantly felt the heat as much as the glare. That meant everyone in attendance was staring at him. He was trapped and alone if that was possible, at midcourt, where he gave a military-style salute, intended to mean "at your service."

Maniscalco yelled something at Sasha—clearly the coach was angry. He moved toward the Croatian, but Sasha flipped the microphone back to Trevor, who had staggered to his feet.

The pass from Sasha seemed to awaken the quarterback's instincts. Trevor faked left and backpedaled to the baseline, his coach pacing after him in pursuit. Layla stepped in front of the coach with her mangled guitar and red wig, but he shoved her out of the way. A new refrain of boos sounded. Layla let loose with a barrage of profanity, tossed her useless guitar down and ran under the bleachers.

Sasha took her place, stepping in front of his coach. Maniscalco knew better than to get physical with the Croatian, so the coach hopped in place, as if desperate to deliver an important play to his quarterback. Two security guards appeared, and Sasha barred his arms to hold them all at bay, five yards from Trevor.

Mooney wasn't in Trevor's line of vision, so he flapped his arms as if to say I'm open. But Trevor stopped again, staring down into his own hands, as though he had no idea how a microphone worked or how he'd come to possess one.

"Wake up, Trevor," Mooney finally yelled. "Here I am."

Sasha roll-blocked two other security guards, but that gave Maniscalco an opening, and he moved unobstructed at his quarterback. He grabbed Trevor's left arm, but Mooney flared to his right to give his quarterback a better passing angle. Trevor pivoted, planted his feet and spiraled the microphone to his professor.

The throw was high, but Mooney read it instantly, jumping to snag the microphone with one hand. The crowd burst into applause. Maybe the spectacular catch could bring everyone around to his side if he acted quickly.

"Check, check," Mooney said. Loud and clear. He tugged at his striped pep band coat. Bits of Layla's broken guitar were strewn along the sideline, like a trail of clues left by a hippie Cinderella. Maybe she'd escaped to freedom, unlike Braverman.

"Please cut the TV lights again," Mooney said, "and give me the spotlight." He noticed Sasha whisk Trevor under the bleachers and into the shadows. A moment later, his wish was granted, leaving him alone but illuminated in a protective aura. Maniscalco and the security guards remained frozen in the dark.

"How many of you," he began, "love Coors State as much as I do?" Miraculously, his pep band cap appeared right at his feet, and he paused to Frisbee it into the stands, where a horde of kids wrestled over it. "I'm Professor Eugene Mooney," he said, "and I can no longer in good conscience allow our fine university to be a sports factory whose sole purpose is to entertain us with winning teams."

Mooney hadn't been booed since the faculty meeting over a year ago, and he was surprised by how much it hurt. His diplomatic instinct was to backtrack, maybe even apologize for his poor choice of words. He wished Braverman were there to push him onward, instead of what he was probably doing this very instant—biting security guards, snarling like a caged pit bull. Thinking of Braverman's loyalty filled Mooney with the needed inspiration. His fallen comrade had sacrificed himself for the revolution. Or for friendship. Or both.

"I've got a list of demands that will help us get our priorities straight." Mooney was conscious of the fact that he was walking forward as he spoke, but he kept on. Going forward was the feeling he wanted. Soon he was standing under the basket, in front of the pep band. Just as he was about to recite the demands, the crowd roared, and Mooney felt his chest fill with pride and courage. But then the school fight song began—those bastards in the pep band, didn't they see one of their own brothers, in uniform, struggling to be heard?

Mooney waved at the band and slashed at his own throat— Cut it! He backpedaled to the top of the key, waved again at the musicians. But the basketball team had emerged at the opposite end of the court, and they jogged into their lay-up lines to get loose for the second half. A half-dozen security guards moved toward Mooney, although not as fast as the lanky players were approaching. He halted. He could try to escape under the stands like Layla, but if his arrest was imminent, he might as well be a martyr and let all 18,000 fans witness the awful injustice of his arrest.

Instead of fleeing, Mooney simply held his ground under the basket.

The Coors State team loped along both sidelines, while the security team was marching right up the middle of the court. Just as security, brandishing handcuffs, got near, Mooney thought of Dr. King, and his inner strength, even under the threat of violence. He stood tall, his back to the pep band, the traitors who'd screwed up his speech with their damned fight song. His head was under the hoop. This was his last stand, and a wave of anger washed over him like at the football practice protest. He had an impulse to honor Braverman by sucker-punching the first cop, but that would have distracted from the revolution, so instead he raised a fist.

Mooney sensed one of the basketball players flying full speed at the basket. He glanced up just in time to see himself get dunked on. The player literally jumped over him—or almost. One bony knee caught Mooney on the forehead, knocking him back. He slammed his head on the hardwood and everything went dark.

Chapter 22

Mooney was upset about his incarceration at first. Did "incendiary speech" warrant cuffing an unconscious professor? The next morning, Criminal Justice also tacked on "contributing to the delinquency of a football player." That stung because it was obvious the player was one he truly cared about: Trevor Knighton.

But he quickly adjusted to his holding cell underneath the Criminal Justice classrooms, which was far cozier than a concession stand. The modern amenities included a queen-sized bed, reading lamp, and wall-to-wall carpeting. Professors from Hospitality and Tourism cleaned his cell and changed the sheets every week.

To resist or attempt to escape felt pointless. Instead, he composed a complex letter asking for change, like Dr. King had done from the Birmingham jail. Mooney requested copies of King's speeches from his guards, but instead he received press releases from Coors State Football and the latest edition of *Rocky Mountain High*. Mooney befriended his guards anyway.

He was not put on trial—he was simply declared guilty by Criminal Justice, in association with the football coach, and the entire process was done and dusted with a half-page memo, affixed with a rubber stamp of the head coach's signature. But what was his sentence? Nobody seemed to know. He stopped asking. This was a war of attrition, so he'd shut up and do his time, and, when he got out, he'd make some carefully considered decisions.

Braverman's story would be entirely different. He'd have clawed at his captors until he was beaten into submission, awakening bruised and bloody to howl protest songs from his cell in solitary confinement. Soon Mooney would likely get a scrawled message from him on toilet paper. Or maybe a tapping on the pipes in prison code. Mooney hadn't had much of a hearing, but Braverman would be better off without a trial. He'd wind up bound and gagged, like Bobby Seale of the Chicago Seven. And where was Braverman being held? Mooney kept his ears open for any loose talk.

After a week, Mass Communications brought him his own television. The TV couldn't pick up a single channel. But it looped Coors State football and basketball games from the last few years. They're trying to brainwash me, Mooney thought. He laughed at the absurdity. He began to enjoy the games, however, especially the just-completed season in which Trevor and Sasha played so well. At first the tapes ran silently, but during the next month the sound gradually emerged. Mooney was glad about that, especially during football, which had so many more names to track. He complained to a security guard about not knowing every player and soon he had a stack of old programs. The various Shakespeare stickers stuck to the covers were wing-dingers:

God has given you one face, and you make yourself another.

It is not in the stars to hold our destiny but in ourselves.

And his favorite:

As he was valiant, I honour him. But as he was ambitious,
I slew him.

Mooney peeled the stickers off diligently and pasted them to the mirror above his toilet.

The food was fine, even healthier than he preferred. Just hanging around watching football he lost a little more weight. He got in the habit of busting out calisthenics during time-outs and halftimes, copying what he'd seen the athletes do during warm-ups. It reminded him of high school. The adulation he received from his pals during Monday morning's homeroom still stuck with him today. Why did he punt that away? Maybe he never would have been good enough for a major college, but what if he had been? Mooney decided it wasn't too late to at least drop all the way down to playing weight.

One morning, Mooney read a *Rocky Mountain High* side column called "Other Football News." That's how he learned Braverman was being considered for promotion.

But how could Braverman be awarded tenure if he was incarcerated? Nothing made sense anymore, but if the coaches who dominated the Promotion & Tenure committee allowed Braverman this upgrade, fine.

In June, Mooney was moved to a new holding cell. He spent the next three months in a converted office next to the varsity weight room. He was blessed with a massive new flat-screen television and a picture-window view of the entire workout area, which was pretty quiet in July.

During this probationary summer period, Mooney met daily with a strength and conditioning coach named J.T. McClure, one of the fifty that Football now employed. McClure was a clean-cut twenty-something who seemed to have nothing better to do than to train, feed, and educate Eugene Mooney. They'd spend hours together, not just weightlifting but stretching, discussing diet, and football philosophy.

Mooney grew to be quite fond of J.T. McClure. It wasn't a case of Stockholm Syndrome, as the coach didn't torture or restrict him in any way—rather, he helped Mooney reach his full potential by maximizing his strength, reducing his percentage of body fat, and improving his eating habits.

McClure also used convincing arguments in support of the lofty status of Football and Basketball—spreadsheets, pay-stubs, canceled checks, donations, charts—a mound of paper evidence that proved academics were no longer viable without Football and Basketball. Any sane person would conclude that the only sensible path was to continue downsizing academics until nearly every department would be on-par with minor sports like field hockey and swimming. This confused Mooney at first, but he slowly began to evolve. Each afternoon, the strength coach would bring along more stats and figures, in addition to a delicious low-carb-mango-protein drink.

Most days were stress free, but occasionally Mooney would wake up in the middle of the night, half dreaming about the Black Panthers movement he'd messed up. It seemed the single mistake in his life he could never atone for.

Mooney was excited for the new season at Coors State. By August he'd occasionally help McClure spot a player on heavy bench presses. The team seemed poised to have another great season and make up for their Fiesta Bowl flop. He wondered why Trevor and Sasha weren't lifting weights, but he didn't ask.

McClure informed Mooney one day he'd been given visitation privileges. He could meet with one person each week for fifteen minutes. Mooney was tempted to select Layla—he missed being around women. But Mooney's visitor choice was, as the coaches liked to say about everything, a "no-brainer." He wrote "*Tenured* Professor Peter Braverman" on the visitor request form. One prisoner requesting visitation from another? Perhaps Football would allow it.

That afternoon, with the flat-screen looping another Silver Bullets victory, he focused in on the team's offensive sets, the precision and beauty of their collective movement. At one point, Trevor Knighton faded back to pass, dodged a tackler, rolled to his left and threaded a perfect fifty-yard spiral for a touchdown. Before he realized what he was doing, Mooney sprung to his feet, yelled *Yes* and did a little hula-hula dance.

Braverman showed up in a silver-gray sport coat, matching necktie, tasseled loafers, and a spiffy haircut. The professors tried to outdo each other with stagey double takes before finally embracing. Mooney buried his face into Braverman's shoulder and detected patchouli and smoke. Marijuana. How was that possible? Braverman had probably picked Layla to be his visitor, and the patchouli and weed smell had come from spending time with her.

Mooney said, "Less of me to hug, right? What's with the monkey suit?"

Braverman's giddy grin turned serious. "Never mind me. What did they do to you?" He moved around the cell, flipping through some DVDs before he tossed them back.

Mooney waved him over to the exercise bench that served as furniture. The men sat knee-to-knee, straddling the bench as if to begin an exercise in tandem.

"Making you wear a business suit," Mooney said, "is a form of psychological torture, you know."

"I got released within an hour," Braverman said.

"What?"

"It's a long story. I can't go into it now." Braverman fidgeted nervously before clasping Mooney's hand—as though Mooney was on life support, not an adjustable bench for dumbbell presses.

"I'm fine," Mooney assured him. "I understand better now. This is how things at a big-time university work." Mooney shared all he had learned from his strength coach. If Football or Basketball didn't do well, the entire university suffered. Ticket revenues had grown dramatically. Boyce Billman, an alum who'd made millions from his Taser-style security baton, had donated half his fortune to Football, the biggest single donation since Coors kicked in their billion dollars.

Braverman didn't dispute these claims, but Mooney wondered if he was truly buying in. Braverman switched gears— he said he was sorry.

But sorry for what? Mooney knew relating his new-found happiness was one thing, but Braverman would have to attain fulfillment and peace on his own. Every man traveled his own road when incarcerated, did his own time. He'd learned that during lockup. Mooney could only share his knowledge, hope it stuck.

"Listen," Braverman finally said. "I've convinced Football not to fuck History over. Concessions are gone, but we won't wind up living in tents in The Hamlet."

"Why would Football listen to you?" Mooney wondered aloud.

"Like I said, it's a long story, but I'm pushing for you to be released soon. I'll explain everything when we have more time."

Mooney was confused, so he changed the subject. "What's going on with our friends in English?"

"I haven't had time to check on them yet," Braverman said. "We can worry about English later, but I've already come up with the first step of my plan for History." Braverman looked around conspiratorially, then said, "You and I are going to co-author two new books. First, *The Glory Years: A History of Coors State Football*. And a companion book for basketball the following year. We'll sell tens of thousands of them. Maniscalco can get us a lucrative book deal."

"My strength coach says..." Mooney began, but the words he wanted to say got lost.

Before Braverman could speak again, a security guard appeared to say time was up. When the door closed, Mooney yawned. Despite his new exercise regimen and diet, he was sleeping a lot more. Those protein shakes made him drowsy. Maybe he needed more carbohydrates. His bed—an old training table—was beckoning to him, so he sprawled out.

In his dream, Mooney drove the bus.

He kept asking the players to quiet down, but when he checked the rearview mirror, it wasn't a football team at all. The bus was filled with Mexican *bandoleros*, straps of bullets crisscrossing their chests, smoking up a rebellious storm of marijuana. Mooney kept reaching back, hoping someone would pass a joint, but they ignored him. In the midst of the riders were Pancho Villa and Emiliano Zapata. They argued back and forth—or, rather, Villa yelled at Zapata for refusing to smoke, which was hypocritical because everyone knew Villa refused to drink. Why the judgmental attitude toward Zapata? On they rode until soldiers at a checkpoint waved Mooney to a halt. All the passengers got off, but Pancho Villa paused to put a hand on Mooney's steering wheel.

"*Viva la revolución, Pancho*," Mooney said with his gringo accent, and he saluted the legendary leader. A new group of riders were waiting for Villa to disembark.

"*Cállate, panzón!*" Villa shouted joyously in his face. Whatever that meant. He smiled agreeably until Villa pulled out a pistol and pointed it at Mooney's head.

Just then, Martin Luther King climbed up, and he put his hand on Pancho Villa's wrist to slowly lower the gun. Villa spat in Mooney's face and stormed off the bus.

Dr. King flashed his Coors State ID as a bus pass.

Next came Tommie Smith and John Carlos in their tracksuits, each wearing one black glove, Olympic medals around their necks where they belonged ever since 1968.

Mark Rudd, the old radical SDS leader, also climbed on board. "Where's Peter Braverman?" he asked in a conspiratorial tone.

Mooney recognized this ruse. Distract the driver. He demanded Rudd's bus pass, but before he could object, Fred Hampton came up the steps decked out in full Black Panther regalia, beret, and all.

"I'm glad you're alive again," Mooney said. Had Fred Hampton heard about Mooney's high school screw-up? Mooney was about to get the bus back on the road when Braverman and Layla Sillimon wedged in, laughing as if they were in love.

"Have you forgiven me?" Braverman asked.

Before Mooney could answer, Layla asked, "Would you leave without us, Eugene?" She leaned in close enough to give him a hug, but instead she licked his ear.

As the bus picked up speed, his ear felt cool and refreshed, and that allowed him to tune in on exactly what everyone on the bus was saying. He steered with his knees as he searched a Spanish/English dictionary for what Pancho Villa had shouted, although it no longer mattered. He had fresh passengers and a new destination, while Villa was on a different quest, to kill the rich Mexican landowners.

Okay, here it was. *Cállate.* Shut up? And *Panzón.* Potbelly? Shut up, Potbelly?

Why, of all the nerve—and he'd lost so much weight, probably thirty pounds. He looked down at his gut—but somehow he'd gotten much fatter than his old self. That's how Mooney figured out this was a dream.

"This isn't me," he announced into the wide rearview mirror, and everyone on the bus went silent. Mooney felt a bulge in his pockets—chocolate bars? The more he pulled out, the more seemed to be stashed away. He ripped one open and bit off a chunk. It was heavenly, with almonds and raisins. He kept munching, but he'd have to be careful not to let the wind sweep the wrappers out the window. Mooney hated litter.

They arrived at the Coors State stadium, and when the bus hit a massive speed bump, it shook Mooney awake.

"I'm the bus driver," he said, and he sat up, trying to figure out who and where he was. He began to tell Braverman about the dream, but nobody was there. Mooney scratched at his nose and stopped. His fingers smelled of chocolate.

Just before the new school year commenced, Mooney got a memo from Coach Maniscalco. Today was his release date, but he'd be on probation and closely monitored. Mooney could resume his professorial duties that fall, but he was required to attend all football games, and he had to buy his own ticket. The memo also said what Braverman somehow already knew, that History would not be working concessions. Foreign Languages was teaming with Hospitality and Tourism. So Braverman had been correct. In a way that was better, Mooney thought, less pressure, and they could focus on their new book project. The advance, the subsequent royalties, might take the sting out of losing concessions. Maybe Trevor Knighton could write the introduction.

Mooney's release coincided with the weekend of Football's home opener. He signed a liability waiver and J.T. McClure gave him a manly handshake and a pile of junk mail.

Football game tonight was the subject line of the first email Mooney had sent in months. He wondered if his old pals could score tickets. Braverman emailed back within minutes, said he had access to five seats and hoped they could all sit together. He mentioned that Trevor and Sasha had been punished, forced to sit the year out. Rather than transfer, they had decided to stick around and count it as a redshirt year, meaning they'd practice with the team, but not play in the games. They'd focus on their classes.

That afternoon, Mooney froze on the front steps of his own home—his door was swinging open in the wind. He'd been slipping into near-hallucinations lately just before he fell asleep, spinoffs of the crazy bus dream, as though somebody was pointing a remote at his brain and changing his channel. But this situation was different, and it frightened him. He balled his fists and rushed in, only to find a frail young woman in his kitchen.

Turned out she was a professor from Gender Studies, assigned by Football to clean his home before his release. "Please don't tell the coaches I hadn't finished," she said. "I'm swamped. I still have to clean four of their homes today."

Mooney set down his book bag and helped her tidy.

Their tailgate picnic was at Trevor Knighton's old pickup truck from high school days—he'd had to return the freebie from football.

On his stroll across campus, Mooney realized he hadn't seen The Hamlet since his arrest. At their little tent city, only the men, Dodo and Wolf, were visible. "What are you guys reading?" Mooney shouted as he approached.

They held up football programs and yelled, "English."

Mooney joined them in their lawn chairs.

"Interesting rumor about Peter's promotion, huh?" Dodo asked.

"His tenure?" Mooney asked.

There was a rustling of a sleeping bag. "Let's not talk about Braverman," Wolf said quietly, gesturing at one tent. "President Cardly is here."

That didn't make sense to Mooney, so he asked, "Is Cardly still, you know, attached? It's nice to see people pair up," he said, mostly to himself.

"The truth is they're not a couple anymore," Dodo said.

"Who dumped who?"

"It's a committee of three," Wolf whispered. Then he winked.

Whale, President Cardly, and Buffalo were a threesome? Wow, Mooney thought. He stood to leave. "Everybody have a good game," he said.

Trevor's truck was the same silver as last year's model, but it was a 1995 Nissan, half the size of the sparkly Silverado. Layla's unpredictable reclining chair was propped up on the bed of the truck, where Sasha was holding court.

Mooney didn't recognize Layla initially because she'd cut her dreadlocks. She looked older, but also younger. He'd never seen her tiny ears or how blond her now-inch-long hair was. The short hair gave her an athletic appearance, which seemed fitting when she hurdled the beer cooler to greet him with a long hug. A minute later she brought out trays of tofu ribs and tossed them onto the little grill near Sasha's feet. She pointed to the spinach salad, the cashews, the pomegranate juice, and told him to dig in.

Trevor had grown a goatee. He'd lost weight, too, and looked more like a basketball player. The roommates' grocery deliveries had stopped soon after the basketball halftime speech. Buffet privileges and weekly steroids had been canceled, too. The Name, Image, & Likeness endorsement deals that were now legal, and that their teammates were now enjoying, had bypassed them, at least for now. Sasha had been struggling to keep his weight steady by upping his intake of organic Half & Half. Trevor said he was impressed with Mooney's weight loss, and he cracked open the cooler full of Coors.

Mooney vaguely recalled Trevor's halftime speech. The quarterback was supposed to say he was quitting. Sasha spoke instead, but did he say anything important? Mooney wondered aloud if the quarterback's plan was still to quit the sport.

"We're sitting out the year," Trevor said without being asked. "I was pretty disgusted with what Coach had done to Sasha, and Dad wanted me to transfer to Knox College. Transfer anywhere, really." This season, Trevor's father was paying his tuition, and Sasha's as well. None of their teammates walked away from football, though—few of them would have had a parent with the bank account of Ben Knighton. The roommates were on probation and if there were no more behavior problems, Maniscalco said they'd likely get their full scholarship, and all the benefits, back in a year. That is if they agreed not to talk to the media about the halftime ceremony. But there'd been a price, besides the loss of endorsements and organic steaks, Trevor explained. In the meantime, the laundry service, the clothing allowance, their radio show—all gone. They even had to clean their own bathroom and change their own sheets, all the while still practicing and lifting weights with the team. This would be a difficult year for the roommates.

"It's hard to comprehend," Layla said, "but not playing football this season was a sacrifice that needed to happen. Sacrifice can be metaphorical, literal, or both. Although Peter was pushing for a more literal sacrifice."

Mooney sensed more earth-shaking news was coming, and here it was: Sasha, enthroned in his recliner, said he'd officially declared Poetry as his major. He was now writing exclusively in his second language. Poems in English would have been unthinkable a year ago, but his verbal skills had flourished. Now when he misspoke or dropped a malapropism, he did it deliberately, making fun of his old self, as though there were two Sashas these days and everyone in their crew knew the difference.

"The Croatian Sensation"—that's what Layla called Sasha, insisting it was a poetry nickname and not a sports moniker. Layla was championing him as a brilliant young poet ready to burst onto the scene. Sasha spent his free time in her office, flopping back in his recliner, devouring Allen Ginsburg and Elizabeth Bishop. Also, he'd gotten contact lenses, dropping his Buddy Holly-meets-the-Hulk look, and his formerly shaved head was now a flattop.

Mooney said, "I hope you two can regain the correct mindset and support the Silver Bullets in a big way next year. What about you, Trevor? You settled on a major?"

"I'm still undeclared," Trevor said.

"Trevor did his basketball game protest to support me," Sasha said.

"And Sasha is staying at Coors State for me," Layla said. "He can take the year off from playing in the games, but he can't leave his poetry mentor. It was totally an academic decision, but we're all still interconnected, Eugene."

"I would miss her too much," Sasha admitted. "Now Trevor stays here because I stay. We are three peas in a pod."

* * *

Peter Braverman arrived at last, still wearing his shiny silver sport coat. It wasn't long before the toasts began. Nobody asked questions about either history professors' punishment, but Mooney told his story anyway, how he was not tortured, not in the least. He only had to watch football and basketball games eight hours a day. It was a pleasurable few months. He boasted he'd lost weight but nearly doubled his bench press. Neither player seemed to know J.T. McClure, but with fifty strength coaches on staff now, how could they?

The Silver Bullets' schedule featured tough matchups against national powers, but the names were new to fans, as other big state schools rebranded. In October, the Silver Bullets would face the University of Foxconn, who used to be Wisconsin. When Mooney saw that on the schedule, he did a little research and noticed Connecticut was making a push for big time status by becoming Cigna University. Same with the former Washington State University, whose new deal rebranded them as Costco State University. Even the struggling Northern Illinois University had made a move, taking on the name Walgreens University.

This season Coors State was opening with lowly New Mexico State. That wouldn't matter so much to the fans—it was easier this way to celebrate a new season, to dance to the blatant on-field destruction of a school that held no hope of competing. Sasha said, "An easy win against cupcake team is important because we have new quarterback."

"They're going to play again in their senior season, and it'll be even more dramatic," Braverman said, nodding at the two players, "but they're milking the sports machine for two years, and they'll help us by working within the system."

None of this quite made sense to Mooney, but he was mum, like a kid in the back row of the classroom who had forgotten to read the assignment. "Why on earth would anyone quit football?" he finally asked. "And, hey, how's the Volvo running?"

Braverman stammered until Layla put a hand on his knee. She said softly, "I told him we needed to make a sacrifice. I'll explain it again later, but if you want Eugene to forgive you, you're going to have to be patient with him."

"We have plenty of time," Trevor said, "to come up with a more complete plan."

"A plan for what?" Mooney asked. The group got quiet. The strains of the violins playing the school fight song at another tailgate floated in the air. "Our team needs you two," Mooney went on, "and it'd be a shame to ever let them down."

"Which team?" Sasha said.

Mooney said, "Football."

Layla said, "We think the Volvo will be returned soon." Then she tapped Braverman on the knee. "Tell him now, Peter," she said.

"Eugene, I have an announcement," Braverman began, "although everybody else here knows. When the candidate from Coors' corporate office turned down the job, Maniscalco appointed me as the new president of Coors State."

Chapter 23

Layla Sillimon had never seen Eugene Mooney look so confused. All the blood had drained from his face, as though he were on his deathbed. She would have to help soft pedal this new development. "Technically," she said, "Peter is interim President Braverman."

"That's right," Braverman added, "although Coach made it clear that interim President is a permanent position."

"But you just got tenure, Peter," Mooney said. "You can't simply leapfrog to the president's office. There's no precedent for..." But the idea must have lost traction in his mind. Since his release, Mooney sometimes couldn't finish his own sentences.

Layla gripped Mooney's arm in reassurance. She explained how after their awkward fast-roping and Trevor's wayward speech, the second half had been delayed by more than ten minutes for cleanup. That badly disrupted the television broadcast. And plenty of parents took their children home before the second half got underway. A week later, at the next home game—when Mooney was still incarcerated—attendance had fallen off by 800 fans. Had Mooney's message made an impact, even a small one? Maybe, but evidently the dip in attendance had spooked Maniscalco, really got his attention, and that might have been the impetus behind the move to conscript Peter Braverman to join his administration.

All morning Layla and Braverman had been rehearsing their

big revelation to Mooney, and she'd feared it might get funky. She smiled now and said, "Peter's promotion is being announced Monday at the department meeting for Criminal Justice. We wanted you to know first."

"We'll get a big audience at the press conference," Braverman said. "There will be free Coors, of course. Eugene, the thing is, I know exactly what Coach Maniscalco is up to. He thinks he's using me. Can you imagine? Keep your friends close and your enemies closer—know who said that? Fidel Castro, I think. Now I'm like a double agent. You always emphasized changing the system from within. And at long last we can, because I'm number two on campus, right behind the football coach."

Layla had already adopted the habit of keeping their new president's ego in check. "Peter," she said, "the basketball coach also outranks you."

"Only during basketball season," Braverman said with a shrug.

"I was wondering about your sport coat and necktie," Mooney said.

"I can get you a set just like this," Braverman said.

Layla knew that wasn't what Mooney meant, but she let it go. "Tell Eugene about your other idea," she said. "Besides the football history book."

"Remember how Cardly started that raffle," Braverman said, "where a student would win a thousand bucks. She'd win if her name was chosen?"

Layla caught a look from Braverman and knew his use of "she" and "her" was supposed to show how enlightened the new president was.

Mooney said he recalled something about that raffle.

"That's exactly what we don't want Coors State to portray," Braverman said, "a crass commercialism. So, my first act as president? Check this out—whatever lucky student gets his or her name drawn automatically earns straight 'A' grades for the quarter. Grades instead of money. Get it? We tie in academics and athletics."

Mooney said, "What if—?"

In the pause, Braverman kept on. "I'm embracing the big picture, like you always suggested. I wanted to tell you all this at the weight room, but I had meetings to get to."

Layla noticed Eugene Mooney's mouth was hanging open. She reached out to squeeze his arm again.

"Here's another idea," Braverman said. "In terms of our revolution—" he lowered his voice and said, "I've figured out how to make nearly every department financially secure. Guess how. Go ahead, guess."

Mooney was quiet for a moment. "I had a dream," he said.

"This has nothing to do with Martin Luther King," Braverman said.

"I mean, I had this dream about a bus, and I was the driver," Mooney said. He didn't look at all healthy, Layla thought. Had he lost too much weight? She poured him a glass of water.

"Okay, here's a clue," Braverman said. "I'm meeting with a potential corporate sponsor who is interested in branding our History Department."

"Under Armour?" Mooney ventured.

"The History Channel," Braverman said. "Naming rights. We'd be the History Channel History Department. I mean until the revolution. But that might be a decade away, and we need to survive, with concessions gone, until we get a cash advance on that book."

Mooney leaned back in his lawn chair. "A decade?" he finally said. "You and I will be retired."

"True, and that's the long arc of justice Martin Luther King referred to," Braverman said. "I'm flying to New York next week, but The History Channel wants to change our pedagogy and curriculum. No more lectures or even online classes. They want every class to broadcast television programs produced by their network. They've got hundreds of shows already archived. We'd have practically no work—we'd just sit back and say, Roll 'em. And you know what? We'd spend what used to be our prep time preparing for the revolution. The students will be entranced, and we'll be sitting in the dark, plotting. We'd have to reduce the size of our faculty, but you'll keep your job, Eugene. I've got your back."

"Thanks, comrade brother," Mooney said.

Layla could see the shock of all this was too much for Eugene Mooney—she'd never heard him call Peter "comrade brother." They should have waited, and now it was too late. She'd done a lot of thinking about her own future. Should she be applying for other jobs? Mooney and Braverman were too close to retirement to make a career move, but with university teaching experience on her resume, should she test the waters? In the end, even after looking over job ads, she couldn't do it. Coors State was home now—and she was close enough to the new school president that they were doing yoga together every morning. Where else in America could she count on being friendly with the guy in charge? "Tell Eugene about your Tenure and Promotion plan."

"Right," Braverman said. "I've convinced Football to put me on the Tenure and Promotion committee. So I'll be in a position to make certain Layla's job is secure."

"That's partly why Peter accepted this promotion. For my sake," Layla said. "See? We really are interconnected, all of us."

"Next," Braverman went on, "I help revive English. Martin Cardly is pressuring me to hire Whale as my assistant, but that's complicated. I've got to find their department a real job to generate revenue, one they won't object to. Then? English will buy their way back into Coors State with a one-time donation to athletics. So, here's my idea. You know those Greek statues, right? The Nike goddess, the discus thrower, Athena, and the gladiator dude? English will do a calendar with their four professors posing in the nude. They'll sell them from The Hamlet, twenty bucks a pop. That's just the initial step."

"Excellent idea," Mooney said, but he wasn't even looking at Braverman.

"Eugene," Layla said soothingly, "do you need another glass of water?" She understood this news must be quite a leap for Mooney—from working to take down Football to interim President Braverman? She still had trouble getting her head around it.

"To get back to Trevor and Sasha," Braverman said, nodding at the players, "it's best that they redshirt this season, but play again the following year." The decision was difficult for them, Braverman said. A popular restaurant chain known for its all-you-can-eat buffet had offered Sasha a pretty sweet endorsement deal. And a sporting goods franchise had headhunted Trevor.

"The Coors State sports machine will function just fine without them," Braverman continued, "so what's the value in them walking away, the payoff for our movement? They might as well play the next year when we'll have a well-considered plan in place. No more knee-jerk stuff. We're so done with that, right, Layla?"

Layla loved when Braverman articulated his commitment to a rational strategy. Soon, they would have to tell Mooney about the slight turn their relationship had taken, although it was not like they were sleeping together. They were just hanging out an awful lot, and she felt safe and secure around Braverman. She fixed the collar of his shiny sport coat. "Peter hasn't sold out, Eugene," she said, "so don't even go there. Look at him, he's conscripting the dress, language, and mindset of the enemy. That's what Nelson Mandela did. And when Mandela became President of South Africa, he invited his jailers to the inauguration. Do I have that correct?"

"That's why Layla cut her dreadlocks," Braverman added. "It was a tactical move to disguise her radical bent. We have to learn from our mistakes."

Layla still obsessed about those mistakes. The Poetry Riot was pointless. Then their ridiculous march onto the practice field? Trevor's basketball game speech, the fast-roping in band uniforms? All counterproductive and ill-advised, like her mother and her hippie friends who once thought getting stoned and not showering would help end the war in Vietnam. Maybe that's why she hadn't talked to her mother since Christmas, although it wasn't a conscious decision.

"After months of conditioning, film, and a healthy diet," Mooney finally said, "I realize now the value of what these athletes go through. It's marvelous, the dedication these boys have to improving our university." When nobody else spoke, Mooney continued. "It's much purer and more authentic than any hoity-toity academic research. Football is important, quantifiable, and real. You can't keep score at a History Department meeting. Besides, everyone would come out a loser if you did." It sounded as if Mooney were a hostage reading from a teleprompter.

A gaggle of music professors approached their tailgate, busking for tips. Mooney requested the school fight song, stuffed a twenty into their tip bucket like it was a jukebox, and the group played the march over and over. The quartet was soothing and not loud enough to drown out conversation.

"What about you, Layla?" Mooney asked. "Any big news? Nothing as dramatic as Peter's, I'd wager."

Layla said she'd sold the movie rights to her book, *Self-Portrait in a Funhouse Mirror*.

"Poetry can be optioned to film?" Mooney asked.

"You can make movie about anything in America," Sasha said. "Remember *Flight 93*?"

Layla admitted the movie option had only netted her five-hundred-bucks. It wasn't like she was financially set, despite the huge sales of her debut book, because of the unusually flimsy contract she'd signed with her press. She might someday sweat getting tenure, too. "I very much want to stay on here at Coors State," she said. "I'm almost forty and I don't want to go on the job market. That's why I supported Peter's career move from tenure track to fast track. I need allies on campus. I got called a sellout after my first book pubbed, so I understand the pressure Peter might face soon."

She'd finished the sequel to her first book, but she was anxious about the quality of the manuscript. She was a lightning rod for controversy in the world of poetry—being championed by a pop star once was great for the *People* magazine crowd, but poets in academia dismissed her. How could this second book, which was more experimental, top her debut?

"The sophomore jinx," Mooney suggested, as though reading her thoughts. Braverman reminded Mooney of what they'd learned at the basketball game. Program sales had been taken from Poetry, jeopardizing Layla's position on the faculty. He knew a one-person department would be short lived. "That's why I convinced Criminal Justice to add her."

"Poetry and Criminal Justice don't mix," Mooney said.

"I've already designed a new class called Poets in Prison," Layla said. "We'll focus on the works of Oscar Wilde, Paul Verlaine, and Jimmy Santiago Baca."

All of this anxiety caused Layla to think she might never get another job, raising the pressure on her to secure her tenure within Criminal Justice. She said she feared her second collection would be a flop.

Trevor said, "Until the bowl game, I actually had a better sophomore year. In football, I mean."

"And in a moral sense," Braverman said. "You too, Sasha. You guys almost shook the world."

"Aw, shucks, fellas," Sasha said in a cornpone Southern accent.

"As interim president, I'm in a position to calculate our best actions over the next few years," Braverman said, like he was reading from a script, too. "And my new base salary will count in a big way toward retirement. We need to discuss all this in the next few weeks, but I'm up to my ears in meetings. After I meet the History Channel folks, I'm going to Easton, Pennsylvania, to meet with the Crayola Crayon brass. I'm going to pitch them corporate sponsorship for our Art Department. Crayola's VP is one of our graduates."

"All of the arts are going to be a priority for Peter's administration," Layla said.

"Next week I'm going to award Coach Maniscalco an honorary doctorate of offensive innovation," Braverman said.

"A journalist found out that our coach never graduated from college," Layla explained to Eugene.

"A doctorate trumps everything and would shut down the naysayers," Braverman added. "We've all learned hard lessons about the nature of revolution."

"Right on," Layla said. "We'll strategize. Nothing spontaneous, and I'll have to remain in the background until I get tenure. Maybe tonight isn't the time to talk about all this." An hour ago, she had been so happy to see Mooney, but it was difficult now to gauge his reaction. She needed to distract him. "We should be celebrating Eugene's freedom," she said brightly.

"Here's to my favorite prof," Trevor said, raising a can of Coors.

"Better self-control," Braverman added, and Layla stifled an impulse to hug him. She'd been laying out ground rules about their relationship and what it meant to her, and she didn't want Braverman to get the wrong impression.

Mooney checked his watch. "We'd better hustle inside if we want to see the kickoff."

They stopped at the Art professors' face-painting booth outside the gates. The kids' line was endless, but the adult line was moving fast. Layla got her face done. She managed to talk the artist into putting peace symbols into both "O's" of the Coors State logo. It looked so good that Sasha and Trevor agreed to do the same. "Let's get a photo," Layla said. One artist snapped a group shot.

The television lights and the body heat kept the stadium warmer than the tailgaters' parking lot. A Criminal Justice major in a neon-yellow vest, armed with a Taser in his belt, ushered them in. Environmental Studies was already setting up recycling drop-offs for cups and cans.

"Did you ever find a replacement for Wilson Keats?" Mooney asked.

"I'm waiting for approval for a teaching line from Maniscalco," Braverman said. "But for now, Layla is part of the Criminal Justice Department. If we hire another poetry prof, she might have to wear more than one hat, like, maybe she could be an expert in sports metaphor or sports biographies."

"Good idea," Mooney said.

Braverman's new seats were near the north end zone, a dozen rows up, not far from the pep band. The game quickly became a lopsided runaway as Coors State blew through New Mexico State with ease, racking up a 76-0 halftime lead. Just as the Silver Bullets' were about to score again, Braverman patted Layla's knee, then left his hand there. She kept her eyes straight ahead, but she sensed Mooney had noticed. It made her surprisingly skittish.

"Why don't you two get us all popcorn," Layla suggested.

Chapter 24

Eugene Mooney was not bothered by the crush of the halftime crowd. In fact, he was happy to absorb the game day atmosphere again. Without a word, the professors instinctively headed toward their old concession stand on the opposite side of the stadium. Foreign Languages had expanded concessions in novel ways that History would have never considered. About twenty yards down the concourse was "French Kiss," a pastry-and-croissant stand run by French professors. "Munich Munch," a German sausage vendor, was next. The Chinese language profs had a dim sum stand around the next curve. It seemed a very good sign for the university until Mooney saw the Spanish profs had declined to participate—here they were, two Latinx profs with picket signs on the concourse, evidently insulted their colleagues had proposed selling burritos to keep afloat. That was too bad, Mooney thought.

The array of choices was enticing, although Mooney still had no appetite. He'd only had a few bites of Layla's tofu ribs. It was shame to go off his diet now. "I'm down to my high school playing weight," Mooney said, holding his hands over his head to show off his withered belly.

"You didn't play in high school. And we're only getting popcorn," Braverman assured him. "Easy on the butter."

There was hardly a line at their old location. Naturally, the current vendors were not selling copies of *Hell No! We Won't*

Go! Or Mooney's *Arriba, Amigos.* They weren't selling books at all, just popcorn and soft drinks. One day, Mooney knew, they'd carry *The Glory Years: A History of Coors State Football.*

A professor behind the counter sneered at Braverman but smiled with genuine joy at Mooney. "Welcome home," he said.

"Five extra-large popcorns," Braverman said.

Mooney whispered, "That guy mad at you?"

"Who gives a damn? I've got something better than tenure. They'll find out next week."

The giant bags were practically the size of tackling dummies, and Braverman pushed them to Mooney. "I'll carry the Cokes," Braverman said, pulling a plastic bag from his back pocket to load up the cans. He tossed down a hundred-dollar bill and left the change on the counter. "I get a concession stand allowance on game days," he said. "Spend it or lose it. It's one of the perks."

Mooney could barely get his arms around all five popcorn bags. Yet, by encircling the three, he could wedge the other two in between, like a circus juggler about to perform a difficult trick. But when he squeezed the bags into place under his chin he could barely see where he was going. "You'll have to lead the way," he said. "Like Trevor used to."

"We subsisted on this stuff last year, remember?" Braverman said. "Stay close to me. By the way, I have to talk to you about another topic."

Mooney tried to look up at Braverman, but the bags slipped a bit. Dropping the popcorn would be a mess, so he tucked his chin tighter into the middle bag to keep it from sliding and squeezed his arms to stabilize the others. He breathed in deeply. His nose touched the popcorn, and he could have used his tongue to gobble some up. Manners, he reminded himself. He shuffled forward, following Braverman as best he could with his limited vision. He inhaled deeper and deeper as he walked, taking in the aroma—the fake butter and the tortilla-roasted corn smell was comforting. Mooney's mind drifted back to his family kitchen where he was raised in Chihuahua City, Mexico. He quickly corrected himself: he'd never even been to that town, he hadn't grown up there at all. Chihuahua City was Pancho Villa's headquarters for the Mexican Revolution. Mooney laughed to himself. He was having an aromatherapy vision. Or was he hyperventilating? Ever since that bizarre bus dream—Mooney inhaled again, long and slow. Had they switched to genetically modified corn? He hoped not. He held his breath until he got dizzy. When he exhaled, he felt nauseated. His gait became irregular, like he'd been pounding down tequila. He sucked in more air. Deep down in the bag he saw himself and Braverman hustling popcorn and books and soft drinks, Braverman in his camouflage pants and slouch hat. Mooney inhaled again and his own voice played in his head, reading off their list of demands that he never got to articulate at the halftime ceremony, or on their disastrous march onto the field, that gridiron Gettysburg. He bumped into a wall but straightened himself out. He felt lightheaded and weightless, but strangely peaceful. Inhaling deeper still, he held it in yet again. He thought he heard the rattle of a bus starting up, and Dr. King's "Been to the Mountaintop" speech came into his head—but it wasn't King's voice, it was Braverman's. And yes, that was the sound of a bus engine.

The next thing Mooney knew he was flat on his back, covered in popcorn.

How long had he been unconscious? Gawkers circled them, and Braverman shouted for folks to step away, for Chrissake, give a man time to come to his senses. He dragged Mooney by the collar until his back was against the wall. The bottleneck busted and the crowd streamed by again, crunching on the carpet of spilled popcorn until it was a fine yellow dust. Mooney was still covered in kernels. "Our snacks," he said weakly.

"Here, drink this Diet Coke, comrade," Braverman said. "You're probably dehydrated. It's a common symptom with newly released political prisoners."

"What a waste."

"We can buy more," Braverman said soothingly, his face inches from Mooney's. Mooney realized they were alone, more or less, for the first time since their weight-room chat.

Braverman said he had two important things to discuss. "I'm starting up a new department," he began, smiling. "Academics have been shrinking. Well, now we're expanding again, and the ball is rolling on our new—get this—Sports Marketing Department." Braverman detailed the plan, inspired by the new upcoming NCAA players endorsement deals looming. He planned to hire thirty new professors, and they'd raise their own salaries by earning a 15% agents' fee off commercial opportunities for their best athletes. Television and radio ads, Lions Club luncheon speaking engagements. Sponsored podcasts, Instagram, and YouTube channels.

"All the things that the NCAA says are now legal," Braverman went on. "But don't you see, Eugene? On the surface, it seems like just another instance of football and basketball taking over, but look deeper. You and I know different. Because we're expanding the faculty by thirty professors, and—" Braverman lowered his voice, "—we're doing it right under the coaches' noses! The infiltration has already begun. Thirty new professors."

"Interesting," Mooney said. "It's the first new department on campus since Online Studies. But doesn't this one make football and basketball more powerful?"

"So that's good news," Braverman said, "but there's one other thing I have to tell you." Braverman's smile disappeared, and his face went dark. He put his forehead on Mooney's chest and said he was sorry. He was so sorry.

"Sorry for what?" Mooney asked.

"I sold you out. I apologize."

"You did what?"

Braverman said, "I told Criminal Justice you threatened to block my tenure and forced me up on to the catwalk at the basketball game. I blamed the poetry riot, the march, the fast-roping, Trevor's speech, everything—on you."

Mooney stared at him blankly.

"I was terrified," Braverman went on, "that they were going to torture me or deny my tenure. You did extra time, Eugene, my jail time. I was a traitor."

"I served your sentence?" Mooney asked evenly. "You outed me?"

"That's how I got named president, in exchange for testifying against you, admitting that you were at fault. It was a straight-up trade-off. Their plan was to cripple our movement by using me as a spy. I want you to forgive me. One of us needed to be free to keep things going. I know that's a lame excuse and I'm sorry. But as interim president—"

A kid munching on a donut stumbled over Mooney's foot. Mooney said, "Excuse me," and he lost track of their conversation momentarily. He asked Braverman to repeat everything slowly. Braverman had gotten Mooney in trouble, but for the right reason? That made sense, didn't it?

"It's nothing to grin about, Eugene," Braverman said.

"This means the Panthers can forgive me now," Mooney finally said. "For high school. We're even. Like you say, it's a trade-off and everybody is all squared away, in the historical sense."

"The Panthers? Eugene, you're confused. This is a university, not a high school, and we were never the Panthers. We're the Silver Bullets."

"After all these years," Mooney said, wrapping his arms around his friend. With one hand on the back of Braverman's neck, he forgave him. Their foreheads touched until Mooney leaned back. "I think I'm awake now," he announced.

"We're not giving up our quest," Braverman said. "No surrender. That's what I was trying to say before." Braverman's voice fell to a whisper. "I suspect you're playing possum, too. You're keeping a low profile. We both are."

Mooney looked up at the mercury-vapor lights, patted the cold concrete beneath him. He was low profile, he thought, quite literally. He wanted to brush the popcorn off his sweater, but he couldn't lift his left arm.

"He who fights and runs away," Braverman said, "lives to fight another day. Remember that one by Bob Marley?" He leaned close to Mooney again and said, "We've been planning. Layla and me, I mean. Wait until you hear what's next, way more than getting the History Channel on board and the new Sports Marketing Department. We're going to get corporate sponsors for every department until we out-fundraise Football. In our lifetime, Football will be obsolete, and Basketball, too. Do you have any idea the affection people in this state have for Electrical Engineering?"

"Are you in love with Layla?" Mooney asked.

"No. Of course not," Braverman sputtered. "Yes. I mean, yes, of course, I am. Aren't you? But not in the romantic sense. And that's not what we're talking about." He picked kernels of corn off Mooney's chest and tossed them aside.

"You and Layla are about to run off and leave me behind," Mooney said, an accusation and a question, but he wasn't at all sure what he meant. Behind, as in lying here on the cement concourse of the stadium? Behind, in terms of finding a new best friend? Or starting the revolution again, without him? "Are you and Layla an item?" Mooney asked. "A couple?"

Braverman got red in the face. He wiped at his nose with the sleeve of his sport coat. "You were locked up, Eugene. I've kept the revolution alive by penetrating the power structure, and over the next few years we'll subvert it. Don't you get it? Listen, I've made sacrifices, too. I gave up tenure when I accepted the interim president position. You won't believe the new office I have, by the way. And Football might provide me with the use of a free motor scooter until they locate my Volvo. Anyway, Layla and I were crazy with regret. We've been meeting a lot, yes, but we didn't concoct anything you couldn't be a part of. And to answer your question, Layla and I are not a couple in the traditional heteronormative sense. I think she looks up to me. Besides, I don't ever want to rush into rash decisions ever again."

"Why not?"

"Why not which?" Braverman said. He got on one knee in front of Mooney and gave him a firm slap on the face, like a corner man coaxing his fighter back onto his feet to get beaten up for yet another round. *Uno mas, amigo*, Mooney thought he heard his friend say. Braverman glanced around then said, "Wake up, Eugene. We've discussed other options, too, but who knows when the hell we'll act? We're certain of this much—we need you. The bus is useless without our driver."

Mooney felt dizzy. He swallowed hard. It was that damn artificial butter smell. He staggered to his feet, pushing himself up with the arm that still worked, and patted down his shirt and pants, knocking the last remnants of popcorn to the cement. "Where did I leave that bus?" he asked.

"The bus? There is no bus," Braverman said, "that was a metaphor. Layla has encouraged me to use more metaphors. Come on, the second half has started. We can map out our new plan with Layla later." Braverman crammed a fistful of kernels into his mouth. "Owza bedda," he said. He took the Coke can, downed a swig and coughed.

"Say what now?" Mooney asked.

"Ours was better," Braverman said and gathered up the scattered plastic bags, whipped knots into the tops, and thrust them one-at-a-time back into Mooney's chest. "Jesus, Eugene, you're white as—hey!"

Mooney found himself laid out on the concrete again. "Go on back to Layla," he said, waving. "I need a minute to get my balance." But his friend refused to leave, and that heartened Mooney. He started to push himself up once more until the glare of the mercury-vapor light above blinded him, and the light was approaching slowly. Had he hit his head again? He felt a clutching pain in his chest. He couldn't lift his arm to cover his eyes, so he closed them.

Chapter 25

Layla Sillimon had recited poems in strange places before, but never over a casket. Eugene Mooney would have objected to a church ceremony or a large crowd making a fuss, so she arranged the funeral to take place outside of town, the mountains as backdrop, in front of a dozen friends and History profs.

The night before, in order to test the poem out, Layla phoned her mother in Belfast. Although she couldn't finish reciting it without choking up, it led to the best talk they'd had in years. She told her mother all about Mooney and Braverman. Her mother, for the first time, shared details about Layla's father.

It turned out Layla's father had been wounded twice in Vietnam. Today, he lived in a Mexican town called San Felipe, not so far from the VA hospital in Yuma, Arizona, where he scored his meds for hepatitis C. He'd done a short time in jail in 2007 for his role in an Iraq war protest, where he tried to start a police car on fire with lighter fluid and a book of matches. When the charges were dropped, disgusted with America, he'd moved south of the border. Layla's mom shared his mailing address, too, but she wasn't certain it was still valid. Layla figured she'd do some research after Mooney's funeral.

Layla opened the ceremony with her new poem, "Hector the Hero," which compared Mooney's courage to the slain warrior of the Iliad. Their friends the English professors—all except

Wolf, who had stayed back to guard The Hamlet—sat silently with Cardly, and they raised clenched fists after the poem, as Mooney had done in his final act of protest at the basketball game.

Whale spoke next and said The Hamlet took great inspiration from Eugene Mooney's patience, and they'd calculated it could take nine more years to overturn big-time sports. Their little tent city had been in existence for one year, and nine more would make their quest equal to the length of the Trojan War. The Hamlet, she said looking at Martin Cardly, was in it for the long haul, although they were going to have to relocate soon because yet another Coors-themed pub was going up in their current spot.

Next, Trevor Knighton and Sasha stood together at the makeshift podium. Everyone knew that Sasha had declared Poetry as his new major. Today, though, he declined to read his own work, but surprised everyone by reciting from memory Dylan Thomas's classic "And Death Shall Have No Dominion"— in the defiant voice that suited the poem and the circumstances.

Then Trevor Knighton stepped forward to say he had an important announcement to make. He didn't want to take any attention from Eugene Mooney, but he thought this was the right time to say he was switching his own major to History, where he'd focus on Mexican and African American courses.

Trevor called up the afternoon's final speaker, and he presented Peter Braverman with a half-sized wooden shield that Sasha had fashioned. Emblazoned across the shield was Sasha's cartoon drawing of Mooney stabbing a football with his sword.

In the days since Mooney's death, Layla had struggled to interpret Braverman's moods. He had assured her he would be fine giving the final eulogy, but at the podium, the shield clutched to his chest, he fell to the ground—just as Mooney had done at the stadium near their concession stand. She hoisted Braverman to his feet and held him as he shook. He seemed more angry than sorrowful. It must have been an incredibly stressful week for him, being introduced as the interim president of Coors State on Monday, having his best friend cremated on Friday, giving a eulogy on Saturday. Braverman finally composed himself to speak matter-of-factly to close the ceremony, promising to learn from the thoughtful Mooney, to make his friend proud.

When the service ended, Trevor and Sasha approached Layla and Peter Braverman to ask to speak to them privately. "There's more to my announcement," Trevor said. "Sasha and I have decided to never play football again."

"What about our team?" Braverman asked, but Layla shushed him.

"I want to honor Professor Mooney's life," Trevor went on, "but also his vision for changing Coors State. We're not going to tell the coaches or anybody, though. We're going to spend our redshirt year practicing with the team, gathering evidence, and working on a strategy. That's what Professor Mooney would have wanted, don't you think?"

To Layla, hearing a plan from the football stars was the most powerful part of the funeral. It was something tangible. A strategy. Still, it did not feel much like closure. Not yet. On the short drive back, she told Braverman that she wanted to be a lot more than simply the face of the movement.

That evening, Layla, President Braverman, Trevor, and Sasha sat together, leaving one seat empty to honor Eugene Mooney.

Coors State was approaching a 30-point lead when the public address announcer told the fans it was time for the Groundswell, the fans' version of the Wave. Because of their location, Layla's section would be last, and the cycle would end—and start up again—with the pep band a dozen rows below. Emotionally exhausted, she wondered if she had the energy to leap to her feet each time the human wave wound around the stadium.

"Look at these sheep," Braverman said as the ritual began. "As interim president, I've decided to sit this one out."

"Will people take notice if the president doesn't stand?" Trevor asked diplomatically, echoes of his history professor in his voice.

"The Groundswell looks different from here," Sasha said. "Players secretly watch, you know." He paused, then added, "I hope we don't mess up. We might get called for offside."

Layla said, "I'll admit I have no patience for this shit today."

"Is that your first decree as a leader of the movement?" Braverman asked. He studied her for a long moment until Layla said, "Not exactly. Maybe?"

Braverman took that as a "yes," because he announced, "We're not standing. Layla just made that decision."

"I'm not trying to shame anyone," Layla said. "I'm just tired. Maybe I better stand. I don't have tenure." The Groundswell was now directly across from them. They had less than a minute before it came around.

"It's difficult to influence the world by not participating," Trevor said. "That's what Professor Mooney would say. Will anyone notice if we don't stand? We're just four people out of a hundred thousand."

"We're five," Sasha said. He pointed an index finger and counted out loud in Croatian—*Jedan, dva, tri, cetiri, pet*—as if to be certain of the math.

Layla knew who Sasha was including. "What about this?" she said to Braverman. "Let's all stand at the wrong time. Just to see what happens. We'll test the waters."

Trevor turned to explain this to Sasha. But Sasha did not understand—or did he?—because he relayed the plan to the people next to him, who continued passing it on. Folks from down the aisle leaned forward to see where the directive had come from. Two long-haired kids stood and flashed a peace sign to Layla. She recognized them immediately—Gerald and Jerome, the real band geeks. They weren't sitting with the rest of the musicians. Perhaps they'd quit in protest or gotten in trouble for losing their uniforms. And right next to them was the entire women's volleyball team. Could that have been a coincidence?

Braverman whispered something to Trevor and gave him an enthusiastic slap on the back, like a coach. Moments later, the former quarterback brought out his booming on-field voice. "Listen up, section 110. We'll be jumping to our feet when I say jump. Everyone follow my signal."

"Just a minute, Trevor," Layla said in such a conciliatory tone that she wondered if now she was, in fact, channeling Eugene Mooney. "We still have time to discuss our options." Folks all around them had already turned to hear Trevor call the play, and the Groundswell was nearly at hand to trigger their public subversion. She leaned toward Braverman and asked what exactly he'd said to Trevor.

Before Braverman could answer, Trevor crouched above his seat and yelled his quarterback cadence. "Set. One-ten. Set, one-ten. Jump!"

The entire area stood, hands to the sky. This caused the folks behind to jump up at the wrong time, too, and an alternate wave rushed up the stadium rows, then back down, until it fizzled next to the pep band. The musicians turned and jeered section 110.

"Fuck you, band geeks!" Braverman yelled, a vicious edge in his voice that Layla hadn't heard since he'd been named president.

"Be cautious of that kind of rhetoric as an administrator," Sasha said. Another echo of Mooney, Layla thought.

"No, no," the PA announcer cried. "Fans, wait your turn for the Groundswell."

The official wave lost momentum and nearly died until the pep band started in full force again. Taunts from nearby fans rang out again as the official Groundswell moved on to section 111 and began to circle the stadium again.

"Maybe we'd better cool it," Layla said, "pick a more opportune time, and perhaps begin this as a campus-wide proposal. Or with a letter to the Dean."

"Security to section 110," the PA announced. "Security to 110."

Two yellow vests appeared moments later at the end of the row. "Everyone stand at the correct time," one of them yelled, "or you'll be subject to arrest."

Braverman stared straight ahead and sneered, "Ignore the fascists."

Trevor cupped his hands to holler at the ushers, like a quarterback communicating to an unhappy coach on the sidelines. "We'll try harder next time," he yelled, and he flashed a thumbs-up. But Layla knew it was a fake, a decoy. The wave was again across the field in the opposite end zone. She could feel her pulse pounding.

"Let's concentrate on our timing," Braverman said.

"Agreed," Trevor said. "Let's really screw things up. I've been reading about the land reform movement of Mexico, and how long it all took for their revolution to take hold, to catch fire."

Layla started to caution them, but Braverman gave his quarterback a nudge. Trevor went into his cadence, and it was apparent to Layla that their timing would be so totally off this time it would utterly ruin the ritual.

Trevor yelled jump, and most of their section—several hundred folks this time—stood and laughed. The Silver Bullet benchwarmers turned to watch. A moment later, a Coors State defender lifted his head from the team huddle and pointed. His teammates turned to witness the rebel Groundswell flat-line and die just before it got to the pep band. Their opponent saw an advantage, hiked the ball, then ran though the Silver Bullet distracted defense for their first touchdown of the game. Maniscalco strode to the end-zone to scream at 110. The entire section was still on their feet, but Braverman was the only one standing on his seat, dancing to a nonexistent beat, a soundtrack that ran through his head, and his head alone.

Layla tapped Braverman on the arm. "Uh-oh," she said.

The security guards at their right were edging towards them, and a few people down the row twisted sidesaddle to let the goons pass, but they got stalled in a commotion not ten yards away. Layla realized a Coors beer vendor was blocking the way—Martin Cardly, sporting her red wig as a disguise. She turned back to Braverman and said, "Peter, I can't get arrested. And neither can you, you'll lose your new position."

"I'll protect you," Braverman said, and he jumped down off his seat.

"You've got to run, this instant," she said. "Protecting me isn't a plan. We said we'd have a strategy, one that might take years to unfold. What about all the things we've learned from Eugene?"

Braverman reflected for a moment. "The Movement needs you," he said, which wasn't an answer to her question at all.

"Needs me?" Layla asked.

Sasha leaned forward in his seat. "Not me," he said gravely. "We." It didn't make grammatical sense, yet somehow Sasha was right on.

Braverman turned to the two former players. "Sasha, you stall the cops. Take a wide stance, get a low center of gravity, keep your feet moving, but hold your ground."

Sasha pivoted in the aisle to face the guards, who had pushed past Martin Cardly and his beer tray. They kept pressing forward. Poised behind Sasha, Trevor followed his lead, got in a crouch, and said, "Make a run for the border."

"What border?" Braverman asked.

"Figure of speech," Sasha said. He twisted shut their bag of popcorn and pitched it back to Braverman. "Go!"

Braverman cradled the popcorn bag between his hip and forearm. "We'll be in touch in the morning," he said to Trevor's back. "Use your new email account and phone."

The quarterback nodded. Layla was seated again and could no longer see past Trevor and Sasha, but she sensed a blitz of security closing in. The entire row—except her—was standing, and the pursuit was coming from a single direction. She feared something really bad could happen. Or maybe something really good. She breathed in slowly and held it, let go of the tension in her upper back, and tried to visualize Mooney. He wouldn't flee like a teenage shoplifter—but wait, there was that football practice protest. She stayed seated, innocently scanning a game program, her bouncing leg the only clue that adrenalin was roaring through her veins. She decided she would remain in her seat, and after Braverman disappeared, she'd explain to the authorities how she was simply in the wrong row at the wrong time when everything went bananas. She'd deny Peter Braverman was involved. At worst? She'd end up being subjected to the same treatment as Mooney—watching hours of football in a holding cell and working out with a strength coach to reduce her percentage of body fat. Would that be so bad? She'd have plenty of time to write, although she'd miss her poetry students.

Braverman yelled, "Coming through," and a path cleared on the opposite side from the security guards, but before he could split the gap he looked back at Layla.

Something pulled at her—a sense of loyalty, perhaps. That must have been it. But loyalty to whom? To Eugene Mooney or Peter Braverman? Her hippie mother or renegade father? To a hopeless cause? Sure, why not, maybe loyalty to all that. Mostly, she didn't want Braverman to abandon her. Mooney, if he was still alive, might have objected to an impromptu show of dissent, but he also might have said, *Join us, Layla, we need you.* Now, President Braverman needed only to parrot what Mooney would have said, aloud.

Before Braverman could extend the invitation, Layla asked, "Can I?" She jumped to her feet and scooted past him into the opening, leading the way, high-stepping down the row until they vanished into the crowd.

Acknowledgements

Thanks to my fantastic friends who have helped me edit, revise, reconsider—and to not lose faith—in the Coors State University story.

First, Robert Boswell and Antonya Nelson, my mentors and the best teachers a still-struggling writer could hope for. Their advice, friendship, meals, and beers have been unwavering since 1994.

Barry Pearce is a fantastic writer, editor, and friend. So is Mike Austin, who has taught me so much about dreaming big.

Other friends have also been hugely helpful with the novel: Phillip Hurst, Jessica Powers, Dave Bachman, Margaret Malamud, Connie Voisine, Daniel Smith, Lee Merrill Byrd, Jonathan Coleman, and Tim Loperfido.

This book project began when Dr. William Eamon at the New Mexico State University Honors College awarded me time and space to write. Thanks, Bill.

Two of my favorite poets also had smart ideas about the novel in its early stages. Sadly, they're both gone. Bobby Byrd was as much a hero to me as a friend. He was a remarkable poet whose laugh could fill the stadium at Coors State. Tony Hoagland was a brilliant thinker whose ironic edge, sense of humor, and insights continue to influence my work.

Plenty of others helped, directly and indirectly: the great Chicago journalist John Conroy, Jonathan Eig, Jesse Washington, Jim Whitesell, Irish legend Kieran Donaghy,

Dennis Daily, Tom Spieczny and Kitty Spalding, Pardeep Toor, Dan McGrath, Gina Colantino, Neal Adelman, Modzel "Bud" Greer, Keith French, Mark Rudd, Alexander Wolff, Ben Osborne, David Shields, Don Johnson and Scott Peterson of the Sports Literature Association, Andrew Blauner, Ellen Bryant Voigt, Sheila Black, Jon Ferguson, Alex Shakar, Rick Burton, Joe and Jill Somoza, Amy and Beto O'Rourke, Yuval Taylor and Kara Rota, Arne and Karen Duncan, Shawn Harrington, Dagoberto Gilb, Casey Gray, Kathryn Willms, Jon Billman, Mary Willingham, Casey Owens, Brandon Hobson, Berni Smyth, Paul Rouse, Myles Dungan, Ross Marks, Amy Lanasa, Chris Burnham, David Brower, and the late-great New Mexico writers we all lost recently, Lee K. Abbott and Mark Medoff.

Big thanks to Steve and Tracy Yellen, my partners with "Basketball in the Barrio" for 32 years.

Thanks to University of Chicago basketball coach Mike McGrath for discussing the gutsy 1939 decision by their president, Robert Maynard Hutchins.

Thanks to my wife, the poet Connie Voisine, and my daughter Alma Bradburd for their unwavering love. And thanks to Arnold, Julia, William, Kenneth, and Amy Bradburd.

Special thanks to David Meggyesy, whose book *Out of Their League* got me thinking about all this as a teenager. Thanks also to Michael James, Sean Tuohey, Gareth Harper, Dave Cullen, Casey Blue James, Doug Harris, and especially David Zirin at *The Nation*.

Finally, thanks to everyone at Etruscan Press: Amanda Rabaduex, Pamela Turchin, Robert Mooney, Steve Oristaglio (Go Bucknell!), Janine Dubik, Aaron Petrovich, and Logan Rock. And especially, thanks to Phillip Brady, a fine poet, essayist, musician, thinker, and editor at Etruscan. Thanks, Phil, for taking the leap.

About the Author

Rus Bradburd is the author of four previous books, including *All the Dreams We've Dreamed: a Story of Hoops and Handguns on Chicago's West Side*. He spent 14 seasons coaching college basketball at UTEP and New Mexico State, followed by 16 years as a university professor. He lives in New Mexico, Chicago, and Belfast. Learn more at rusbradburd.com.

Books from Etruscan Press

Zarathustra Must Die | Dorian Alexander
The Disappearance of Seth | Kazim Ali
The Last Orgasm | Nin Andrews
Drift Ice | Jennifer Atkinson
Crow Man | Tom Bailey
Coronology | Claire Bateman
Viscera | Felice Belle
Reading the Signs and other itinerant essays | Stephen Benz
Topographies | Stephen Benz
What We Ask of Flesh | Remica L. Bingham
The Greatest Jewish-American Lover in Hungarian History | Michael Blumenthal
No Hurry | Michael Blumenthal
Choir of the Wells | Bruce Bond
Cinder | Bruce Bond
The Other Sky | Bruce Bond and Aron Wiesenfeld
Peal | Bruce Bond
Scar | Bruce Bond
Until We Talk | Darrell Bourque and Bill Gingles
Poems and Their Making: A Conversation | Moderated by Philip Brady
Crave: Sojourn of a Hungry Soul | Laurie Jean Cannady
Toucans in the Arctic | Scott Coffel
Sixteen | Auguste Corteau
Don't Mind Me | Brian Coughlan

Wattle & daub | Brian Coughlan

Body of a Dancer | Renée E. D'Aoust

Generations: Lullaby with Incendiary Device, The Nazi Patrol, and How It Is That We |
Dante Di Stefano, William Heyen, and H. L. Hix

Ill Angels | Dante Di Stefano

Aard-vark to Axolotl: Pictures From my Grandfather's Dictionary |
Karen Donovan

Trio: Planet Parable, Run: A Verse-History of Victoria Woodhull, and Endless Body |
Karen Donovan, Diane Raptosh, and Daneen Wardrop

Scything Grace | Sean Thomas Dougherty

Areas of Fog | Will Dowd

Romer | Robert Eastwood

Wait for God to Notice| Sari Fordham

Bon Courage: Essays on Inheritance, Citizenship, and a Creative Life|
Ru Freeman

Surrendering Oz | Bonnie Friedman

Funeral Playlist | Sarah Gorham

Nahoonkara | Peter Grandbois

Triptych: The Three-Legged World, In Time, and Orpheus & Echo |
Peter Grandbois, James McCorkle, and Robert Miltner

The Candle: Poems of Our 20th Century Holocausts |
William Heyen

The Confessions of Doc Williams & Other Poems | William Heyen

The Football Corporations | William Heyen

A Poetics of Hiroshima | William Heyen

September 11, 2001: American Writers Respond |
Edited by William Heyen

Shoah Train | William Heyen

American Anger: An Evidentiary | H. L. Hix

As Easy As Lying | H. L. Hix

As Much As, If Not More Than | H. L. Hix
Chromatic | H. L. Hix
Demonstrategy: Poetry, For and Against | H. L. Hix
First Fire, Then Birds | H. L. Hix
God Bless | H. L. Hix
I'm Here to Learn to Dream in Your Language | H. L. Hix
Incident Light | H. L. Hix
Legible Heavens | H. L. Hix
Lines of Inquiry | H. L. Hix
Rain Inscription | H. L. Hix
Shadows of Houses | H. L. Hix
Wild and Whirling Words: A Poetic Conversation |
Moderated by H. L. Hix
All the Difference | Patricia Horvath
Art Into Life | Frederick R. Karl
Free Concert: New and Selected Poems | Milton Kessler
Who's Afraid of Helen of Troy: An Essay on Love | David Lazar
Black Metamorphoses | Shanta Lee
Mailer's Last Days: New and Selected Remembrances of a Life in Literature |
J. Michael Lennon
Parallel Lives | Michael Lind
The Burning House | Paul Lisicky
Museum of Stones | Lynn Lurie
Quick Kills | Lynn Lurie
Synergos | Roberto Manzano
The Gambler's Nephew | Jack Matthews
American Mother | Colum McCann with Diane Foley
The Subtle Bodies | James McCorkle
An Archaeology of Yearning | Bruce Mills
Arcadia Road: A Trilogy | Thorpe Moeckel
Venison | Thorpe Moeckel
So Late, So Soon | Carol Moldaw

The Widening | Carol Moldaw

Clay and Star: Selected Poems of Liliana Ursu |
Translated by Mihaela Moscaliuc

Cannot Stay: Essays on Travel | Kevin Oderman

White Vespa | Kevin Oderman

Also Dark | Angelique Palmer

Fates: The Medea Notebooks, Starfish Wash-Up, and overflow of an
unknown self |
Ann Pedone, Katherine Soniat, and D. M. Spitzer

The Dog Looks Happy Upside Down | Meg Pokrass

Mr. Either/Or | Aaron Poochigian

Mr. Either/Or : All the Rage| Aaron Poochigian

The Shyster's Daughter | Paula Priamos

Help Wanted: Female | Sara Pritchard

American Amnesiac | Diane Raptosh

Dear Z: The Zygote Epistles | Diane Raptosh

Human Directional | Diane Raptosh

I Eric America | Diane Raptosh

50 Miles | Sheryl St. Germain

Saint Joe's Passion | J.D. Schraffenberger

Lies Will Take You Somewhere | Sheila Schwartz

Fast Animal | Tim Seibles

One Turn Around the Sun | Tim Seibles

Voodoo Libretto: New and Selected Poems | Tim Seibles

Rough Ground | Alix Anne Shaw

A Heaven Wrought of Iron: Poems From the Odyssey | D. M. Spitzer

American Fugue | Alexis Stamatis

Variations in the Key of K | Alex Stein

The Casanova Chronicles | Myrna Stone

Luz Bones | Myrna Stone

In the Cemetery of the Orange Trees | Jeff Talarigo

The White Horse: A Colombian Journey | Diane Thiel

The Arsonist's Song Has Nothing to Do With Fire | Allison Titus
Bestiality of the Involved | Spring Ulmer
The Waw | Jacqueline Gay Walley
Silk Road | Daneen Wardrop
Sinnerman | Michael Waters
The Fugitive Self | John Wheatcroft
YOU. | Joseph P. Wood

Etruscan Press Is Proud of Support Received From

Wilkes University

Ohio Arts Council

The Stephen & Jeryl Oristaglio Foundation

Community of Literary Magazines and Presses [c|mp]

National Endowment for the Arts

Drs. Barbara Brothers & Gratia Murphy Endowment

Founded in 2001 with a generous grant from the Oristaglio Foundation, Etruscan Press is a nonprofit cooperative of poets and writers working to produce and promote books that nurture the dialogue among genres, achieve a distinctive voice, and reshape the literary and cultural histories of which we are a part.

etruscan press
www.etruscanpress.org
Etruscan Press books may be ordered from

Consortium Book Sales and Distribution
800.283.3572
www.cbsd.com

Etruscan Press is a 501(c)(3) nonprofit organization.
Contributions to Etruscan Press are tax deductible
as allowed under applicable law.
For more information, a prospectus,
or to order one of our titles,
contact us at books@etruscanpress.org.